DANCING WITH THE YUMAWALLI

A combination of Roots and The Odyssey, Dancing With The Yumawalli is a charming, mature, picaresque novel. Alick's prose is clear and pure as the waters of a Caribbean cove. If a tale that includes mysterious drownings, black-hulled yachts piloted by sketchy skipper, ayahuascan-induced visions, quests for Amazonian diamonds, and characters with names such as Trueblood and Soulages don't interest you, then, by all means, don't read this book.

If you do, by all means, join decent, clear-eyed, brave Godfrey Soulages on his wanderings.

Bryan Di Salvatore
Author of A Clever Base-Ballist

I've been a fan of Claude Alick's fiction for more than twenty years, since he first started writing his cycle of works about the Caribbean. The world he portrays—with fine writing, bone-deep knowledge, and passion—is not the glossy stuff of tourism, but the far richer and more powerful life that he himself grew up in. Strong men who wrested a precarious living from the jungle they fought to turn into farmland, or from the treacherous sea; stronger women who quietly carried the burden of holding everything together; children striving for opportunity that too often was bitterly denied; all infused with the mysterious presence of the spirit world, with the sinister yumawalli always watching and the alluring ladablais haunting dark paths late at night.

Dancing With The Yumawalli is fascinating, unsettling, and from the heart.

Neil McMahon
Author of Blood Double and Lone Creek

DANCING WITH THE YUMAWALLI

CC ALICK

iUniverse, Inc.
New York Bloomington

DANCING WITH THE YUMAWALLI
inspired by true events

iUniverse books may be ordered through booksellers or by contacting:

*iUniverse
1663 Liberty Drive
Bloomington, IN 47403
www.iuniverse.com
1-800-Authors (1-800-288-4677)*

*Because of the dynamic nature of the Internet, any Web addresses or links contained in this book
may have changed since publication and may no longer be valid. The views expressed in this work
are solely those of the author and do not necessarily reflect the views of the publisher, and the
publisher hereby disclaims any responsibility for them.*

*ISBN: 978-1-4401-4505-6 (pbk)
ISBN: 978-1-4401-4506-3 (ebk)*

Printed in the United States of America

iUniverse rev. date: 6/10/2010

ACKNOWLEDGMENT

I must give thanks to a generous group of people: Neil McMahon, Dennis Held and Barbara Theroux. They read the manuscript at various stages and gave me encouragement. Annick Smith allowed me to hang around Yellow Bay Writer's Workshop and participate in those great, yearly adventures. William Kittredge, who introduced me to the arc, and allowed me to benefit from his immense knowledge of the craft of writing. And my eternal gratitude to the late, Jim Crumley, who always advised to do it my way.

DEDICATION

This book is dedicated to Anzilla Peters. Jean (Happy) Strater and the late David Strater.

I'm just a soul whose intentions are good… Oh Lord, please don't let me be misunderstood.
  Bennie Benjamin

CHAPTER 1

Just four days after carnival the bacchanal seemed to leave the streets of Saint Georges and floated across the bay to the beach at Balis Ground where a number of people were making preparations to launch a vessel. The steel band, the food and the drinks, all sat in the shadow cast by the big wooden hull. The craft stood in the bright sunlight, a colossal mass of wood, caulking and tar, surrounded by a jamboree.

The results of my silence on that day still reverberate like dry thunder. A premonition was gnawing at me, skulking like a stray dog. Yet, I said nothing, not even to my friend and confidant Karrol Lagrenade. All these bits and pieces still reminding me, the sea, the sand, winds moving through the leaves of trees, even the frantic laughter of neighbors. And for a variety of reasons an anxiety toward all these familiar things refuse to let me go.

My friend, Karrol, was a scamp and an instigator of the best kind. He saw opportunities in places that most of us would look straight through. So when he approached me that Saturday at the launching of the vessel, I was a little doubtful. But we slipped away from the gathering, leaving the food and the celebration back on the beach. He enticed me to follow with a promise of money and a silly idea. It had something to do with the heat of the sun and an old man's fruit trees. "Should take less than ten minutes, man," he argued. "We'll be back in time to watch them drag her into the sea."

1

The day they launched that vessel, *Miss Irene,* the world, as I knew it ceased to exist. I crossed over into matters arcane, mystical, and do I dare say murderous? Our run-in with the old man turned out to be the first sign. This was nothing new for us. Papa Pouchete sat in an easy chair inside his house, near a glass window. A fan blew air across a big chunk of ice melting in a washbasin near him. We strolled by casually, made a circle, and came back to his fruit trees at a place far from the house.

The prevailing wind wrangled in the leaves, dried the sweat and seawater on our skin, leaving white streaks. Perfect day to remain close to water. We crouched in the goat weed, and looked down on the fruit trees scattered behind love-vine and barbed wire. He slapped me hard on one shoulder, choked my neck, winked, and pointed.

"See. See. What I tell ya?"

I hated it when he was right. Clusters of color nestled between green and yellow leaves: mangoes, guavas, and those little oranges with red innards, all of them ripe in just three days. We moved out of hiding. I carried the empty crocus sack and we crept between the love-vine and the barbed wire entwined along the wooden posts.

Karrol grabbed a limb and pulled himself up into a mango tree near the fence. He moved quickly, scampering up the main trunk to a place where the tree forked. He wedged himself in, and began shaking the branches. Mangoes began hitting the ground. I dashed about filling the sack, and then I moved to the oranges, snatching the small fruits off the branches by the handful, completely ignoring the thorns.

We saw Papa Pouchete a little late. He came at us with his machete brandished high in the air. I shouted at Karrol, dashed for the fence, and threw the sack over. My fingers gripped the top of the fence post and I hurdled, came down hard on the other side. I looked back just in time to see Karrol's feet hit the ground. His ankle twisted, but he sprung up. He and the old man squared off. Karrol had lost the angle, and the momentum to scale the fence. I should have warned him about my strange feelings, I thought.

He hobbled from the first tree, crouching, and dodging. His head moved like a chicken pecking corn. The old man kept after him, slicing at the air, and muttering words laced with spit. Karrol made no sounds with his mouth, but his bare feet stomped and scuffed the dry dirt, raising little dust clouds. He kept drifting away from the spot where I stood. Only his get-up-and-go kept him away from the blade. An urge hit me: jump back over the fence; pelt the old fool with rotten fruits. But then I grasped Karrol's plan.

I grabbed the barbed wire and pulled it apart by resting my bare feet on the bottom strand, and yanking on the one in my hands. The love-vines stretched and snapped, pealed off the barbed wire and the post. Karrol saw the opening and took off. In spite of his limp, he left the old man behind. He lunged and scrambled; his shirt snagged and tore as he crawled between the barbed wire. I snatched the sack, threw it over my shoulder, and we dashed for the bushes.

"Too close," Karrol said, tongue sticking out, panting like a dog, big smile on his face. He enjoyed the whole thing. He fingered the rip in his shirt. "Ah, shit! My mother will…"

"Look over there. Who's that?"

"What? Where?" Karrol spoke and turned. A boy, about our age, slid behind the trunk of a tree. Good thing we didn't see who he was; we would have to beat his ass. Must have seen us and told the old man.

I focused on Papa Pouchete pacing near the fence, hair and beard white and coiled as lamb's wool. I swear there was a smile on the old man's face. We knew he would complain to no one. He was a solitary person who spoke only to people paying to pick a basket of his fruits; he only left his house to buy food, and even then, they say, he would just hand the shopkeeper a note. People said he was the last of his kind. What kind they meant exactly, I had no idea.

Karrol and I moved down the ravine under the remains of the evening sun. No limp to his steps now. The bag of fruits dangled on my left shoulder. Karrol's younger brother, Ian, appeared on the road ahead of us, just behind Tante Rose's house, where the ravine came up against the cane field.

"Where you been? Listen to the music." He spoke breathlessly as if he had been running. "They ready to move…" then he looked at the bag. "What's that? What's in there?"

"Nothing," Karrol said. And we continued to walk.

"I'll tell if you don't…"

"Say a word and I'll give you a fat lip." Karrol balled his fist and moved toward his brother.

"Ian, here." I stepped between them, reached into the sack, and pulled out two bruised mangoes and three little oranges.

"Don't give him all that," Karrol said. "Little toad will tell anyway. Can't keep his mouth shut."

"If you tell, we'll say you helped us," I said. Ian looked at me and then he took the fruits from my hand, bit into a mango as we moved down the road.

We planned to sell the fruits to the shipwrights, and their friends down on the beach-for movie money. But things were looking doubtful, first, Ian, now my girlfriend, Yvette. This sack could be empty by the time we reach the beach.

She came at us, up the road, from the edge of the cane. Her approach struck me like an ambush. I pulled back from the brothers the moment I saw her. All three of us waited, looking at her as she approached. She brushed past Karrol, clouted Ian on the back of his head. Her braids dangled near her cheeks.

"You think these two thieves can save you," she said. "What's in that bag? And don't think you can threaten me," she stood in the space between us as if blocking an escape.

"Karrol, take this," I said. "Go on down. I'll be there in a minute." I took two mangoes out of the sack, and stuffed them in my pocket. Yvette would not be as easy to cajole as Ian. Karrol came back to us, looked at me, and then at Yvette. He reached out and took the sack. "Don't sell anything for less than twenty-five cents, you hear."

He winked again and laughed out loud. "And the baby, that's three," he shouted. Then he and Ian ran off down the road, their laughter hanging in the air. His antics left me mixed up. I had no guts to broach the subject of sex with Yvette. Fear of her answer kept me in check.

"Fresh boy," Yvette said. "Feel like slapping his face sometimes."

"Why?"

"You know why. Making suppositions about us and laughing like a jackass."

"You calling us names, girl? You know you want one of these." I pulled my hand out of my pocket and showed her the mangoes without offering.

"You two. Always taking advantage. One of these days that old yellow man will pull a gun," she said.

4

"They real sweet. Have one." I offered her.

"You stole that. I don't want it." She wrinkled her brows and shrugged.

"Why you always like that, Yvette?"

"Like what? You mean I can't speak my…"

"That's not what I mean. You know what I mean."

"No. I don't."

"Damn, you so hard-headed, girl."

"Now who's calling names?"

"What we doing here? Let's go." I gestured in the direction of the music. "We can watch the drunks pulling on the ropes, see which of them slip and fall on their face. See who break a leg, or almost get crushed by the hull. Might be fun."

"That's fun? Bunch of drunken fools, making all that noise. Acting as if that vessel means something to them. What's that going to do? Tell me that. Am not going…"

"Yvette, I witnessed the entire thing. From the keel up, raw wood against tools, sweat into-you don't expect me to…?"

"I don't expect anything. Go, have fun. Always talking about sweat and tools. Go on." She waved her hand as if brushing a fly, and then she turned her back on me and walked off. Through speech or action, Yvette always got the last word.

The music drifted up the road. The steel band completed the melody, *"If I had the wings of a dove."* It was getting late, so I ran toward the celebration. Through an opening between the cane tops, and the coco branches, I saw the vessel, *Miss Irene*, afloat for the first time. I felt cheated. The unpainted, wooden hull sat high on the water, near the just completed Grenada Yacht Service. The big rough hull dwarfed the sleek yachts scattered here and there around the lagoon.

My toes slammed into a root protruding from the sprawling manchineel tree. Pain shot up my leg, and I stumbled onto the sand. Ian came running away from the crowd, a chunk of breadfruit dappled with isolated scraps of Callaloo in one hand. He slowed down beside me, gnawing and yammering through the mouthful of food. "You missed the oildown, Godfrey."

He slid the last portion of the breadfruit into his mouth as if to deliberately deprive me. We strolled back down the beach. He chewed, looking nasty, with scraps of white mush dangling from his teeth. His mouth made moist noises.

"Where's Karrol? You guys sold any?"

"Over there." He pointed. "Where did he go? We were playing on those." Two masts and a bunch of booms sloshed about in the waves off the beach, near a cluster of mangroves where the earth was littered with woodchips and shavings. We came to Karrol's ripped shirt, pants beside it on the edge of the sand.

The waves followed each other, slapping at the shore with a common beat. A steady breeze buffered us. The new vessel stood at anchor. The people on the beach seemed scattered now, not bunched as they had been before we left to raid Papa Pouchete's fruits. It was easy to tell. In a few minutes, the pan-men would take their instruments to the truck-the food gone, the rum gone, the party is over. Down the beach stood a group of boys, but no Karrol in sight.

Realization struck me like the echoes of a bird's wings and that premonition was itching at me again. Could Karrol be under water, in the sea, right there? Where would he go without his clothes? I stripped off my shirt and pants, and plunged in near the spars. The group of booms slammed into each other, creating a hollow and garbled noise. I groped about, awash in a soft muck of sand and seaweed still settling-debris scoured by the keel of *Miss Irene* as they dragged her across the dirt and sand into the sea.

Rough granules slapped at my face, and collided with my eyeballs. I groped around in the gray water near the bottom, wondering what I would do if I found him. My feet contacted something solid, but as I turned a lump of coral came into view, and I was out of air. I pushed up toward the surface and misjudged my position under the booms. My head glanced off the edge of one chunk and a sharp pain poured into my skull. I tried to stand, but my feet found no bottom. Kicking and gasping for air, I reached out and grabbed one of the booms to steady my self and catch my breath. "Ian, go. Go tell somebody." He looked at me for an instant and then he ran toward the people remaining on the beach. I filled my lungs with air and plunged back under water, anxiety pounding at my ears. Why didn't you say something, Godfrey, why didn't you say something to him?

CHAPTER 2

Throughout that night, every groan of the bed springs entered my head as something else. Since none of us had found him underwater I held fast to the delusion that Karrol could have gone into the woods and simply fell asleep under a tree. It was like waiting for two things, both concrete, but worries made them shadowy. I wanted to fall into a deep sleep and be awoken by a knock on the door.

Creatures revile the night. Hooting, barking, and chirping, every sigh brought hope. But eventually the pale dawn squashed all that, and I was left embracing a single nagging question. What happened to the sack of fruit we stole from Papa Pouchete?

My father and I left the house without eating breakfast. Sydney and Xudine, Karrol's uncle and aunt, they stood near the shore, shrouded by the last remnants of that long night. Like two congenial and expectant spirits, they waited near my father's fishing boat, the boat we called *Lucky Joe*. Sydney leaned on his walking stick and shifted his weight as we approached. He spoke first.

"Good morning, Ethan."

"Morning, Sydney."

"I don't envy you."

My father grunted; a deep sigh came out of his nostrils. A little silence loitered between them.

"A ladablais could have lured him into the woods."

"But we know better," my father said.

Their manners, the weight of their words, the morning, dry, bothersome and cold-we climbed into the boat. The water appeared thick; the oars slid through, slapping the water like the tongue of a dog. The goose bumps on my arms tickled like bites from a swarm of insects. I sat with my back to my father, facing Sydney and Xudine, and the stern of the boat.

Their gaze and the disparity of their features made me anxious. I knew these people through Karrol and from a distance. From yarns and supposition whispered about the place they came from and what might be chasing them. Sydney wore a droopy straw hat. Flattened, crooked lips hid the cavity that was his mouth. His raspy breathing came out of two openings at the ends of what remained of his nose. His cheeks looked like leather, but gouged and pitted in places. When he blinked, hairless pleats of skin moved with his eyes like a reptile's. Skeletal fingers clutched the smooth briarroot that he used as a walking stick.

Xudine wore a red shawl that covered her hair. She looked strange wearing that green dress that I remembered so well. Their eyes never left me. What if I catch this disease that did those terrible things to Sydney? My father seemed unafraid. Xudine, the Arawak from South America, she lives with Sydney as husband and wife; her reasons for lying with this mangled bag of bones eluded me.

Their continuous stares burrowed into me. Although the goose bumps were gone from my skin, tightness remained. I looked down, away from their eyes, but the curves of Xudine's bare toes splayed out on the floorboards of the boat caught my attention. Those same toes had left prints in the damp sand. Does Sydney know that Karrol and I often watched his wife as she swam naked near the peninsula at Mon Pandy?

The first time we snuck into the rocks to watch Xudine, something changed between Karrol and me. We had known each other all our lives, and few things of importance had ever come to light for us. I had seen naked women before, but Xudine was another substance, something like warm buttered bread with guava jelly.

Once in between the rocks we could go nowhere by land. We would be trapped by anyone coming into that far corner of the beach. Behind our backs, a vertical finger of rock extended up and then out into the sea. We waited with mounting anticipation for Xudine to come down the beach. We knew she would come because for months we had seen her going down there, faithfully, each morning. No idea what took us so long to fix on this adventure.

The sea deposited an array of relics between the rocks and along the sand below the precipice. Dry seaweed and shards of worn, smashed glass, bits of rusted wire, and rope from fish pots smashed rough seas. We waited amid the debris and the whiff of brine. The screw pines and the sea grapes down along the sand shimmered with beads of the morning dew.

Xudine came around the bend, stepping gently over the clumps of sea grapes. The color of her dress, so close to the pale green bulbs scattered here and there along the white sand. I leaned on a cold rock, trying to find a better view, and to quiet the trembling in my knees. Her bare-feet left prints in the sand.

The sight of those prints alerted me. She might be aware that we were about looking at her. Our prints also remained on the sand, just below the high-water mark. She showed no signs of concern. She stopped twenty yards away, reached down for the hem of her dress, and heaved it over her head. Her strands of straight black hair went up with the dress and then settled back around her neck. She wore no bra. Brown breasts the size of large grapefruits jiggle slightly on her chest.

I looked at Karrol; his jaw was slack, as if caught in the midst of almost speaking. A rush of air left our nostrils in concert. Small waves slapped at the shore. She removed her underwear and placed it near the dress, on a chunk of driftwood abandoned by high water. She moved into the waves, up to her knees, and then she plunged in. The cheeks of her ass remained on the surface as she kicked and swam out into the deep.

An urge to bolt gripped me. A stupid grin on Karrol's face gave me courage. We settled among the rocks, silently, staring down at the woman in the water. This was better than any movie we had ever seen. Even that restricted one we had snuck into, with Laurence Harvey and Kim Novak, the one called Of *Human Bondage*.

Xudine swam way out toward the end of the peninsula as if contemplating a swim back to her home in South America. When she finally came back to the shore and started scoping the rocks, I thought we were caught. But she climbed back into her clothes and walked back down the beach. We sat there waiting for her to get far off the sand, and I weighed the prospects of returning to that feast without getting caught.

Amazing how the mind seeks refuge. I had no idea that I had embraced the conclusions reached by my father and Sydney, and started hiding from the possibilities all at once: *a ladablais could have lured him into the woods. But we know better.* Were those words uttered for my sake? I wanted the sun to rise right then and warm the world.

"Okay. One at a time." My father's voice nudged me out of my reverie. He lifted one oar out of the water and pulled hard on the other, twirling the boat, stern to shore.

Ethan eased the boat onto the sand where Cyril Ogilvie, Yvette's father, waited with one other man. The unpainted hull of the just-launched vessel stood there like a giant toy. No masts, no stanchions, no booms. No one associated with *Miss Irene* stood on deck. Cyril caught and steadied *Lucky Joe*, and Sydney, Xudine, and I disembarked. Cyril and the other man took our places. Several groups of people were moving down the path to the beach. They looked a little festive in the soft glow of the morning. I resented their presence.

Karrol's mother, Anna, she stood with the first group to reach the sand. She looked frantic, eyes red. I avoided her face. My gaze drifted to the sprawling branches of the manchineel arced over the water, and there, between the small leaves that dangled into the top of the waves, was the sack that had contained our loot, empty in the shallow.

Everything felt quiet. The tree stood there witnessing. A gust of wind worked up the leaves, as if the old noxious tree needed to shed some memories, about the time Karrol and I went diving for the white urchins around the reef off Balis Ground and came upon that school of dogfisk.

The small sharks moved slowly, down, around and over the reef. Their tails fanned the spines of the black urchins wedged into the fire coral. I should have warned Karrol about my intention. I brought the spear gun out before me, sighted down the shaft, and pulled the trigger. The spear hit the shark, and it ran straight for Karrol, struck him on the calf, and bit in. He shot to the surface like a cork released from a bottle, bubbles climbing with him as he let out a gurgled scream.

The sound exploded the moment his face broke the surface. His shriek may have been heard on the shore and beyond. He scrambled into the boat with the small shark still attached to the back of his leg. The spear stuck straight through the leathery skin and protruded. I wedged a blade into the small slits on the side of its head, but that didn't make the thing release its grip. Karrol's blood mixed with the blood of the shark, flowing across the floorboard, and into the bilge as I rowed for shore.

Cyril Ogilvie, Yvette's father, and Mr. Collins Peters, another shipwright working on the vessel, pried the jaws open with a crowbar. The shark left a perfect double row of teeth marks on Karrol's right calf. That's how I first recognized his body.

After all this time, I still recall some details of that morning as if witnessed in a dream. A ship sounded its horn in preparation to leave port at Saint Georges across the bay. The unpainted hull of the just-launched vessel stood off shore. No name on the hull.

Nothing cast a shadow. The rising sun stood right over Richmond Hill, exactly over the prison, shrouding the beach in a fresh, low light. Everyone had made it down to the sand now, and they stood looking at the small craft bobbing on the water between the shore and the vessel. Cyril and Ethan attached long ropes to themselves and the gunwale. They dove into the water repeatedly, coming back to the surface for air. When they found him, they pulled his naked body to the surface with the rope tied around his waist. They allowed his body to linger on the surface as they climbed into the boat, then they lifted him out of the water. The man at the oars began rowing.

For just one second, the world stood still, for just a second. But Karrol's mother, Anna LaGrenade, she got it started again with some words that sounded like a final shriek. "Cyril! God punishing me, Cyril!"

The moment bounced like a ball falling out of nowhere. Anna doubled over, her hands clenched into fists, pounding at her chest as if to expel despair. She tried to dash into the waves, but Tante Rose and Miss Olga grabbed her.

Sydney and Xudine stood next to me, staring at the boat floating toward shore.

Karrol's body was placed on a tarp under the old tree. The siren from an ambulance blared in the distance as if speed had some importance. Anna LaGrenade went limp as the two women took her away. Many things hit me in that little moment: the wind, the sun. Everything moved around me and accused me, like the look on Anna's face. Karrol would still be alive if you were on time. Why did you remain there like a fool, bickering and teasing Yvette?

Karrol's puffy face fastened to my mind.

The incident hung suspended as one big flash. I wished it would end and allow me to see clear again. A dull ache at the back of my neck made me cringe.

Sydney stood next to me. The fingers on his left hand clenched hard on my neck as if he thought I would run if he released me, which was exactly what I wanted to do. I wanted to run, hide and let the strange pain pour out of me, through my eyes, out my mouth, into the ground: bitter bile. But Sydney held my neck tight. The urge to knock his hand off made my stomach gripe.

Xudine stood to his right as if stricken by paralysis. Her hair stuck out around the edge of the shawl. Tears slid down her cheeks; her chin rested on her chest. She held her husband's right hand, the same hand with which he held his stick, and a low murmur, something resembling a prayer, escaped her lips.

We stood in an open circle looking down at him. People pushed to get a better look. Ethan and Cyril stood close to the body, as if guarding it. The open gash down the left side of his temple looked water-soaked, raw in the middle, and turning white along the edges. The seaweed and white sand in his hair resembled mock adornments. I had a sudden urge to reach down and slap him, see him jump up, shake that stuff off and make a fist, ready to fight. But that urge just hit me like a fly stopping and then quickly moving on.

What was left of his body did something to me. The gnawed skin at the end of his shriveled penis, the bare chewed flesh at the tips of his fingers and toes. One night under water and the sea creatures had already eaten his eyes. Two fleshy holes remained just over his. When they covered him with a second tarp, it seemed rude. I wanted to shout at them, but his mother's bawling trampled everything, forced me to keep my mouth shut.

The ambulance appeared on the road above the beach and started to reverse down the narrow path. When they reached the edge of the sand, two men jumped out, opened the back door and took out a stretcher. Ethan and Cyril moved aside to give them room. I expected them to left him gently, but they grabbed him like a sack of flour, hoisted him onto the stretcher and moved him into the vehicle.

People began to scatter the moment the ambulance turned on its siren and began crawling up the path. I looked around, lost and dazed about the irrevocable. I saw Ian standing away from the crowd with Yvette. She held him as if to keep him standing. Our eyes met. They lowered their gaze, turned and started moving away. I knew they blamed me for what happened to Karrol.

CHAPTER 3

The vessel sat out there on the water as if it had zilch to do with anything, but on land it had started. The rumors came out of the trees, vines and nettles in whispers and conjectures. Tante Rose and Miss Olga, the two women who had prevented Anna from charging into the sea, they led the procession of words.

They sounded like this: "De boy's soul was taken for dat vessel. Ah know dat for sure. New vessels must have ah strong soul to guide it over de seas. De soul could come from anyone who built de vessel. She could have received ah soul from ah shipwright, but no accidents happened. So, de soul had to come from someone who witnessed de placement of de new keel. We knew something like dis would happen wen dose two boys started playing around dat vessel. We warned Anna."

The talking took on differing forms. It was the biggest thing for a while, and people kept on. I took it all in and bemoaned the days we wasted around the skeleton of *Miss Irene*. They had been building the craft for more than six months, a bunch of Vincentians from Bequia, and a few Grenadians. Every day after school, Karrol and I went down to Balis Ground to swim and play. In the early stages, we wandered down to watch the shipwrights set the keel. We admired the array of tools: clamps, adzes, augers, caulking irons, hammers, saws, spirit levels, and the various planes, smooth black steel, the tools of shipbuilding.

The day Cyril and my father retrieved Karrol's body from the sea, everything changed for me. Pleasures became pain, stealing ripe fruits, fishing and diving in the sea, even the movies. The world took on a different tinge, spoke to me in a somewhat new way, and the belief that Karrol Lagrenade couldn't have just drowned infected me like a disease.

CHAPTER 4

In one hand she held a basket covered by a white cloth and in the other she held her remaining son, Ian. The basket was full of freshly baked bread. Anna Lagrenade stood in our yard, three days after we buried Karrol under the sapodilla tree near his grandmother's house. Ian looked as though he would rather be someplace else, give him one chance and he might pull away and bolt. My father went outside and spoke to Anna. He came back and told me we were going to make a trip up to Jan Anglais.

We went to the home of an old woman who lived in a wooden house off the main road, just up from Papa Pouchete. Her place was also cultivated with fruit trees. It was rumored that no one messed with her fruits because she had the power to give you more warts on your ass than God gave to the Crapo. The old lady's place had many trees-mango, sapodilla, oranges, ugli-fruits-all laden and ripe. I wanted to ask her for some; Ian and I could have had a good time with some of those. But everybody looked so serious, even that pretty girl, the one the old woman called Alma.

We sat on wicker chairs in a small room. A bird chirped in the trees outside. Our breathing became rhythmic. I heard the shuffle of feet and realized they were mine. The old woman sat on a chair in the middle. A small red and white statue of the Virgin Mary rested on a shelf, near a bouquet of dead flowers. Dozens of vials of different sizes, all containing dried whole leaves adorned every shelf in the room. Alma brought a basin with water and a white towel. She placed the container on the old woman's lap, and left.

The place emitted many wet smells, herbs, candle-smoke, nameless essences triggering tenfold questions. The old woman sprinkled powder on the surface of the water. The stuff spread out across the surface of the liquid, leaving a thin film. She placed her hands in the water, and then suddenly yanked them out. Sprinkles hit my faces.

An odor rose out of the basin, sweet-scented in my nose, but it made my eyes water. I looked at Ian-nothing moved, not even his head or shoulders. His mother still held his hand and was speaking as the old woman finished with the white towel and tossed it to the floor, where she had placed the basin of water.

"Mama ah lost Karrol, meh son, ah lost meh first born. Wat's happening to me, Mama? Tell me, meh children." The reek of rum on Anna's breath mixed with all the competing scents in the room.

"Ah heard about your troubles, Anna. Ah wish dis were easy for you. Dis world is not our home; we all just passing through. Your son left his marks everywhere. If you came to me before, ah could have tried to prevent some of your pain, but now... Ah can't turn dat back. Ah sorry, Anna. Ah keep seeing dis man with blood on his hands, just standing deer. Ah can't see his face. Dat vessel is in de way. Did dey really call it *Miss Irene*? Named it after a woman?"

Mama Viche paused and looked around the room. She examined our faces in silence, as if our expressions could tell her something or take her beyond this place. When she spoke next, she spoke to Anna and my father as if dealing with one person.

"You two brought dese boys here for clear reasons. Let me see your hands, Ian."

The old woman opened her palms and presented them to Ian. He hesitated and his mother bumped him with her elbow. Ian's hands flew out, trembling. He placed them in Mama Viche's. The old woman took a deep breath, and then the air came flying back through her mouth as if someone had slapped her on her back. She spoke as she caught her breath.

"Oh Lord! Anna, dis boy will help take Grenada apart and put it back together again." She laughed out loud as if someone told her an excellent joke. "Don't worry about him, Anna. He'll be fine. De spirits real strong in him. Just mourn your lost child. Don't worry about dis one." Ian glanced up at his mother as the old woman finished speaking, a refreshed smile barely visible on his face. I knew that look. It was relief.

Mama Viche licked her lips with a pink tongue, and then turned to me; my heart shuddered. There was something about her face, about her eyes, a solid thing.

"Godfrey," she said. My eyes twitched at the sound of my name. "Your father doesn't believe in any of dis mumbo jumbo. He brought you here because Anna is his friend and he needs to put her heart at ease." She smiled and shrugged. "Give me your hands anyway," she said.

I hesitated, but then I remembered Ian's reaction. I didn't want to appear foolish or cowardly, so I leaned forward and placed my hands in her palms, hoping for nothing. She gently folded smooth, cold fingers over my hands, and I felt a sensation, like the tingle I felt after touching the two poles of that rectangular transistor battery to my tongue.

I looked deep into the old woman's eyes this time and my skin shivered. She was looking into me as I was looking into her. I tried to disconnect from her gaze, but I was stuck there. I felt a calm wash over me when her eyelids folded shut. But her next words sounded like she meant to curry favor with me.

"Godfrey, you know it's possible to call things by name and still not recognize dem. For instance, your father calls dis mumbo jumbo. Dat's de name of de protection spirit for sure. It followed us all de way from Africa to dis place. De white people know it by name. Dey printed it in dat big book of captured words and meanings. Your father calls dat spirit by its name and he doesn't know it. You're filled with dat spirit, but it's hidden, like water below. You know people see you as mud. Dat's all you allow. You buried within de old shades, light within and light outside." She paused and looked at me as if seeing me for the first time. "But take care now, de two old spirits knows your name.

"Listen." She paused as if waiting for a sound. She still held my hands and I felt awkward, because I was waiting for more about the old spirits that knew my name. "You will come across some new spirits wearing skin," she said. "They will open doors, invite you inside. Be careful of their offerings." She nodded her head as if enticing me to agree with,

I don't know what, but then she was speaking again about something else. "What you see wen you walk in de spirit world?" she asked. "Have you ever told your father about de snipes you see dancing around his shadow in the water?" She paused again, waiting for an answer. When I said nothing, she spoke softly, as if to let me off the hook.

"It doesn't matter," she said, "what will be, will be."

The old woman sounded doubtful of her own words, and that gave me some courage. One question sat on the tip of my tongue, and I decided to ask it before the opportunity withered.

"Mama, I want to know what happened to Karrol. You know what happened to him?" The words left my mouth and everyone stopped breathing, or it felt that way. The old woman released my hands and pulled back, a mixture of surprise and amusement on her face.

"Godfrey, not everything in dis world has clear answers. Sometimes not knowing can be a blessing. Ah don't have wat you need. But if ah did, wat good would it do? It wouldn't bring him back."

Her response left me baffled and speechless. "Remember, de cutlass cuts both ways, and all of us must own our scars," she said. "Your memories, your ancestors, all of dem will lead you. Be careful where you let tem take you. If you ever need me, I'll be right here." She paused and turned away from me with an air of conclusion. "Anna, thank you for de bread," she continued. "Ethan Soulages, send me two pounds of fish de next time you have ah good catch. And will you clean dem for me? Alma is kind of squirmy about pulling out de gut. De fate of your son is in his own hands, Ethan. Keep his feet on de ground. Dat's all you can do. My concern is always about de living. Not much we can do for de dead." My father nodded his nearly baldhead as the old woman spoke and dug into her pocket. "Take dis." She handed one vial to my father and another to Anna. "Crush dem in warm water. Man better Man. Don't let dem drink it. Let dem take sponge baths with it for thirty days. Every night, before bed."

The meeting ended, and I felt as if I had caused this with my abrupt question. But what else could I have done? Everything about Karrol's death appeared far too filigreed. I had questions for Ian but was afraid of the answers. On the way back home, Ian and I walked far behind my father and his mother. Long skinny shadows danced on the ground at our feet. I wanted to clear up what the old woman had said.

"What did she mean when she said you would take Grenada apart and put it back together?"

"Who knows anything about all that obeah?" Ian said, "I like that mumbo jumbo though. Always nice to have a guardian. But what about you? Is it mud or is it water? And two spirits knows you name?" He looked at me and laughed. "That stuff she sprinkled in the water though-" He went silent as we caught up to our parents.

I placed little stock in what the old woman had said. I knew spirits. They hid off the road in bushes. They flew across the night as balls of fire; they wail and cry, scaring the hell out of man and beast. But none of them have skin. If spirits had skins, someone would have found one already, just like they find snakeskins and drag them home for use in no-good spells. No one has ever seen a spirit skin as far as I know. So, what is she talking about?

"-Did you smell the stuff? It tickled my nose," Ian continued just before we got to the juncture where we would part company. "It was eucalyptus," he said. "Uncle Sydney said the Indians in South America used it as medicine. But spirits with skin? I don't know what to tell you, brother. Such a world, how are we suppose to tell fish from bait?"

My father said nothing to me about the visit to the old woman. My regret and disdain at the whole thing was compounded by his reaction. He treated the whole thing like some kind of entertainment. Two days after we saw Mama Viche, he took a job on a vessel, heading north, and I was left chewing on all my suspicions and doubts.

CHAPTER 5

I started avoiding my friends, Yvette, her sister Yoelina, Cosmus, and Ian. We usually walked home together after school. They couldn't begin to understand the trouble in me, even if I explained it a thousand times. One evening they took their usual road home and I went off alone in search of satisfaction. My lie worked well. I told them I was going to the fish market to collect some money owed to my father. None of them offer to come with me. Too many flies and the stink of rotting fish guts. Persnickety bastards, afraid of a little stink.

The moment they left, I headed down past the Anglican Church and Barclays Bank. A policeman dressed in a crisp uniform and white gloves directed traffic, extending his palms, and beckoning like a marionette. All flowed around him. Drivers honked at each other, disembodied voices filled the cobblestone street with a chorus of discord. I crossed the street near Palmer School and headed up Gran Etang Road toward the police station. I figured I could tell the police about Karrol and they would help me do something about his death. A policeman dressed in a dark blue uniform and a hat with a red band, stood behind a counter as I came into the station. The fellow looked barely older than I. There were pictures on the wall: the Queen and the prime minister, Eric Gairy.

"Can I help you?" he asked, looking at me with stony eyes.

"Yes. I want to be a policeman," I said. "You solve murders, crimes?"

The man struggled to keep the corners of his mouth from curling. But he could not hide the little amused twinkle; it made his eyes shine. He reached for a pencil and one sheet of paper, hand poised over the page to start writing.

"What's your name?"

"Godfrey Soul-ages."

"Where do you live, Godfrey?"

"Belmont, the Mang."

"How old are you?"

"Seventeen."

He dropped the pencil.

"Godfrey, you must be twenty-one to join the Royal Grenada Police Force, and even then, there's all the training. What's all this about?" He glanced at the paper. "Are you a friend of that boy who drowned in Balis Ground?" He looked at me directly. "Do you have some information to give us?"

"I've a feeling. A hunch as they say in the-"

"Godfrey, this is no movie. We work with witnesses and information. Now, I've your name and where you live. If anything, we'll let you know. And about joining the force, come back when you're twenty-one."

I walked away from the police station feeling a little foolish. That young policeman must be laughing still. The vehicles still swirled around the traffic police. He looked at me inadvertently, the way one might look at a bug. On the other side of Gran Etang Road, near the edge of Tyrel Street, I saw a man painting something on a wall. I found it remarkable that the man could sit there and concentrate with all that racket-cars and busses speeding by, horns honking, radios blaring, people shouting.

At first, I thought he might be deaf. I had seen him from a distance before, but never ventured close. This time, I decided to inspect. The policeman shouted as I dodged a bus and darted to the other side of the street. I came up behind the man. He was painting an advertisement on a low wall.

His feet were bare, toes spread out on black asphalt. They gripped the surface as if unsure of gravity and were trying hard to keep him attached to the earth. Dungaree pants rode high on his calves; his shirt had no sleeves. When I looked at his arms, my heart bounced. Two small limbs protruded from his shoulders-black featherless chicken wings covered by ashy black skin. He held a small brush in the crux of the small appendage where an elbow should have formed. I had a full view of his face from where I stood. Above his wide nose sat eyes the shade of newly rusted steel and his hair was bleached red by the sun. He worked looking over his right shoulder, his mouth twisted by a strange frown.

I couldn't believe what he was doing. He applied the paint slowly, delicately. I figured that if a man with no arms could do such work, why not me? I have arms; thank God for arms to carry my schoolbooks. Can he swim? Can he eat food? How does he take a piss or wipe his ass? Lord, have mercy.

I stood and watched. The advertisement gradually took form. The man sat on his wooden toolbox close to the wall; three containers of paint rested on the asphalt near his feet. Smoke rose out of the cup he had already drawn close to the can he was now creating on the wall. The smoke looked wispy, as if it could move.

He glanced at me sideways as he filled in the space around the cup and can. I had an idea about what he might be thinking: *Go on boy get de hell away from here before ah vehicle run your ass over and dey blame me. Wat de hell you standing dere looking at?* But no words crossed his lips. Must be a mute? Finally, he wrote the words: *DRINK OVALTINE.*

The man stopped daubing the paint as if I had interrupted. He stood, toppled the box he was sitting on with one foot, and began using his toes as if they were fingers. He opened the toolbox and placed his brushes and paints inside, and then he fastened the two clasps with his toes. He sneered, kind of bemused, when he saw me gawking. But then he tilted his head, motioning toward the box. He wanted me to pickup the box. I grasped the handle and lifted the box, expecting him to take it from me. It was heavy. He just turned and started walking toward the Carenage. I followed him, the heavy box in my right hand and my bag of books in the other.

Is his voice like his body? Men do sound like they look. A man walked by and shouted, "Fins! You found a helper, boy!" The man chuckled and moved on. Fins said nothing, but I liked what I heard. A helper. Yes, I can be that. I left him near a gate with his box. A piece of board attached to the gate read, FINS SIGNS.

The next evening, I faked a detention to get away from my friends again. Fins didn't acknowledge me when I walked into his shop on the Carenage. He sat on his ass applying a viscous solution to an old sign, and then scraping a multi colored goop off the wood. He then commenced to sand the section of board with sandpaper attached to a piece of two by four strapped to the sole of his feet with two strands of rubber. It looked like a strange shoe. Fins cleaned the board in a matter of minutes, and then he picked up a thin blade with his big toe and its near neighbor, began carving a segment of cardboard into various shapes.

His shop looked messy. Paint cans, pieces of wood, sawdust, and mildewed signs with flaking paint, all this littered his surroundings. A closed door and drawn blinds stimulated my curiosity about what lay in the space just off the shop. I decided to make myself useful. The old straw broom standing near the pile of scraps in the corner beckoned to me like a new friend.

People came to his shop from time to time, picking up stuff and giving him money. After pursuing him and cleaning his shop for nearly a week, he finally spoke to me. He looked at me and spoke as if something standing between us had finally collapsed.

"Call me Ezra. Dat's wat my mother called me, God bless her soul. I hate the name Fins. De place looks good since you been cleaning," he said. "You doing ah good job. Take this." He handed me two-dollar coins, money enough to see several movies.

"I don't want money," I said. "I want to learn this."

"You want to learn dis, huh? Take de money, boy. Dis is no child's play." He stood with one hand extended holding two coins.

I thought he might be offended by my refusal. I took the money.

"Don't pay me any ... Just show me how to..." I pointed at a big sign with a list of provisions and prices, all tidy and bedecked on a black background with small white flowers.

"Okay so you want to learn?" Fins smiled and cocked his head to one side. It reminded me of the way Karrol reacted to jokes.

"Wat you know about patterns?" He asked.

The question caught me by surprise. "You mean what women use to sew clothes?" I said.

"No. No. Not tailoring-in music, in de waves on de shore, in plants, and fruits. As babies, we learn life by identifying patterns-like ah mother's face. Takes determination. Concentration, good eyes, good eyes." He glared at me and gestured at his face with the tip of his right fin. "You need all dat. If you have dat, ah can teach you to make ah decent living with lines and light. Capture some of dose patterns. Make dem do what you want dem to do. Wen you see dem trying to lie, well, treat dem like a child."

He smiled, exposing worn, jagged teeth. I imagined him using them to move objects. I could only think of him as Fins. Ezra just didn't fit. Now that I had him speaking, I decided to venture, try to contrive.

"What you think of people from Saint Vincent?" I asked.

"Wat?" The word left his mouth traveling on a fine spume of spit. He looked at me with a vexed face. Oh shit, I thought, I wrecked this already. "Everybody knows how ah feel about Vincentians," he said. "Doctor who gave meh mother de pills," he waved both fins, "came from Saint Vincent. Why you asking me?"

"Bunch of Vincentians killed my friend. They made it looked as if he drowned, but…"

"You mean Anna's boy. Dey killed him, huh. Wicked. Wat you going to do about it?" He spoke and stuck out his lips as if pointing at me with his mouth. I knew I had found an ally.

"Haven't figured that out yet," I said.

Fins shrugged and puffed out a modest laugh as if he might offer a suggestion. But then he spoke sideways.

"How's Ethan? He's ah good fisherman. Sometimes he brings in more dan fish you know."

He spoke, and swiped his tongue over ample African lips. The new slant of his words made me uneasy. I listened without comment.

Days turned to weeks, and Fins introduced me to straight edges, triangles, and squares, the rulers of illustration he called them. Start little and work towards big. Exactly what did he mean by making a living with lines and light? Removing old paint, sanding and painting shop signs, all this became boring after a short time. He must have noticed, because he did something that altered our relationship just slightly.

He fed me salt-fish souse and tight-bread that day. We washed the food down with orange Fanta. After the meal, he invited me into the section where he lived. I felt uneasy when the door closed behind me. The place smelled like wet dogs. But in the room, and down along the walls sat the meaning of lines and light. I had seen drawings and paintings before, in churches, on the walls of the library, but nothing like these.

Fishermen in rowboats, large-breasted African women dancing wildly, colors and light liberated everything. Pan-men in a road-march, twisted, curious smiles, as if they had to hold their mouths in a certain way to bang the notes out of the steel. The fruits and the crops, the bright yellow of ripe bananas, the deep brown of cocoa and nutmegs with the red of secretive mace barely peeking out; the brilliance, everything shouted and dazzled me. For an instant I felt dizzy; but there was more.

Off to one side, in a corner stood one big canvas depicting black slaves fighting a battle against soldiers and white farmers firing guns. It looked unfinished. Large empty patches dotted the canvas. I moved closer to it and Fins came up behind me. If he had hands, I imagined that he might have rested them on my shoulders, but if he had, it would have made me very nervous. God, how could he have done this without hands? What would he be if he had hands with fingers?

"Fedon's Rebellion," he said from behind me. "History, boy. Dese must be appreciated with more dan your eyes."

Near the slave-revolt canvass stood another big blue picture. It looked like a depiction of seawater stretching to infinity below a high bluff. But as I looked closer, a drama unfolded. Native Indian figures were looking down on the rough sea crashing into the rocks below. Some of the figures were airborne, off the cliff in mid air. Others were tossing smaller figures-children I presume-down into the rough seas and rocks below. Further into the painting, and out across the water was a bright red spot.

"What's that?" I moved closer and pointed.

"Don't touch," he shouted as if I were a young child about to stick my hand in fire. "Kick 'Em Jenny, de jail of de two old spirits. You never heard of dem? Teachers don't teach you children anything in school dese days." He smiled and moved between me, and the painting as if protecting it. "Dis is a story. Not in words but in lines, colors, and light. De Caribs were already here with deir spirit, Mabouya. De white men thought it would be easy to make slaves of dem. Dose natives had other ideas and ah war started. De whites killed dem quickly with de guns. De last ones decided to deprive the white beasts of food. De Caribs were cannibals, so dey supposed de whites were also. Dey got rid of each oder just like dat," he gestured at the depiction of the natives being thrown and jumping off the bluff.

"De white men went to Africa and brought us Africans here, in chains, in de belly of ships, so our spirit, Dambala, came with us. After ah time, Dambala and Mabouya quarreled over who should rule dis land now dat de Caribs were gone. De fight lasted for months. Drought came in hard on everything. Wind almost blew all de dirt off of dis rock. Dry thunder cracked all night. Everyone hid inside wen de cane fields started to burn. Dambala knew dat if dis continued, all would be lost. So, he decided on a sacrifice. He tricked Mabouya into meeting him on de bottom of de sea for an agreement. De moment Mabouya arrived Dambala made de earth fold around dem. De heat from de long fight created ah boiling soup of rocks under de ocean. Ah volcano. We call it Kick 'Em Jenny. Right out dere, under de water. One day, Dambala and Mabouya will escape dat jail and swallow all of us, just like everybody believe dey did to dat vessel, de Island Queen. Ever heard of her?" I stood there, looking at him, expecting more. His tales staggered me, left me intoxicated. He looked away. "Dey should teach you children more about this Grenada."

Everything about the place and the man left me mystified, dreamlike. I wanted to ask him, about the vessel called the Island Queen and much more. But he was talking again, motioning with his little fins, and moving toward other pictures scattered along the wall. "Meh sister in Miami. Ah send her a few of dese every month and she sells dem. De history paintings hardly sell. People want to buy pictures of de fisherman, de cocoa and de nutmeg, sweet colors, decorations. Dey can't connect to de blood and de tears dat sanctified dis place. So, I give dem wat dey want. Den ah draw de oders for me-very little color, sometimes one or two. Very little light or shadows. Mountain-fog over Gran Etang. You look at it and it begs you to interpret. Take a look at dese for instance."

Other drawings leaned on the wall down near the floor. Different breeds entirely, depicting sheer misery. A dead dog in the middle of a black asphalt road, eyes oozing out of bloody sockets. Seagulls twisted up in fishing twine; the naked torso of a woman rendered in a silver-white pigment, no arms, no legs, mouth and eyes wide open in what could only be an ungodly scream.

The largest of these pictures depicted another naked woman rendered in flesh tones. All her skin pulled tight against jutting bones. Big eyes bulged as though she might be trying to smile, or scream, but was unable to do either. She looked painful. Why would anyone waste paint and time on something that wretched? We left the room; Fins looked as if showing me the paintings and telling the stories had caused him pain. I asked this question attempting to console him.

"Why did you start to draw and paint? How did you…"? The last words refused to leave my mouth. I didn't want to insult him by speaking about his deformity or expressing myself with naïveté. Relief propped me up when Fins answered my unfinished question.

"Ah wanted, friends, people to like me," he said. "Ah would draw something and de kids at school, dey would look amazed and smile instead of calling meh names and looking at meh with scorn."

The look on his face, the sad tone of his voice, and the way he shifted his weight and moved. Fins suddenly became more than a charisma. I had never thought of our arms as a means of balance, wings on a bird, but with Fins it became obvious the way he waddled. His expressions of the needs for love and acceptance made my heart ache.

"But how did you learn to do this; who thought you?"

"Ah didn't have to… It just came to me little by little," he said.

Two days later, Fins started instructing me in a technique that he called picturing. I had to close my eyes and see, visualize a whole design before committing a single line. All this came to me easy. Closing my eyes, I could see details, colors, all the way from beginning to end. This exercise gave me tremendous pleasure. I knew I had found my calling. Nothing else mattered, not even my relationship with Yvette. One day I tried to skip school and skulk around his shop, but he ran me off. "Ah teaching you nothing else until you go back to school, every day," he said.

Learning Fin's trade was not as easy as it first appeared. But my newfound pride in the apprenticeship had given me a new direction from which to approach my suspicions about the death of Karrol

Lagrenade. So, I used every ounce of my common sense on the skills he demonstrated, and applied my visualization to everything in sight.

The sign shop on the Carenage became my place of refuge. I should have known that there would be questions, from Yvette, from my aunt Grace. The belief that I was learning to be an artist appeased my aunt, but not Yvette. I drew a picture of her, and she said it made her look constipated, trying hard to take a shit. I understood what she saw. I should have paid more attention to the eyes.

My father had returned from one of his trips. He did his usual thing: pulled up the floorboard near the bookcase and placed a wad of bills into a metal box he kept there. He asked his usual questions with the box of money sitting on the floor between us. I told him about Fins and my new preoccupation.

"He looks so… how do he do-?" My father spoke, screwed up his face, his eyes raked me up and down. "They say he's more than a sign painter. I saw one of his drawings once, and it sent shivers up my spine. A lone fisherman curled up in the fetal position on the floor of his boat, out at sea, lightening ripping the clouds above him. The figure looked dead. That's what you want to spend your spare time doing, go ahead. Find out all you can, who knows. But be careful." For the first time I had an urge to hug and kiss my father. He placed the box back into the floor, nailed the board into place and repositioned the bookcase.

Fins taught me how to create perspectives, angles, and vanishing points. He spoke about confronting reality. Reinventing it, make it big, rude and bright. Give the picture the power to jump up and slap people on the face. It had been some time since we started the lessons, and I knew that this world would be mine. I wanted it badly. Between lessons, I asked him concrete questions, attempting to smooth things, curry favor, and draw out the man.

"Your parents still alive?" I asked.

"Meh mother pass on ah long time ago. Wen ah was born, my father took one look at me, got on ah boat and we never hear from him gain. He was ah Vincey, too."

"You ever listen to them? They talk funny. And they killed Karrol to give that vessel a soul.

"They killed who? Oh yeah, to give dat vessel a soul, huh. So what you doing about it?"

"Planning."

Fins insisted that I do the small stuff: cut and paste, draw exact outlines, fill the outlines with the proper colors. The cutting and the painting, the billboards and the store signs, all were good for something. Now and again, he would give me money, but that seemed paltry compared to what I had in mind. I wanted to know how to compel my pictures to dance, how to render a soft smile on the face of a woman as if she might be inviting you to kiss her. I knew this could only be done if you get the eyes right. All these things were coming together nicely until one evening a further side of the man came at me out of a bottle of rum. It was as if the spirit in the bottle acquired a physical form called Fins.

It was a Friday, and everybody was out enjoying the start of the weekend. The sun melted into the sea, and left stains of orange smeared into chunks of black clouds hanging low on the horizon. Around 6:30, I decided to go to Empire Theater to see the early show. There was some time to waste, and I knew where to spend it.

Fins hardly looked at me when I entered the shop. I walked across the yard toward him. He sat on the workbench, cardboard scraps all around, a bottle of River Antoine rum and one glass next to him. No water.

He wore no shirt. A pair of sweat-soaked khaki shorts covered his lower trunk. I had no idea that he drank rum. The man grasped the bottle between his two small appendages and poured the rum into the shot glass. He brought the bottle back to the bench, and set it upright. Then he reached down low for the little glass of rum, and cradled it all the way up to his lips. There was a suckling noise as the liquid left the glass slowly and entered his mouth. He didn't spill a drop. He licked his lips and brought the glass down to rest on the bench.

"What you doing here?" The question left his mouth with wickedness. He looked wounded, nothing like the man who had shown me the pictures and told me stories. My teacher and friend had turned into this churlish jumby.

"You sick?" I asked.

"Sick? Sick fuck." The words left his mouth like the hiss of a snake.

"You want to go? Ah was going to de movie," I said.

"Movies. Ha ha ha. Dey have arms, all of dem."

Dabs of white foam sat at the corners of his lips. He extended a pink tongue and licked, first the left, then the right side. His eyes looked wet and miserable.

"Come with me. It's a serial, with Richard Widmark," I said.

"Ah hate 'em, ah hate 'em all. All dose white people, dey holding each other, and crying looove." He pursed his lips. "You know wat… women enjoy de touch, de feel of arms and big fingers, on de skin, and holding… Only whores allow me to touch, and even whores."

He hacked deep, cleared his throat and nose into his mouth and spat at me. I jumped back. The wad of spittle and mucus hit the ground and spread out near my feet. His eyes began twitching and I had a feeling he might start sobbing like a child. So, I refused to look at his face. His bare chest sported clumps of damp hair, his balls squeezed out of one leg of his shorts. Our eyes met again, and that reminded me of another incident.

Karrol, Ian, Checklea and I, we found the old dog Moocher sleeping and dreaming in the dust under a tree. The dog was moaning and fidgeting. A hint of a smile played around the edge of his lips. We found string, tied it around a large rock, and slowly slipped it around Moocher's balls. Then we shouted. The dog leaped up, the knot tightened, and Moocher came crashing back to the ground, rolling and yelping.

My father came up behind us, rapped Karrol and me on the back of the head, and reprimanded us about cruelty and wickedness. Moocher allowed my father to cut the string with his bait knife, but as the dog limped away, it glanced back at us with spite. That same expression now sat on Fins' face and I had no idea why he would harbor any bitterness towards me.

"What de fuck you staring at, jerk boy?" he asked. "You feel sorry for me? Don't be getting sorry for me. Ah kick you in your ass."

Rage boiled up in me. If he had arms, I may not have broached the idea. He came off the bench, swayed and puffed his chest. I saw the chunk of pitch pine out of the corner of my left eye. He kicked a cardboard box and started waddling toward me like a big man-bird. I took two steps back, moved left, and picked up the two-by-four. One hit to the knee; as he crumble, split his head like an egg. No one will know. My thoughts made the air taste cleaner. I felt powerful-God with a piece of board in his hand.

"Get your ass out of here," he shouted. "And don't come back. You hear me? You cockroach." He stood before me as if ready for a fight. But then he slowly split in two, broke up in the weak light. I ran my left hand across both my eyes; my fingers came away wet, and Fins came back into focus.

"Walk!" he bellowed. "Go before ah stomps your guts out. Little chicken shit coward, People killed your friend, and all you can do is plan. Ah planning," he stuck his face close to mine, disregarding the board in my hand. Rancid breath, the aroma reeked in my nose; drops of spit hit my face. My muscles tightened, my fingers squeezed the piece of wood tight, splinters dug into my palm. I clenched my teeth, the muscles in my legs contracted, but before I could strike, I stepped backward and threw the piece of wood. It made a dull clangor where it hit the floor.

"Chicken shit, coward!" he repeated. "No balls. Dey hired me to paint her name. Port, starboard, and stern. Know wat dat mean? She'll be gone soon. Wat you gona do den?"

His words stung me. I turned away from Fins and ran for a moment. Noises spilled from the rum shops, music mixed with loud voices. Seawater slapped against the concrete wharf, everything churning and grinding. The hulls of fishing boats groaned against the tire bumpers used to keep them off the concrete. Slow crushing motions. Fuck you, Fins. Chicken wings, chicken fucker. I'll show you coward.

My guts boiled. All that time I spent liming with a bowlegged Jumpy? I felt like a drunk who had fallen asleep on the ground, came awake, and realized that someone had pissed all over me.

The movies became the last thing on my mind. I moved around the Carenage, searching for a boat with a spare gas can. When I found the one, the can was empty. I went quietly into a shop near the wharf and bought kerosene, and a box of matches. At the inner harbor, near Tanteen, the vessel, *Miss Irene* stood completely rigged. The masts, booms, and stanchions stretched in place, and the hull painted a greenish blue that matched the sea. She stood complete, except for her sails.

I moved around the harbor with the can in my hand. No movement around the vessel. Weekend-no one should be around. The gangway buckled and groaned as I moved onto the deck. All of me trembled. My temples drummed hard enough to cause a headache, the thumping of my temples matched the beat of my heart. At first, I thought of starting below, but changed my mind. If they caught me down there, I would be dead, just like Karrol.

The kerosene smelled foul as I splashed it around the deck while scanning the area to make sure no one was watching. I tried hard to keep the liquid off my shoes and clothes. This kerosene may not be enough for what I have in mind, the thought occurred to me, but I had already started. No going back now.

If she had sails, I might have started it in the canvas. Instead I struck a match, and threw it at the fuel on the deck. The fire jumped off the wood and into the air, a soft blue, iridescent, it followed the trail of kerosene across the planks and illuminated the deckhouse. I watched it for a moment, transfixed. Then a voice inside my head whispered, "RUN! RUN!"

CHAPTER 6

Two days went by and then my past lumped around me only to contract in chunks like a snake loosing its skin.

"Godfrey."

The voice came from a spot off the road, behind a plunk of banana and breadfruit trees. The figure blended so subtly into the bush, I didn't see him until he moved. He stood, grasped a stick and came into the road, limping, but bouncy. I had a suspicion that he might have been waiting for me. He had a look in his eyes that resembled a hunter that had just bagged something. It was Sydney, Karrol's uncle.

I was torn between two desires, catching up with Yvette and her sister, Yoelina, and wanting to know why Sydney waited for me on the side of the road. Since I had been going to Fins shop, none of my friends waited for me after school. The girls were walking behind a group of guys, Ian, Cosmus, and Marsden. I could hear Yvette, if I had caught up with them: *Well look, he honors us with his presence. No Fins today?* The need to know what Sydney wanted took precedence.

"I had no idea you loved him that much," Sydney said.

"He was my friend."

"Kerosene is a slow-burning fuel," he said, lowering his eyes. "Gasoline would have worked best."

"What you talking about? I don't know what you talking about."

"I saw you on that vessel Friday night," he said.

34

A miserable feeling came over me. The words hit me like a rough clout, so much, so fast. I needed him to slow down; give me time to think. His voice sounded like the night howl of a dog.

Two days, two days I didn't see or hear anything about a fire onboard *Miss Irene*. I was unwilling to go down there and look at what I had done. But that Monday morning, on my way to school, there was no going by without looking. I expected to see a derelict, burned and swamped; instead she stood there as if nothing had happened. My failed attempt to burn the vessel made me self-conscious and deliberate. That funny sensation followed me around that day and into the evening. Since there was no more fins shop, I skulked far back from my group, and walked alone.

Sydney strolled beside me in the evening sun. I struggled to find words to deny what he had just said. What will he do? We reached the gap leading up to his house, and we stood under the coconut tree, saying nothing for an awkward moment. I was too afraid to move.

"When's your father getting back this time?" he asked.

"Next week. He went to Saint Vincent."

"Still hanging around with those pirates, huh?" Sydney mumbled. I decided to ignore that remark.

"The vessel is headed to Trinidad next," I said.

"Well, we know what that means," he said. "Come eat dinner with us." He spoke, looked at me, and then moved off before I could reply.

The man limped up the path, leaning heavy on his stick. I didn't want to go to any place where I would have to deal with the memories of Karrol Lagrenade or the consequences of my failure. But I couldn't refuse to eat with them. Not with what he knew. I could see Sydney talking to that same young policeman. They would come and arrest me, take me to jail. Later that evening, around 6:30, I stood at the gap leading up to Sydney and Xudine's house, the place we called the Jupa.

This was my first visit to this place. Like most houses in the little village by the sea, Sydney and Xudine's consisted of a galvanized tin roof and pine-board walls. Its height, roundness, and the story of its construction set it apart. People said it was the fastest house ever built on the island of Grenada. Men came with a bulldozer, posts, boards, and galvanized sheets. In one month the structure was completed, but the death of a carpenter from a fall off the roof bequeath the place a peculiar reputation.

The house looked like a tall, rickety barrel with windows. It sat near a garden cultivated with tomatoes, carrots, pumpkins, and flowering vines that crawled up sticks and chicken wire. Paths made of flat rocks led here and there throughout the garden, around the house and between the trunks of breadfruit and coconut trees. From the outside, the place looked charming and curious; it reminded me of cottages I had seen in books of *Brothers Grimm Fairy Tales*.

Sydney greeted me at the door and we entered the house. On the inside, the house was decorated with braided straw partitions, and mats of various colors: red, green, yellow, and black. The place appeared smaller and tidy. The bed sat behind a straw wall. I could see only one end from the spot where I sat in a chair at the little mahogany dinning table that Sydney had guided me toward. A stronger, black wall separated one other room from the section where we sat. That room was the kitchen where I could hear Xudine humming a tune.

Rumor had it that Xudine would use no straw unless it came from Marquis, up near Grenville. The partitions of colors excited me. I had seen nothing like this before. A shelf made of wattles held several big books. I had no idea that Sydney or Xudine could read. The big wicker chairs where Sydney sat completed the trimmings in the Jupa. I felt very edgy about the kerosene lamps they used for light. It reminded me of the story about the boy who played with matches in the cane.

Dinner consisted of fried fish, boiled yams and buttered rice. Xudine served the food on green clay plates, decorated with little yellow flowers. She told me these were Karrol's favorite foods, and the food lost all taste. We ate deliberately. The spoons clanged on the plates and our mouths made noises. The whole proceeding seemed hurried without the convenience of conversation. The last scrap of food hit my mouth, and Xudine stood, grabbed the dishes, and ducked into the kitchen. What now? Regret gnawed at me, but Sydney rescued me with words that sounded like a dare that could have been thrown down by Karrol, Ian or any of my friends.

"Only truly stout people have the nerves to ask," he said. "How about you? Most people want to know but…" He looked at me as if he might wink. I had no idea what that dreaded question could be. "I could stub my foot, a toe could break off, my shoe would fill with blood, and that's the only way I could tell I was wounded. That's leprosy."

I really wanted to know about Sydney's affliction, but the way he tossed it at me. My back itched, my ass felt hot against the chair. His eyes kept blinking in the dim light. It took a great effort to stay focused on his face.

"People think they know something about this," he continued. "They look at me, embarrassed, and at times guilty, as if they had anything to do with it. They think I caught this in the Amazon, but it happened right here, in Grenada. I was fourteen years old. The thing sat in my blood and waited. It came here with two English missionaries, from Madras, India. They were on their way to South America to spread the word of God. They spread more than the words of God. They had a son, Terrance. You and Karrol reminded me…"

Sydney glanced around panic-stricken, as if he might call out for Xudine, but then he looked back at me. His eyeballs looked glistened, teary. But his voice remained steady, focused.

"Joining the missionaries was as easy as drinking a cup of water," he said. "After my father vanished at sea, Grenada seemed a little, you know. And we needed money."

The light from the kerosene lamp flashed erratically. An abrupt burst of rain-laden wind made the shadows pitch and tilt in a wild dance across the walls of many colors. The house vibrated as if some ghost might be warning Sydney. The wind moved on. I heard it dashing to the sea, whistling through bananas, breadfruits, and palm trees, then silence. An owl hooted into the stillness that followed, and then Sydney's voice seized the moment again.

"Godfrey, at first, it had little to do with religion," he said. "I worked for them. They paid me, and I sent the money home. They schooled me right along with Terrance and the native kids. It took Terrance and I about a year to catch the gist of the Palikur language, a branch of Arawak, but by the end of the second year, we were speaking it as if we were our mother-tongue. His parents were two of the most pious white people I have ever met. How they managed to breed," Sydney flashed me a roguish glanced. "I could never imagine that woman with her legs spread wide," he said. "I guess biology takes its course regardless."

He smiled and both sides of his lips turned up, exposing stubs of teeth. He ran one crooked hand over his hairless face as if wiping something away. Two small puffs of air escaped his nostrils and he dug with one finger into each hole as if trying to dislodge something atrophied inside his face.

"Life is so full of strange dealings," he spoke and brought his hand down into his lap. "Your friend Ezra, the one they call Fins, we went to school together. Kids were so cruel to him. The same drug that made him what he is, it saved me. The North Americans call it thalidomide. His mother used it for morning sickness. They used the same drug on me years later to arrest this leprosy." That urge to interrupt gripped me, but his words made me swallow instead.

"Wicked gossipmongers," he whispered. "So many one-mouths. For a time, everyone around here claimed my mother sold me to those white people. They said that's where she got the money for her house and bakery; now you hearing more of that same old…always talking shit. They saying Anna sold her son to give that vessel a soul, and others going on about how she put a curse on Cyril's wife. The fools even brought the children's name into it. They saying Yolan, Cyril's oldest girl went up to Sateurs, turned that old curse back on Anna." He laughed and shook his head. "You listen to them, and you get the impression. No accidents any time. That's why her husband left her. That's why she lost her son. I hear them. They go silent when I walk by. I feel bad for Anna.

"Don't listen, Godfrey. Anna loves her children too much for that. That asshole Ned, in Trinidad, playing Saga-boy, didn't even show for his own son's funeral. It's a good thing she finds some comfort with Cyril. Jealousy, boy, they all just covetous of her success with bread. The scriptures said: 'Wherefore, laying aside all malice, and all guile, and hypocrisies, and envies, and all evil speaking, as newborn babes, desire the sincere milk of the word.'"

He filled his lungs with a long noisy draw of air, held it for a moment as if replenishing his cells. He exhaled and the wind escaped his nostrils with a slight whistle. A whiff of decay slid under my nose.

"Uncle Sydney, what you think really happened to Karrol?" The words tasted sore as I realized I was asking him the same question I had asked Mama Viche.

Sydney cocked his head; his eyes blinked twice in that strange, lizard way.

"Anything could have happened," he said. "What you driving at?"

"He was a good swimmer. We lived in the sea," I said.

"That could be it. Impudence, and the sea have a way of taking advantage of that. He could have tried to swim out to the vessel, cramped up. Could have hit his head on one of those booms," he shrugged.

"What if he made it out to the vessel and one of those Vinceys got vex."

"Godfrey, you dancing with your double's ghost. Careful what you choose to let in. What you believe becomes you," he stared me down as if looking for something on my face. "But Anna," he continued. "You can always tell with a woman like her. Could never have done what they saying. You see how she kneads that dough, baking it, carrying it around to the shops. I remember our mother doing the same thing. One day, they found the old woman dead on the ground, bread scatted all around, I was deep in the Amazon, didn't hear about her death for almost a year."

He went silent. A muddled moment embraced me. I wanted to hear anything that would lead me to certainty. Xudine came back to us. She carried three cups in two hands. A cotton skirt covered her from her waist to just above her knees. She wore nothing else.

She bent and handed me the cup of steaming, black-sage tea. Her brown breasts hung in my face. Her nipples were the color of ripe plums. Seeing her naked from a distance was nothing. I shifted my weight, brought my legs together to conceal my growing anxiety. I took the cup from her fingers, cradled it in my palms, and took comfort from the heat.

"Drink," she said. "Make you sleep soft, bathe your dreams." She smiled, exposing a mouth-full of stout teeth.

The steam from the cup warmed my face as I placed the rim on my lips. We sat in a nice, final silence. They didn't invite me back. It would be a week before I saw Sydney again. And even then, I had to connive, worm my way in; nothing seemed as vital as staying close to the keeper of my secret.

CHAPTER 7

The gray broth resembled thick dirty water. It sat in a shallow bowl with bits and pieces floating: crushed cloves, garlic, thyme, and chunks of celery with little onions-the rest, half-ripe bananas, bluggoes, and some Jacks. She fed us this meal on the night of my second visit to the Jupa. It looked nothing like it tasted. Her food contained less salt than I was accustomed to, but the tang of the spices compensated for all it lacked. Conversation seemed so necessary.

"Where did your people come from, Xudine?" I said. "I mean in the beginning." The question came out of my mouth sounding clumsy. I knew that no one had uprooted her people and transplanted them far across the world as the Europeans had done to mine.

She perceived my question in a whole new way, and I was relieved. Bit by bit, she spoke, sounding something like this: "'from the claws of the two-headed Vulture King," she said. "One day, a long, long time ago, the two-headed Vulture King came down and was standing near a river, admiring the great creation. We were in the mud that collected on his claws. He flew away from the riverbank, and we fell from his claws, spreading us across the land. That's how we came to be, all of us.'"

She sounded so sure as she continued to speak about gods and ancestors. She mentioned two things that stuck with me: the Hungura and something called, Yumawalli. But then, she suddenly went silent, collected the dinner dishes, and left the room.

"Uncle Sydney, Hungura and Yumawalli, what are they?" He stared me down with funeral eyes, and then he smiled. The expression on his face reminded me of a traveler, satisfied that he had finally reached his destination.

"The beliefs of these people," Sydney shook his head and threw open both his palms, "their religion is not that simple, Godfrey. To appreciate them, even in the slightest, you must first have a basis, an awareness that might anchor your thinking, or you might jump to some hasty conclusions. Like I did, the time I tried to explain to some rumored cannibals the importance of the body and the blood of Jesus Christ. They all sat there calmly, smiling, and then they asked me if my name was Jesus. Their attempt at humor didn't make me comfortable."

The dishes jangled. Xudine hummed a melody that sounded like the tattle of birds. Crickets and tree frogs accompanied her. Down Lagoon Road, the bark of a dog mingled with a car horn penetrating the night from far off.

"Let me tell you about Xudine's brother, the man known among his people as, Azymu, the savior. We traveled for almost three weeks, down the Vaca and into the forest of Brazil. Quite an occasion the day when we met." Sydney looked up and flashed me a quick smile. "Terrance was diagnosed with leprosy and his parents took him back to England. As a servant they no longer needed, I had two choices. I could come back here, to Grenada, or stay with the other missionaries, wait for the new boss. See if we were compatible. I chose to wait and see.

"Azymu came into the mission between the two rivers, the Urukaua and Vaca. Missionaries from our faction came from all over the world, spend their few months or a year, contending for native souls. Azymu came up to me one day and asked me to tell him about the dead Christian called Jesus. He was a stout little fellow with jet-black hair and a face as round as a full moon. I had never heard Jesus referred to as the dead Christian before. Azymu told me an old chief called Iti taught him to speak the words, which Iti had learned from his father, who stole the words from missionaries many years ago. The whole thing sounded peculiar. Stolen words?

"I couldn't remember the story of Jesus from birth to crucifixion, so I decided to relate the account in fragments. I started with the Immaculate Conception, worked my way to Herod's decree, the journey to Bethlehem, and the three wise men at the manger. I filled in with the baptism by John the Baptist, the days of wandering in the wilderness and the offer made to Jesus by the devil.

"When I got to the part about the shores of Galilee and Jesus walking across the water, Azymu smiled a smile that showed all his teeth. I sort of muddled through the section about the loaf of bread and the three fishes used to feed the multitude. When I got to the Sermon on the Mount, a visible glee covered his face. But then I started talking about Judas Iscariot, the incident in Gethsemane, and the run by Pilote to start up to Golgotha, Azymu shook his head vigorously and stopped me by waving all his fingers.

"'They all take this trail. Every time?'"

"His question astonished me. He must have noticed my reaction, because his next words came out with the intention to clarify."

"'All your Jesuses, they get the same… I asked a man in Carapuchi to tell me about the dead Christian called Jesus, and he told me a story of a warrior priest killed by his enemies.'

"'We have only one Jesus, and this happened a long time ago,'" I told him.

"'How do you remember?'" he asked.

"'We have the book. The Bible.'"

"'Many have told me of the book and read to me from this book. I need to know. I listen, I see beyond shadows. Like looking into water. You look past your own face. In moments of calm, you could see the face of the messenger who spoke to us long ago, telling us that we are mortal. Could that be the same one?'

"For the next three months, the man lived around the mission. He would disappear for days at a time, but eventually he would return. I knew no Bible student like him. He always seemed to have questions, and as he perused the simple tracts, more oddities surfaced from his inquiries.

"The man had the soul of a poet. The way he forced words to conform to what he wanted to convey. Everything he said formed pictures. He spoke in allegories, in tales. He forced me to listen with more than my ears. He once warned me of the river of blood that flows from the ancestors to the spirits and then to the God who dwells in the great hut in the sky, the one whose footsteps are thunder.

"Day after day he stuck with the religious studies as if something more than saving his soul might be at stake. In that time, I knew he had the story of Jesus straight, but he still took off on small tangents, attempting to convince me of other aspects of Jesus as it related to his world.

"He once compared Jesus to the Hawk Spirit, who helped to bring back the world after the flood. Another time he told me Jesus is the same spirit who lives in man, animals, and trees, often lives on the wind, and in the rain, but can also hurl the fire of the sun.

"One night we sat admiring the stars. We had become good friends. So his silence troubled me. I pestered him out of his contemplation, and the words that came from his mouth hit me like large drops of rain on a bright sunny, day."

"'We have a custom…the same as your Jesus and crucifixion,' he said. "'We know the importance of body and blood. My people came out of blood. They had to shed blood when they stole the words from the mouths of the others. So, like the long time ago, blood will be shed. I am chosen.' Godfrey, there was a look of ecstasy about him, the kind that can only be conveyed through the testicles."

Sydney smiled.

"It's getting late, Godfrey. We're going up to Grenville for a couple days. We'll see you when we get back."

I held back my sudden urge to protest and shuffled home that night, cuddling my expectations. The next morning, on my way to school with some of the guys, I spied Sydney and Xudine, waiting near the Botanical Garden for the bus that would take them into the countryside. They stood very close, like two blind people. They reminded me of the morning my father met them on the shore to go search for Karrol. I waved quickly and they waved back. I walked on in the company of my friends, looking back only after the screech of the brakes. The bus stopped and hid them from my view.

CHAPTER 8

That evening, my father came back to Grenada from his trip north. He walked up to the house with his old grip in one hand. He had grown a beard. The boat was headed south, to Trinidad, so he was through with that job. What came next was a familiar ritual for the small Soulages clan. Every time my father return from an extended trip abroad, Tante Grace would cook dinner at the old house and bring it to ours, along with my two cousins, Julian and Alister, the most well-behaved boys on earth. I always thought she might be beating them, but I saw no bruises. We were at the old table on the veranda, looking at the yacht *Ring Anderson* move smoothly through the channel into the lagoon. Tante Grace was saying lots to my father. I moved closer to hear their conversation. She moved the food, from the pot to the plates, and then onto plates.

"Come and get your food. This is not a restaurant," she turned and saw me listening. "They see everything, they hear everything. Those two. Olga and Rose remind me of God." My aunt laughed at her own irreverence and continued to speak. "The rumor about them must be true," she said.

"Who cares? People always talking shit," my father replied.

The dinner consisted of fish cakes, rice, and sliced ripe plantains.

My aunt always brought out her religion at mealtime, insisting that someone prayer over the food. She pointed to my cousin Alister. He looked at his brother and me as if we could rescue him, and then he made the thanks too short. His mother looked at him as if she would make him do it over. But the three of us dug into the food. Then my father's voice blended with the jangle of spoons and forks.

"I hear you spending time with Sydney and his wife. What you doing over there?"

"He's telling me about South America. Xudine is a good cook."

Tante Grace looked at me quickly, but then she went back to eating. "Be careful, there's lunacy there." She spoke with the food in her mouth.

"Sydney sounds fine to me," I said.

"He's not the one am talking about," said Tante Grace.

"Most crazy people don't know they are crazy." My father looked straight at me. I avoided his gaze, and concentrated on his beard and mustache. This was a new look for him. I didn't like it. It made him look cruel.

"What's he telling you?" My father continued to speak as he shoveled a spoonful of white rice into his mouth. One grain fell from his mouth, and lodged conspicuously in his beard. "Some say, he never made it past Angel Falls." He spoke as he chewed at the food.

"What's the matter? It's just a story. A bunch of words," I said.

My father swallowed. "Godfrey, words have a life of their own."

"You can say that again, brother. In the beginning was the word." I had a feeling that Tante Grace, instead of Rose or Olga, must have told on me.

"You getting where I can't keep an eye on you all the time." He spoke as if he had kept one eye on me all my life. "Everyone tells the truth, or lie for a reason," My father said.

"What can be his-?"

"Who knows? Might want you to spread the word that he's a great explorer or something."

"People around here talking about him like that already," Tante Grace said.

To my surprise, the conversation changed tack without them giving me any don'ts. I was relieved. Although I recognized the scraps of truths in their words, I resented their meddling. I knew repeating what my father had said would be a kind of betrayal, but I intended to say something to Sydney anyway. We ate the rest of the food as my father and his sister laughed and spoke about stuff from abroad.

The next day, the sky looked so clear you get the impression that if you stared straight up, hard enough, you could see all the way to heaven. Yachts sat tugging on their anchors in the lagoon near the Yacht Service. Ian and some of the guys had invited me to go hunting, but I cried off, planning to spend some time with Yvette. We went to the beach at Mon Pandy, and then I promised to show her how to fly a kite, knowing that this was a sure way to get very close to her. But in spite of these clean and tidy moments, my true desires hinged on Sydney and Xudine.

We stood in the center of the field just down the road from Yvette's house. A big bamboo kite sailed high in the sky above us. I knew the flyer, a fellow from up near Springs. He would frequently surprise us by swooping down like a vulture, cutting strings, forcing us to pull our smaller kites from the sky. We called him the kite bully. Whenever he was up there, we kept our eyes open. I decided to show off for Yvette by placing a blade in the tail of my kite. I could hear her talking as I gauged the wind, preparing to launch.

" . . . He's liming with those trouble makers," she said. "What's those Rastas teaching him? Leading him astray. Giving him all that ganja. Smoking up his brains."

"Nobody making him do anything. Ian is a man. And I think Anna is his mother," I said.

She let fly an angry glance and continued to speak with nimble determination. "Anna looks so sad, drinking rum, cursing everybody; hope to God I don't end up like her. Bunch of children with no father. No husband. Ian needs a big brother. Instead, you're gone all the time. First Fins and now Sydney. You have some kind of attraction to those Jumbie people."

The cord tingled the palms of my hand as the kite gathered the force of the wind and shot into the sky. Her question got me. But I said nothing. Yvette made a noise by sucking air through her teeth.

"You think people don't see you sneaking over there all the time," she said.

My little bright-colored kite dodged and dragged on the cord I had borrowed from my father's tackle box. It shimmered and shook on the wind. I took back some of the slack and watched the kite climb high.

At the apex of ascend the kite dodged left and went into a steep dive, almost crashing into the branches of a palm tree. Just before slamming into the tree it came out of the plummet, its tail glanced off the fronds, and it shot back into the sky. Instead of responding to Yvette's acumen, I tried to entice her.

"Take this, let me show you." I offered her the string.

"Keep your damn kite." She waved me off with one flick of her wrist.

It was a good thing. The kite bully inched toward my kite with his razor blade. I pulled on the cord, forcing my kite to duck left and climb higher, but the kite bully followed. Yvette stood looking at us play cat and mouse on the wind. There was no way this fellow could cut my string. I saw his handicap; his kite big, unwieldy, my kite small and nimble. I took slack out of my string as if pulling my kite from the sky. But still staying just above him. He saw my strategy a little late. As he tried to adjust by pulling his kite alongside mine, I allowed my kite to duck right, running the tail right over his string. His kite separated and floated away. Yvette looked at me and shook her head.

"Something as simple as flying a kite and you turn it into a war. Men." She turned and started to walk away.

"Yvette," the voice shouted from the edge of the cane and breadfruit that lined the field. "Wait there." She stopped and looked back at her father. I had the impression that he may have been watching us. He threw me a stern glance as I pulled my kite from the sky, intending to hide just incase the kite bully came looking for the guy who cut his string.

"What's happening, Daddy," she spoke softly. He caught up with her and they walked off. She didn't look back at me.

In order to understand what came to pass between Yvette and me, an appreciation of her father and the history he shared with my family is essential. Cyril learned to fish from my grandfather. One day they went out, and the boat capsized in a storm. Cyril was rescued a few days later, alone. From that day, my father remained arms-length friends with Cyril. They only came together in moments of crisis to assist their neighbors. But after Cyril landed the job that my father craved at the Grenada Yacht Service, their strange friendship became even more strained.

The entire village chitchat about Cyril, but never to his face. That's how I learned about the incidents that transformed him, even those that transpired before I was born. The man had five beautiful daughters: Yolan, Yellis, Yvonne, Yvette, and Yoelina. He guarded this brood of beauties with a sharp machete and a sharper tongue. Their mother had died giving birth to Yoelina, and Cyril never remarried. The oldest girl, Yolan, took care of the house. They say, after the death of his wife, Cyril cursed God every night for two weeks.

Before Cyril landed that part-time job at the Yacht Service, people already perceived him as peculiar. They say the love of his children kept him alive during that incident at sea with my grandfather. When he was rescued and brought ashore the look in his eyes scared everyone. They say he resembled an ancient biblical prophet, and sometimes he acted like one. The man would drink strong rum and sit around for hours, talking nonsense about politicians or anything that happened to cross his mind. No one paid any uncommon attention to him, not even when he mentioned specific names and deeds in his diatribes. Like who got rich from the sale of government land, or who might be taking bribes.

I personally witnessed the final conversion of Cyril Ogilvie. By this time, he had turned into an occasional fisherman—a man that fished alone when he felt like it. Each time he had a good catch, he would drink half the money, and bring the rest home to his children. One Saturday night, Cyril came rowing across the lagoon shouting loud. Most of us knew that Cyril must have been drinking with some sailors and fishermen down on the Carenage, but the information he brought came as a surprise because Cyril was no Rastafarian.

"An emperor is crowned in Africa. You hear me? They crowned an emperor in Africa," he shouted. "That woman in England is not your sovereign. Look to Africa. Look to the bosom of your mother. We crowned an emperor. Prince Tafari, Ras Tafari is your emperor. King of kings, lord of lords, descendant of Solomon."

He preached, shouted, and babbled about Haile Selassie, Marcus Garvey, and the *UNIVERSAL NEGRO IMPROVEMENT ASSOCIATION*. He went on for hours, repeating himself, doubling back to explain, like some preacher wrestling with an intricate sermon. Finally, the police came and arrested him. They kept him for three weeks without bail. My father went to see him, and came back with reports that he was fine. However, Cyril returned a changed man. He started talking about Haile Selassie and Marcus Garvey in his sober time, and he didn't shout anymore. He even started distributing a newspaper, called the NEGRO WORLD. Once a month, he would show up with a new batch. I started reading his newspaper and my association with his daughter benefited.

To this day, I often wonder what road my life and Yvette's would have taken if Cyril had refused that job at the Yacht Service. You see, what existed between Yvette and I could hardly be called a romance or love affair. It was more like an unstated promise, and despite our measured situation, I needed to protect myself by befriending Sydney and Xudine.

When they returned from the country, I almost rushed to the Jupa. But I remembered what Yvette and my father had said. I controlled my urge, waited for darkness. A weak stream of light dispersed near the opened door as I approached the house. Sydney and Xudine sat at the kitchen table with two empty plates.

"Godfrey, you like my tea," she rose from the chair as I entered the house. "I make some to drink." And she left with the two plates.

"Well, where were we?" Sydney asked. His voice reminded me of a teacher nudging his student, attempting to reestablish a link.

"The ceremony, he had just told you about the…"

"Oh yeah! The idea of the whole thing. Jesus! Azymu started talking to me, simple, strait forward.

"'The Paje told me I would come back in the company of a man with the face of night. Always thought it would be a warrior painted with the black paint of the spirit world,' he said. 'But it's you. They wait for us near the place of the old ones. We should be there when the tenth moon cross the jaguar sun.'"

"Godfrey, I had to ask one question, and when I did, he only answered me more of his doggerel."

"'Sydney, the Hawk must seek the sky to settle in the palm of the Great Spirit of Thunder. No man chosen can run and remain the same with the Earth, live within his skin. The Great Serpent would come to torment that flesh. Thirst-quenching rainbows would refuse to touch the ground where he plant seeds. He would drink mud forever, and never see the sun.'"

"A vision of hell, worthy of Dante, Godfrey. Two days later, Azymu packed his few belongings. He had spent no time trying to convince me to go with him. He had only mentioned that one thing about the man with the face of night. Nevertheless, there he was standing before me like a man ready to catch the bus.

"'Ready to go?'

"'No. Not yet. Tomorrow.'" I stalled for the remaining hours, hoping that some great insight would come to me, something to help me sway him or defy his devotion. When nothing materialized, I said to myself: *Jesus, take me into thy care*.

"I was twenty-four years old, full of piss and vinegar. I had to see this, this ritual, these people, try to understand. A few of the missionaries knew of my intentions and tried to talk me out of going.

"Three of them cornered me in my little room, and one fat fellow with a German accent did the talking. 'Sydney, many people go into the bush and never return,' he said. 'I think your friend came from a group thrown out of this tribe many years ago. They murder some missionaries. Fifteen of them stole a Bible and a short-wave radio. They assumed these were the objects we used to speak to God. The elders banished them deep into the forest of Brazil. One priest, a father Montoya, made contact with them many years ago, but when he went back to the place where he had found them, the village was abandoned. Just the skeleton of one person remained. Father Montoya said in his journal that he thought they might have eaten that poor soul. We hear rumors from time to time about some bastard form of Christianity being practiced out there. You will be risking your life, Sydney. Animals, disease, hostile natives, no Eldorado or Garden of Eden out there.'

"They just succeeded in pissing me off, Godfrey. After all, we have our religions and these missionaries were just trying to grow it. All the things that Azymu said to me sounded like religion. What kind of danger could I be in? Azymu spoke English, his whole tribe must also, I assumed. I was a free man; free to do whatever I wanted. I saw the whole thing as a big camping trip from which I would return with stories to tell. Little did I know.

"I secured a few Bibles and some tracts. This was nothing new to me. I had spent time in the bush before-a whole week one time. I had maps of the area we would travel. A Brazilian called Rondon had traveled and mapped the area many years before. He even constructed telegraph lines and stationed soldiers to guard and repair them. I was not headed to a place where no man had gone before. The missionaries held a prayer service for Azymu and me. The other Indians who lived near the mission and attended the school looked at me as if I was crazy. Actually, I felt like one of Christ's disciples.

"We caught a flat-bottom ferry the next day. The old diesel-powered craft, full of rubber tapers and other assorted river rats carried us for four days down a brown channel swelled by rains. The first part of the journey was uneventful. We picked up passengers along the way, dropped cargo; we encountered hazards in the form of floating logs and branches that we dodged successfully. Finally, we docked at a little muddy settlement at the confluence of two tributaries.

"Azymu left me to stand guard over our provisions. When I saw him next, he was painted red and paddling a dugout against the current. He pulled into a muddy patch along the shore, and I noticed he wore no clothes just a string around his waist that held a pouch for his penis and balls. Bow and arrows dangled over his shoulders.

"We packed our belongings into the craft. This was not a craft in the stylist sense of the word. It was just a hollowed-out, big, fat trunk of a tree. I wanted to linger near this last scrap of civilization, but Azymu would have none of it. We headed back into the flow of the river. Little houses were wedged into the red hills above the shore and along the banks of the rivers. The structures resembled rotten stubs of teeth lodged in red infected gums. As we moved beyond the settlement the growth along the riverbank thickened.

"The first two nights we pulled into the shoreline, lashed the boat to a tree, took our few belongings out, and moved to high ground. We ate the dried meat and cassava bread we brought along. Daily we traveled with a current that seemed to move faster and faster. At times, I saw the same landmark twice, as if the river had looped around and came back to the same place at a different angle. It was quite disconcerting. Azymu handled the dugout through rapids and around boulders that seemed to appear out of nowhere. We had been on the move now for a week, four days on the ferry and three days in the canoe. Since I had no way of measuring distance, I was left with darkness and light as my only gauges in this dimension.

"Godfrey, on the fourth day, it began to rain heavy. Bugs came out in droves, tiny black flies, small bees that came at my face. They scared the hell out of me, until I became aware of their only interest- the fluids in my eyes and my mouth. They were more of a nuisance than dangerous, but a few of them flew down my throat and the result? Coughing till my guts hurt. The cold evening rains and the lack of sunshine were simply miserable, hot and wet, refusing to dry. I had no idea that this would be the norm for some time to come.

"Most nights, after erecting the tent, we would sit in the glow of a fire. We made one every night, for cooking food, to keep animals away, and to drive back the relentless darkness. Recently, we had been making an especially large fire to dry my clothes and take the cold out of my bones. I couldn't understand how Azymu could be so accepting of the weather and the unrelenting insects. Nothing seemed to bother him. One night, I pitched a question, attempting to pry at some parts of his belief.

"'How can you be so sure? About all of this, what are you thinking?' A prolonged smile lingered on his face. Azymu looked at me as if I was some small child asking a rude question.

"'This is the way of my spirit, Sydney. My travels, my learning, I will give them all my wisdom. The chosen surrenders his body, becoming one with the earth, the rivers, the trees, and the birds, down to the smallest blades of grass and the smallest insects in the grass.' He looked at me through the glow of the fire. His face was set as stone. What could I say? I hid in silence.

"On the seventh day in the dugout, the current picked up speed. It hurled us along like a car on a road. Azymu had warned me that if capsized swim for shore. Forget everything. Search for it later. His warning sounded ridiculous. What could I do otherwise? I had no idea that he was warning me about the water it self, not the snakes or caimans.

"Around the middle of the next day, I heard a slight rumble. It grew louder as we came down the river. In the distance, I saw a bank of mist rising toward the sky. Azymu moved the boat toward shore, into the shelter of some rocks that formed a small bay. By this time, the noise in the gorge was so loud I could hardly hear his voice. He was trying to tell me how we would get beyond this mountain of water and what lay ahead.

"Godfrey, just imagine this. A volume of water, deep as the lagoon and the outer harbor combined, moving fast and plunging into space. Thick mist bellowed up from the place where the river plummeted.

"We lashed ropes to the boat, began dragging it and hacking the thick bush in front of us. The moment we were out of sight and sound of the river, it occurred to me that we could do this forever, hacking and dragging the load. We traveled until dusk that day and before we went to sleep, Azymu told we should be among his people in no time. I knew that 'no time' had a different meaning for him.

"Grenada seemed a million miles away; could have been on another planet. Would I ever make it back? They might kill me right along with him. Can Bibles protect me? Why should they give a damn? My faith and resolve slowly deserted me. If I knew the way, or had the slightest notion that I could travel this bush alone I would have turned back immediately. I knew that Rondon's telegraph poles were somewhere to the west. But what's between the place where we stood and those telegraph poles? Another story entirely.

"The next day we found the river again. We lowered the boat down a steep incline littered with sharp slivers of rock. We climbed in, and instantly the water swept us along, down a gorge that narrowed, steep cliffs on both sides. Azymu told me nothing of what lay ahead. I had no idea if he knew. We traveled like that for the rest of the day. Then the day paled, turned to night, and I remained in mortal fear of running into rapids or careening over another waterfall. We used a flashlight to try and maintain our position in the stream. But then the moon came out and illuminated the walls of the canyon and the flowing river. Early the next morning, tired and hungry, we were abruptly flushed into a pristine lake at the bottom of a large valley.

A smoldering flame on the far side of the lake caught my attention. On further inspection, I noticed the fires were just remains of a village burned to the ground. Azymu skirted the lake, moving away from the village. This could not be his village. He looked at me, "'No need, Sydney, long gone. Men paid to kill. The white skins want the land. They pay men with guns.

"From that point, we started traveling by foot, moving away from the burning village. We had to hack our way in, penetrate the dense undergrowth along the water's edge. We came out of the undergrowth, into stands of very large trees, so many of them, and they all looked different, as if God stood, hands full of an assortment of seeds and just threw them.

"I stumbled over roots covered by fallen leaves, the earth dry and hard under my feet. We came into an area far from the edge of the river, and Azumy suddenly stopped, turned, and pulled me behind the trunk of a tree. He put one finger to his lips and then he pointed. A figure came stumbling toward us. Truly elated to see another human, I almost jumped out of hiding, but Azymu held me back and shook his head. 'Yumawalli,' he whispered.

"The figure came to within some feet of us and just stood there, panting. Air left his nostrils, raspy and loud. His eyes were fierce, disparate. He looked around as if he could sense our presence. It was a man, bitten by all the insects in the forest. He must have lay down in the wrong place to rest or to sleep. His clothes was torn and frayed. Every exposed piece of flesh, including his face, looked raked, bumpy, and oozing. He was a dripping lump of scabs and pus. He wore one boot. The man was obviously lost and on the brink of starvation and death. After a moment, he stumbled on without seeing us.

"'We could have helped him, Azymu.'

"'No, Sydney. He is between, not dead, not alive, not yet. Any help we give him only make us weaker and closer to death. We can't take him anywhere. We can't show him the way. We can't carry him. Leave him, to the forest. He's a part of this now.'

"Godfrey, I felt for the man way down in my guts. That cliché, *'There for the grace of God, etc,'* came to mind. All my fears about falling over a waterfall, or being eaten by fishes, cannibals, or water lizards, all that seemed so painless after seeing the man. For an instant, I almost fell to my knees, beseeching Azymu not to leave me. The sincerity of my predicament struck me like a stone thrown by some unseen wicked boy. It was all so cruel, so heartless, could this be hell. The thought made me smile.

"We came out of hiding and Azymu continued leading the way as if nothing had happened. A scream came out of the trees where we had seen the man. Something deep and harsh, a primal screech, sounded like a final plea for deliverance. We stood for a moment and listened, and then we moved on.

"For the next few days, I kept expecting to see other people. The man came from somewhere, right? But no one else turned up. We continued moving through brush laden with cobwebs. They covered me from head to toe. Azymu kept looking back at me, smiling and hacking a path with the machete. The image of that man by no means left my mind. I wanted to ask Azymu about him, where he came from, who might he be? I thought better of molesting that ant's nest. What if I made him vexed and he walked off and left me? I kept my mouth shut.

"One evening we pitched the tent on the eastern brink of a peak that seemed to jump out of nowhere. I had no idea we had walked uphill. The forest stretched out below us, a solid green all the way to the tip of a horizon, near the sun. The orange orb sank into the trees, and the clouds boiled, instantly releasing a mist that turned everything slightly gray. The air became still, and darkness fell from the sky like a stone. We started a fire, began cooking some food. My legs, my back, my neck, everything ached. Azymu looked at me and began rummaging in his pack.

"'Eat. Will help you to sleep. Ease you.' He extended a handful of leaves, motioned me to put them my mouth. A sour taste flowed on my tongue as I chewed and finally swallowed. 'You looked troubled today, in the web of the Great Mother,' he said.

'The Great Mother? What did you just give me…?'

"'The spider, the web.' He handed me the container of water. I took a mouthful and swallowed. The pain eased away. His voice sounded like air; his mouth looked like water. The Great Mother: he was telling me another parable, and all I could think of was that lost man.

"'Spider is the Good Mother of the Earth. She wove the dream that we live each day. She brought life to the Earth; she created all this. Plants, the animals, and at last, she takes care of us humans. She gave us music, words, and when the great water came, she escaped, but returned to help us get back the light. She can change her shape and embrace you in many ways. She's the mother of the Yumawalli. His voice faded.

"We moved deeper into the bush the next day. This part of the Amazon reminded me of that Bible story, about Jonah in the belly of the whale. In the belly of this beast, the sun barely shined. Occasionally, the beast would yawn, and I would catch a glimpse of the sun, only to see it vanish again. I moved through the undergrowth with my head down, fearful that something would poke my eyes. The posture caused terrible stiffness at the back of my neck.

"It seemed like we were in some endless limbo, constantly hacking our way, through dim wet thickets, laboring to breathe air that left a metallic taste at the back of my tongue. I felt a continuous need to swallow. At the end of that day, we came out of the belly of the beast, just above some wooded pastureland on the crest of a hill. And there stood a circle of large rocks, similar to those in England.

"I counted them: 127 forming a rough circle. 'From this place the Ancients spoke to the Gods,' Azymu said. He suggested we pitch the tent in a small grove of trees, away from the ruins. We ate the last of our food in silence. Such distance. Although we sat on the ground, just a few feet from each other, the situation felt like the view across a steep ravine. He stood on one side, me on the other. No bridge.

"Just outside the glow of our small fire, I knew thousands of eyes peered from the blends of vegetation. They were there, and probably thought of us as dinner, but they maintained a numbing silence, a stillness that confirmed the night. The roar of a big cat broke in. The sound sent shivers into my bones. Azymu cocked his head, and listened as the beast roared again. Then he started talking as if in reverence. A strange irritation took hold of me at the sound of his voice. 'This is the king of all beasts,' he said. 'The world sits on the backs of four jaguars.' Shut up, man, shut up. Go to sleep, I wanted to shout. He continued to speak.

"He told me about the endless journey of the human soul, its rebirth in spiritual challenges, and the transforming power of the Jaguar Sun. I've heard many preachers who sounded just like him, only, they warned of the retributions a different God.

"His sermon was brief, and for that, I was thankful. How could he be such a being, yet go willingly to his death? That was my final thought of the night. I can't recall exactly how I slept, but a certain sound had my attention as I came awake. Drip-drip-drip. Drip-drip-drip. It thumped on the piece of canvas we had thrown over the shelter.

"I first thought of rain, but a bright sun shone around the tent. I rose and walked into the light. The trees wept. Dew fell steady. The water streamed so continual I used it to wash sleep from my face. Azymu crawled out of the shelter, stretched, and turned his face up to the fresh, cool water. In a short time we were packed and on our way down into the valley.

"'The Earth Father has spoken,' Azymu said, pointing to the circle of stones. 'The Hungura reminds us of the sacred powers, the powers that belong to the Earth Father, the Jaguar. So we always give thanks to the Hawk for appeasing Jaguar and helping to create this new world after the Great Water.' He spoke as we skirted the ancient stones and found a path that led away.

"We walked into the village late that evening. They all turned out-women, children, young men, and old people; they followed us like a parade through the village of thatched huts. Several roasting animals were sizzling over pits of red coals. The villagers shouted at Azymu and me, touched and retreated as if seeking assures that we were real. We walked to the largest hut in the center of the village.

"A young woman and a bony old man waited at the entrance. The old man appeared frail in his huge feathered robe. His greeting sounded like the chatter of birds. Azymu and I followed the old man into the hut where a circle of other men waited. They made some introductions and salutations. Azymu stood before the small gathering with me at his side; all the others men sat on mats on the floor. The old man turned out to be Iti, the old chief that Azymu had mentioned. The woman was Xudine, Azymu's sister. She remained at the entrance as if guarding the proceedings.

"The old man took a seat on a big wooden seat against the wall, and all eyes turned on him. He settled himself into the feathers and furs, cleared his throat, and vocalized what sounded like the distant call of an owl. The others in the hut responded ceremonially, and then the old man started speaking almost perfect English.

"'In three days we give, as we always have. We will perform the Hungura and give to the Yumawalli. We hear you carry words of a God captured in a bag. We know those words. Many years ago, we killed the people who brought us the words. Made it our own. That's why we speak it today. Our brothers judged us wrong and chased us away. Like the children of Oiapo, we had to run from the lands along the Vaca. We are still Palikur, but we know the power of blood. Man with the Face of Night, you came willingly. Azymu, you brought voices and the gift.'

"Azymu stuck his hand into his bag and brought out a package.

The old man threw back some furs and exposed an old radio and the most decrepit Bible I had ever seen. Azymu tore open the package and what appeared to be batteries fell into his palm. He spoke next, without looking at me.

"'For the voices from Mikene, and the man with the Face of Night for his body and his blood.'

"My stomach flipped; my heart started pounding. The betrayal struck me like a closed fist. A storm roared in my head, blowing away all words.

I was afraid to run and afraid to stay. Escape, that was my first thought, but the image of that man, lost in the bush. Death here would be preferable. I stood there, unsure of everything. They acted as if his declaration of me as the sacrifice was just so ordinary. I stumbled backward to the entrance of the hut. All eyes fixed on me as if asking a single instant question. Xudine came and took my arm. I couldn't help but wonder about the radio and the Bible. The missionaries back on the banks of the Vaca were right. I was in the company of deranged murderers. My legs felt stiff; my head swam. Xudine introduced me to a group of people who offered me food and drink. They looked innocent, commonplace, like some of the Indians back at the mission.

"Godfrey, I was on the brink of shitting my pants. For the first time in my life, I controlled nothing. I tried to eat the food, and it tasted like dust. I sat and watched dancers, listened to boys playing flutes. The whole thing seemed like a weird dream. Xudine finally took me to her hut. I barely slept that night. Her half-clad body next to mine offered no comfort.

"I saw Azymu the next day. He sat in a circle, and the people, especially the children, paid special attention. Their parents brought them and forced them to stay. Azymu told them of the world he had seen: metal birds that fly across the sky, big canoes that moved with no paddles, metal that extend from men's arms and spit invisible arrows. They came and they listened. In the end, he told them that all these things were coming. He spoke like a prophet warning them of pestilence.

"On the third day, Azymu sat down with me. The magnitude of the predicament I had wandered into made me giddy. He sat on the ground all adorned in feathers, looking so content. Since that would be our last talk, I tried to rile him, see if I could talk him into running back into the bush, get to the dugout where we hid it on the edge of the lake, and make a run for it. Save me Azymu, I wanted to say. I spoke words that didn't match my intent.

"'You tricked me, you son of a bitch. You brought me here to be killed. Radio and batteries?'" I felt like grabbing something, and smashing his head. But the look in his eyes…

"'Sydney, no need for fear. They told me. Jesus gave his life for others. I give my life for you and all my people. That's the Hungura, that's the way every time. A stranger come, we give a life for his life. We are who we are. We are not like water in the river. We are not new each minute. Soon, we will follow the sun, cross the river and continue our search for the black lake. The voices from Mikene told me you will take them to the black lake.'

"Godfrey, relief and disappointment gripped me. The mixture of emotions made my next words wilt on my tongue.

"'Take them!' I heard myself saying. 'I'm glad you saved me, Azymu, but… I can't lead them. Where's…what's a black lake?'"

"'No one knows,' he said. 'The lake was formed when the God Oiapo chased his three lazy children away. He hurled the thunderstones at them to make them run far and see the world. One of his children was struck and killed by a stone, and a black lake was formed when the tears of Oiapo fell to Earth. We seek that place, and then we can start the final journey and be Palikur again. Too long we have wondered like those in the book.'

"'Azymu, how can I lead them to a…to a place that no one knows?'"

"'We are wanders Sydney. They will follow you. One day you will see a man with a light at the front of his head. The man will be milking a tree. Ask him to take you home. As for me, tomorrow I will drink the Ayahuasca and join minds with all. One person will plunge the blade, and that person will remain here for seven days. The period of fire and flies.'"

*   *   *

Sydney sat silently as the bell on the Anglican Church across the bay in Saint Georges chimed. I heard every vibe: clang, clang, clang. Waves of disappointment lashed me. Questions buzzed in my brain. I decided to steer clear of the obvious, test his response to what my father had said.

"He said you never made it past Angels Falls."

"Who said that?"

"My father."

"Jesus said this to his disciples after he withered a fig tree. I'll say it to you Godfrey, in our own tongue. *'Verily I say unto you Godfrey Soulages. If yea have faith, and doubt not, yea shall not only do what was done to the fig tree, but also if ye shall say unto this island, be thou removed, and be thou sunk into the sea; it shall be done.'* What do you really believe, Godfrey?"

I felt stunned. Betraying the conversation with my father was one thing, but Sydney's reaction left me disarmed. What kind of promise was that?

"I've questions," I said.

"How I came to understand Azymu is the real story." He stared me down. "The day before Azymu and I left the mission between the rivers, I was standing near a field of grass hoping for some miracle, anything that would help me see the point. Little did I know, the answer was right there, in full view, demonstrated by mounds of ants. The field sat in a low area near the edge of the river. Sediments would drain off and swamp the area for most of the rainy season, but the moment the river returned to its banks the grass would sprout like crazy, grew so fast you could almost see it inching out of the ground. At that time of the year, the people around the mission would graze their sheep and goats down there."

Sydney held me in a fixed stare.

"I was sitting watching the animals graze," he said, "when I noticed a swarm of ants working their way into the grass and crawling up the stems. Great big blanket of them reached the top of the stalks and attached themselves to the blades out in the sun. Just waited out there on the grass as the animals grazed right through. A wind blew across the grass and knocked some of the ants back to the ground. The fallen scurried about kind of frantic, and crazy, and then they started back up the stems. Again and again, the ants would be knocked down, but they kept climbing back up the stems and lodging themselves out there where the animal would eat them with the grass. It took me some time to understand what Azymu and those ants had in common.

"Right after they told me I had leprosy, I started reading books on biology. I wanted to know how this malady lived in my body. In my reading, I came across two microbes, lucent fluke and toxoplasma gondii. Sounds like two characters from a fairytale don't they? These things survived by using other creatures as conveyers to reach their ultimate goal in life, reproduction. In the case of the lucent fluke, an ant is its vehicle to reach the belly of goats, or sheep. Toxoplasma gondii, is another story, a mouse or a rat is its vehicle to reach the belly of a cat.

"The eggs of the lucent fluke are found in the shit of goats and sheep, where ants consume them. The fluke then hatches inside the ants and makes it's way into the brain of the ants. There it takes over, turning the ants into the crazy climbers I had noticed in the field. The fluke grows to adulthood in the stomach of the animal, lays eggs, the animals shit the eggs and the whole cycle begins again when other ants eat the eggs and climb to the top of a blade of grass to be consumed by goats or sheep.

In the case of toxoplasme gondii, it makes its way into the body of a mouse or rat. There it secretes an enzyme that makes the rodents fearless. Little bastards would stand toe to toe with a cat. Usually, they loose the battle and become a meal for the cat. And that little microbe is on its way to fulfill its destiny.

"Belief has a similar existence. We shun people who might sneeze and infect us with colds and coughs, through the nose or mouth. But this infection goes through the ears and eyes. It enters our brains, multiplies and makes us do all kind of crazy shit. Why else would a group of people create such deceptions, such rituals? Nature is a hell of a thing."

"You blaming nature? I hear the words uncle Sydney, but…

"Call it what you want, the facts remain."

"That may be but…

"Let me wash your face of those doubts. I can show you the magic of two vines, shown to me by the Palikurs. They say some people even get the chance to look into their future, meet their spirit guide. This journey is not without some danger. You must do as I say. Eat lots of food, rest. The Palikurs call it Yumawalli. Karrol didn't survive his encounter with the Yumawalli. You think you have the strength to wrestle with a force bound on devouring your future? If you think you have it, come let me show you."

CHAPTER 9

I agreed to join Sydney in this exploit without saying a word. As I left the Jupa, a sliver of a moon hang to the east, over Richmond Hill. The night wrapped around me like an easy fitting shirt. A dog barked in the distance. Cat and mouse, ants and goats, catch the pouring rain with a strainer. In spite of all my uncertainty, I looked forward to what Sydney might be offering.

When I tiptoed into the house, my father was tossing and snoring loudly in the dark. He always snored loudly when drunk. The little lie I intended to tell him now seemed stupid. After I had been in the bed for some minutes, shuffling the events of the night, it occurred to me that Xudine remained out of sight throughout Sydney's account.

My father made one big flop across the bed, and the mattress and springs groaned under his weight. Frequently, he would make a wet snarl, smacking his lips as if tasting something sweet, and then he would settle into a momentary silence, just before starting the oeuvre all over. His breathing sounded like the folding of waves on the sand.

My father, Ethan Soulages, dwelled outside the events of everyday. The allusions of life and practically never fully engaged him. But he had other sides. One of them was a fondness for insinuations and funny interpretations of the ordinary. For instance, one day we were sitting on the porch, looking down at the lagoon and the yachts from all over the world. He was drinking ginger beer mixed with rum, and I was drinking sorrel. No rum. Out of nowhere, he proposed a challenge. Had something to do with trees and their search for one of their own to rule over them.

"Godfrey, listened to this, listen carefully and when I'm done tell me what you got out of it," he said. "Trees desired one of their own to rule over them," he began. "First, they approached the mighty Silk Cotton with flattery: 'Eminence among trees, your roots are deep in the ground. You stand tall above all else'. But, the Silk Cotton refused, and replied, 'this is where I stand. I've seen devils coming down off white horses, pissing steam at my roots. I know the erratic ways of those planted in the ground. I've stood in the wind. I will not be what you want me to be.'

"Then they called on the Flamboyant, speaking of its beautiful flowers and majesty among all trees, and then to the Calabash, where they spoke of its utilitarian functions and cunning application to music. When they approached the Divi-Livi, they praised its ability to bend with the prevailing winds and its contribution to pollination. All the trees refused. Finally, they came to the common bramble. Bramble accepted, but soon after, he demanded trust, even in his shadow, and leveled a threat of fire if he was not obeyed.' You see? My father asked, and waited. I wanted to say great story, but I knew he wanted more, and I had nothing to tell. I heard vague suggestions in the telling, but the words to convey understanding eluded me. My father looked at me with disappointed. "Don't ever get into politics. You'll never have the guts for it," he said.

I also knew him by way of gossips, legends, and weird little games made-up by people for laughs. They claimed he could dive to the bottom of the sea and have lunch before coming up for air. The first time I challenged that assertion, they told me he could dive into the sea and come back with a fish faster than any man. They said he once saved a baby from drowning, and that he once stood up to be counted as a man and ended up in jail. I think I remembered when he was gone for some time, around the time I was three or four. Then again, I could have heard that from one of our neighbors and just imagined that I remembered it. People seemed to respect the man. All my friends called him Mr. Soulages. The man worked at many trades, and he looked different every time he switched.

Barefoot in his rowboat, *Lucky Joe*, with lines and tackle boxes, he became a fisherman. Rubber boots on his feet, fork on his shoulder, a sharp cutlass in his hand, Ethan was a farmer. And from time to time he would pack a grip, take a job on one of the cargo vessels that voyaged from Grenada to Carriacou, through the Grenadines to Saint Vincent, Saint Lucia sometimes, and even as far north as Dominica. Frequently, I would hear people whispering about Ethan Soulages and what he did on those journeys. The money hidden under the flooring in our house supports some of those rumors.

My father once told me of the men and women who lived on these islands long before the Europeans came. He told me about the Caribs who still live on Dominica, way back in the bush on a portion of land reserved for them. The only piece of land they will ever know. And to think of it, they once ruled all of this. What does that tell you?

I marveled at his various transformations. To me he was like those men in the movies. I loved the objects and the stories he brought back. My father had his limits though. He refused to sail further south than Grenada. The vessels would procure a cargo for Trinidad, and that would be the end of my father's job. He would jump ship, and remain in Grenada, working his fish pots, and cultivating his piece of land. It seldom took him long to find another job on a vessel going north. He had a reputation. Ethan Soulages refused to go south because of my mother. For some unnamed reason, she had left him, and went to Trinidad years ago.

The next morning at breakfast I felt drowsy. My father's voice roused me from my meditation on corn porridge, condensed milk and brown sugar. He had started speaking to me long before I was listening. "The pay is good, and it's her maiden voyage. Everything new-except for the spots where someone tried to catch her on fire. Can you believe it? Why would anyone try to do that?" My toes curled inside my shoes. I struggled to keep my face neutral; the corn porridge tasted like puke in my mouth.

"Haven't been to Dominica in awhile," he said. "We'll be smuggling a group of Haitians into Martinique." That was the first time my father had revealed to me exactly what he did on his journeys.

"You sailing on *Miss Irene*?" I asked.

"Yeah." He looked at me.

"Daddy, those Vincey killed Karrol."

"What you talking about, boy? He drowned."

"There was no water in his lungs."

"How long you have this in your head? You spoke to no one?"

"I spoke to Fins and Uncle Sydney."

"Uncle Sydney? He's not your blasted uncle. And what you doing talking to them instead of to me? No water in his lungs? The fellow who cut him open could have punched a hole in the lungs, the water ran out, and he had to tell his boss no water. They don't depend on us for their jobs or nothing. They tell us anything. Now get your books; off to school so that you don't have to work your ass off like me." His outburst left me upset and speechless. I grabbed my books and headed out the door.

My father had made many such journeys as I grew up. Most of the time I stayed with my aunt, Grace. However, in this little village by the sea all the women became my mothers as time went on. Church on Sundays was always mandatory with my aunt Grace and her family, so most of the time I slept at Karrol's house. The food was always good there. His mother, Anna, always fed us sweet ginger funtay, fluffy bread with meat inside, plumb stew, all of that. But now with Karrol gone, and Ian posing as a Rasta Man, nothing felt the same.

Miss Irene left port that evening and I stood on land watching the crew unfurl her sails. Yvette came up behind me and rested one hand on my back. Her sudden appearance made me resentful, as if she had intruded on a brittle moment.

"Why the donkey face? Your father always…"

"This has nothing to do with him."

"Oh, I see. Karrol. You can't bring him back, Godfrey."

She removed her hand from my back; stood to one side looking at me like somebody's mother. I almost shouted at her, but I held back, and spoke directly.

"I know, Yvette, but I had plans, plans to find out who murdered Karrol and make the fuckers…"

"Godfrey, I know how you… but regardless, if he was murdered or drowned, you still can't bring him back."

"Stop saying that. You think I don't know."

"I hate it when you act so… no comforting you."

She looked at me with her jaws set, holding back.

I stood at this juncture with no ideas about how to proceed. The vessel took more than my father away. My efforts to discover and avenge what had happed to Karrol seemed so futile. With the vessel gone, and no evidence, or persons to accuse, I saw no way forward. I was a kite that had lost its breeze. Even Yvette's attendance didn't lift me. I realized it would take the most fortuitous of events to give me a glimpse of the satisfaction that I craved.

Poor Karrol. Where do we go from here? A void remained where my little plans once flourished. My friends, and especially Yvette, had started to question why I spent so much time with the leper and his wife. I told them there was lots to learn, and proceeded to convey the connection between leprosy, thalidomide, Sydney and Fins. Then I watched their jaws drop. This did not impress Yvette. She kept asking questions, and staring me down with skeptical eyes.

Sydney chose that Saturday to reveal the magic of the vines. Ethan was gone, Yvette wanted to go swimming at Mon Pandy; I told her I had work to do. I was beginning to gather so much doubt about us. She looked at me, turned away, and I thought I saw a hint of regret in her movement.

I waited for dusk before sneaking over to the Jupa. Sydney and Xudine had already prepared the mixture. It looked like a pale green porridge, kind of like soupy callaloo in a brown stone container. It sat right in the middle of the dining table. Sydney's fingers were folded around the container as he spoke. His voice sounded just like my father's, the times he had attempted to instruct me about balance and posture when kicking a soccer ball.

"Relax, don't fight it. It will feel strange, and maybe even frightening at times. Just relax; let it pass. We will both be here. You will know what we know, and we are alive. This is for when you come back. Remember that time will pass; you will be unaware of it. Just focus on our voices. This is best done in natural light. Perfect shade this evening."

He spoke kindly. Xudine said nothing. She took the cot from the corner, moved outside, and erected it in the clearing near the stairs behind the house. Sydney went after her, and I followed. He carried the green gruel clutched in his left hand and his cane in the right.

"Take this." He handed the container to me just as we started down the narrow stairs.

For an instant, I thought of dropping it, just trip and fall down. Fear and doubt, fatigue crawled into my curiosity. My eyes blinked rapidly as my feet came off the last rung and hit the ground. This is it. No turning back now. The cup felt like a giant boulder. We all stood there as if unsure of what to do next. The content of the cup had no exact smell when I brought it to my lips-just a faint herbal hint.

The first swallow was bitter, but the second was sweet, lumpy, and coarse in my throat. It settled somewhere below my gullet and nothing happened. A wave of relief mixed with regret washed over me. They both gestured with little upward motions of their hands. Finish the stuff. I placed the cup to my lips and felt the remains slide down my throat.

"Don't feel anything," I said.

"Be patient, Godfrey," they both spoke in unison. Bright smiles rounded out their words.

"Sit," he instructed. "You will feel a little sleepy. Don't worry. It won't last long. Remember. Listen to our voices. Don't resist."

I sat down heavily on the cot. They both stooped next to me. I stared at their faces and saw only pleasantry. Sydney offered his left hand and Xudine her right. I took them. Their palms felt cold and I felt stupid. They started a low drone that sounded like the buzz of bees. The comfort and beauty of the murmur urged me to lie back; sluggish warmth inched around my chest. The drumming of my heart made me panicky.

Tears gathered at the far corners of my eyes, and spilled out over my eyelids, down my face, hot as scalding tea. I wondered if the tears would burn a trail down my cheeks. I thought of hands, to wipe the tears, but my hands refused to move. Something was clawing into my eyes near the bridge of my nose, exactly where the tears had drained out. No pain, just an itchy sensation that forced me to swallow, and the spittle, dry and sugary, slid slowly down my throat. I melded with the cot.

At that moment, I knew I sat in the right palm of God, at the center of the universe. I knew the world and everyone who had ever lived on it. I knew them all in intimate details. I knew what Sydney and Xudine wanted. And with that awareness came a fear that almost stopped my heart. But in the same instant, all the information was gone, forgotten as if I had never absorbed it. And there I was, in another place, suspended from the tail of a kite. And I knew I couldn't fly. I hung over an ocean as blue as ink, and the tail of the kite slowly slid through my palms. I plunged toward the ocean like a stone, and broke the surface of the ink-blue water. Then everything went backward, to an embryonic stage, like a child just conceived, no definition, just a kind of free-floating mélange.

I seemed to exist in two places.

In one, I was following Sydney down a long corridor of green through which I sensed another me. I struggled to find meaning in a circling vat of disjointed images. A man chased by two painted people climbed into a tall tree and flew off in the form of a bird. I thought I was the bird, but then Sydney became the bird. I struggled to give that world some form, some kind of alignment. I imagined a road, and it was there. An ugly white face stood on the road beckoning. I wondered, is it a man, a woman or a spirit? But that presence became Karrol, and then dissolved like mist.

I came out of the eyes of eternity into another place. No longer in a blue ocean, I was now standing on the bare ground in an empty village. Out of the brush slid a giant horned serpent, but the serpent twisted its head and transformed into a woman standing on two legs, clad in a skirt of woven snakes. I recognized the woman as a younger Xudine. I heard myself speaking with Sydney's voice.

"Who are you? Why? My guide back? They left you for me."

The woman looked at me with a face as sad as time. It moved me to tears, tears as cold as night rain. The sadness peeled opened my eyes. All their pains and pleasures, everything laid bare, viewed from a singular point. It was as if they both walked before me skinless, and I beheld the places where their souls rested. However, all that seemed brief like an embryo dreaming in its mother's womb. Everything seemed liquid, entangled, and inconsistent, passing bits, forever moving and taking, like standing on a high bluff and watching a river rise to flood stage, gouging at its banks, forcing the earth to collapse into its flow.

I felt limp and leaky, like a wet sponge, and before me stood Xudine, in the middle of this elusive tableau of people and noises. But then came the smell and the taste of blood. I felt a hunger that only an exact conclusion could satisfy. The voices were chanting; they sounded like water spilling into empty crevices, the rush to return after some long drought. I sensed it before it happened. I knew it was coming, and it filled me with a revulsion that almost stopped my breath.

Xudine gripped a long, wide blade over a man stretched out on an altar of wood. The blade and her hand plunged into his chest, continued down, and returned with the guts that squeezed out above his skin. Her hands now held two organs, heart and liver, bloody and raw. Her fingers folded around the dripping meat, and she moved toward the flames.

The instances tumbled across my vision as the fire received the meat. Then she moved his head into the flame. The fire burned into an ever-widening cordon fueled by the hair on Azymu's head. I saw his brain bubbling, cooking inside his skull, and I knew it would taste like wet bread. Nevertheless, all was fading fast, and a thirst prevailed, a need for water. I swallowed and my throat was dry as dust.

I knew what Sydney and Xudine wanted of me. I knew exactly what Sydney would ask me to do, and I was sure I would do it. I already knew that, but that sliver of doubt and the need to embrace the comfort of dry voices forced me to choose. So I went with the chants, allowed myself to be snatched up and held suspended between fleeting uneasiness and an innocent joy.

I relished it all for a moment, but that sweet surrender vanished. The crowd and the voices melted, gone again as if doused. Xudine now sat alone, to one side. I focused on what remained of the ruined body of Azymu, stretched out on the bed of wood. Flies began to amass.

The first few circled and landed. They buzzed as they moved to make space. The others came in steady, settled over his exposed remains like a well-fitted coat, and covered everything. They made sounds, low drones that carried, to whistles and grunts, augmented by the growl of an angry jaguar somewhere out in the trees.

The bush spoke in a way that I comprehended with my skin. Then that face from the road was there again, smiling at first, as if it understood something that I didn't. Xudine moved closer and took my hand. "'I'll show you the pleasing paths, but I'm not your guide. He is.'" She pointed to the ugly white face from the road. It was that face, but it was laughing with Karrol's voice.

Xudine and I now rested on a slope near a river, moving together, receiving, and propagating the melodious ecstasy of sweet water music. We slid, supple on that grade with soft ridges, and I slid into that abiding flow of euphoria. Xudine became the Earth, and the river. The river that I floated on came from her, and our voices were the music of that deluge, now striving to consume the world. Noises came from many places, not just our mouths. Our mouths were occupied exploring crevices that held the scent of night blossoms.

She yielded up in adulation, and an element as primal as water washed over us. Then it was all gone, in an instant, wiped away as if a teacher had dragged an eraser across a blackboard. All at once, there was everything and nothing. I could still feel it. The taste remained, but only inside my head this time.

I became aware of my body in a new way. It was there but unaware of itself. Like living in death. My fingers, and toes, they swelled, festered, and rotted away. The sweetness of rot assailed my face, but even that held a delight, like the promise to a suffering man that there will be no tomorrow.

The androgynous being reappeared, however, this time it wore new clothes. I stood before the thing with a machete in hand. I struck at it without knowing why, and it vanished like smoke as the blade went through. But then, I stood face to face with what I knew to be a conclusion. Awareness presented itself like a tease. Tantalizing bits. I remembered it all, every detail. It was like coming back from a long journey through reversal of thoughts. But at the same time, there was an unsettling awareness of a debt to be paid. That singular worry followed me back.

A group of roosters crowed at each other across the night, first one, then another and another, in contesting exhortation. I reached for the sound of the crowing fowls like a drowning man reaching for the gunwale of a boat. Count them; count them. How many? What time is it? And the serenade continued. I lost track of the count, and the whole thing turned into a noisy provocation. Comfort and recognition crept into me. I was on a bed, inside the house, naked, wrapped in a damp sheet. I rolled over into a cold, sticky spot. A wet dream. That moment by the river with Xudine. And with that thought, a heavy dreamless sleep swallowed me.

CHAPTER 10

Long shafts of light penetrated the only window in the room. Could have been any time, any day. I languished in what could only be called, a rational swamp, searching for some kind of traction. The visions remained fresh, the tastes, the smells, my entire being begged for more of everything. Xudine came into the room carrying food and water. I had questions, but no voice with which to ask them. She offered the food and I ate, swallowing gulps like a hungry dog. I brought the cup to my lips, the water tasted sweet and at once my body became mine again.

My clothes itched as I crawled into them. In the yard behind the house, Sydney stood near the garden, immobile. He kept gazing at the plants and flowers sprouting from the neat furrows cut into the soil. I knew he heard my footsteps, but he was slow to acknowledge my presence.

"What time is it? What day is it?" I asked.

He finally looked to me. "It's three o'clock on Sunday," he said.

"Can we do that again? I saw Karrol. I heard him laugh."

Sydney looked at me hard and serious, his eyelids slapping quickly.

"I have to go back. See what I missed," I said.

"You saw all there was to see. Karrol is dead and that is that. No bringing him back. We just wanted you to understand what it feels like to have an appetite with no way to feed it. We need a favor, one that we'll repay. You are young and strong, let us be your teachers."

The words left his mouth, coming at me from a funny angle, because I already knew what he was avoiding. Why didn't he just say it plain? Godfrey I would like you to fuck my wife.

"She knew you and Karrol watched her from the rocks," he continued, "and last night, under the influence of the vines-" He didn't complete the statement.

So, it was no dream. Sydney was still looking at me, a fraction of a smile skulked around his mouth. I knew I would say yes to what he was avoiding, but before I gave him an answer, I wanted something, some kind of assurance.

"What was it, Uncle Sydney?"

"What do you mean?"

"All of it…did it really-"

"What you saw shouldn't vary that much from the story I told you. What did you see?"

I related the experiences from the vision. Sydney appeared to be waiting for some specific details. When I mentioned the white face along the road and Karrol's laughter, he flinched like a man who had just discovered a snake on the ground near his feet. I told him everything except for two details: striking at the figure with the machete, and knowing what he would ask me to do with his wife.

Sydney forced a smile and nodded when I stopped speaking. He reacted as if saying yes to some unasked question. His response stumped me. I wanted to hear more about the white face, Karrol's laughter, and the Yumawalli. But instead of pestering him for more details, my mind remained fixed on the carnal aspects, the part where Sydney would ask me to fuck his wife.

* * *

Sydney didn't really have to ask or say much. It happened one night with absolute simplicity. Xudine came to me, rested one hand on my lap, and looked at me with expectation. Sydney stood just behind us and to the left. I glance at him, and he looked wooden, no expression. He could have been dead.

In the bed, her body felt soft, her belly warm against mine, her eyes held me firm, and a soft moist hand slid between, and grasped my penis, pulling it down and across her thigh. She guided and I pushed just slightly; it was like a closed door swinging open on oiled hinges. So moist, so warm, she moved ever so slightly.

Xudine looked different stretched out on her back, brown breasts spread flat. She licked her lips between short breaths. I wanted to ask her if she was okay, thought of Sydney and didn't. Intoxication, and fear: the combination made me sweat. This was my first time; it took less than the length of a song. But my appetite for Xudine heated up as time went by. Knowing exactly why I was having sex with Sydney's wife seemed unimportant. Twice a day sometimes, she became abundant, not the shape or feel of what I imagined a girl might be. She looked more like somebody's mother. She smelled like ripe mangoes. What I felt for Xudine differed from what I felt for Yvette. With Yvette and me, it was more like cultivating trees. With Xudine and me, it was like she was a tree in the woods and I was the cleaver. It took only six weeks before things began to sour.

My father had returned from the maiden voyage of *Miss Irene*. School was a bore. Fins, that foolish, cripple. I'm never going near that dump he calls a shop. Never again. I had what I wanted. I knew how to draw and paint. The Jupa became my refuge. My father and Yvette suspected nothing, and I intended to keep it that way.

My new circuitous route to the Jupa was working well. And so, I connived my way further into the alliance with Sydney and Xudine even as they tried to push me away. My plan to uncover what had happened to Karrol, that became minor. It sat at the back of my mind. Not completely forgotten, but not as essential as it once appeared.

Sydney began showing signs of impatience with my frequent visits and constant inquiries about Ayahuasca. It showed in little ways. He started avoiding my eyes. He started speaking in short sentences. He acted in a hurry. I could only guess at Xudine's attitude toward all this. Sydney never left us alone, and she seldom spoke. I had to ask her questions to make her talk. She seemed to enjoy herself when we coupled, but in a detached way. She always shouted Sydney's name at her moment of climax.

I assumed she wanted to make sure that I didn't think of her as mine. Still, that didn't stop me. Every time we brushed, I prized her in a different way. The small lines on her face disappeared. She looked young, like the little sister of the snake woman in the vision. The shivering of her thighs and the tremors in her voice left me with the impression that I was in control.

I started fantasizing, and the fantasies invaded my dreams. At night, as I lay in bed, considering the possibilities, I would slide into a shallow sleep that felt like wakefulness; my brain would play these fantasy games. Sydney would be dead and Xudine would be mine. Again and again, in a variety of forms, I had my way. In one disturbing vision, I killed Sydney, held him under water until he went limp, and turned to sand, and a wave washed him out of my palms and through my fingers.

At first, these whimsies were encouraging. I immersed myself in them through the waking hours, and I played with them near sleep. School became worthless. Reading about the Pirate Morgan, Marco Polo, and the Lady of Sovereign, in that Caribbean Reader, so much crap. However, one night those visions changed, turned malevolent.

The dreams cropped up every time I laid my head down. It became impossible to distinguish between dreams, thoughts, and imaginings. I was going crazy. In bed, trying to sleep, everything became copious, ornamental, a finely woven embellishment of past and present, mounting but yielding only chaotic spasms that some-times expressed themselves in the familiar. For instance, the dream that the old woman, Mama Viche, ask me about, my father standing near a waterhole, with a flock of snipes pecking at his reflection in the water. That one emerged frequently. Another one, about a woman who looked as though she had been bathing in milk, the liquid slid off her body in steady drips that covered the ground around her. The visions teemed in my head like red ants on old bread. One thing seemed to sooth calm them. The lessons Fins had taught me.

I started drawing with sticks, in dirt, in sand on the beach. The pleasure of it absorbed me. My obsession with purging the images from my head forced me to steal chalk from school on the days that I attended. I used the chalk to draw on stones, on the walls of peoples' houses. I blended crushed chalk with a mixture of charcoal dust, creating a powder that I mixed with water. I used my fingers and at times brushes to capture the images flowing through me.

My drawings were all berserk and stretched out, as if seen through sheets of tears or thick glass. They were rough depictions of trees, water, or people. And at times, they held a touch of the whimsy, like the time I drew Fins with crab claws instead of his little nubs. They kept me anchored in the now.

In one vision, I found myself on a cargo vessel that I knew was *Miss Irene*. My father was there somehow, and someone was sobbing. I recognized the voice as Karrol's. But before I could reach my dream became Karrol's dream. And I was in, but only watching, unable to do or say anything. Then that dream folded into another and effortlessly merged with a lurid Kaleidoscope of me and my father.

We were moving through a forest of blue-green leaves where it rained yellow, and the sun was shining a dripping light. Our bare feet collected no mud from the ground, or sand from the beach where we boarded our rowboat, *Lucky Joe*. He knelt in the bow and I rowed him out across water, black and smooth, toward a rock that resembled a pregnant black stomach. We came to an entrance, and there we descended stairs of cool smooth rocks, steep and winding as a corkscrew, no light at the bottom. An intuitive feared convulsed deep in my chest.

The need to protect my father and save myself besieged me. But he was ahead and moving down, far and away. He came back, strolling up the stairs holding my mother's hand. She ignored me, and a mixture of covetousness and delight made my heart beat hard. She leaned into my father and laughed as they strolled by. "I will always love you, Ethan," she said. I followed them back up the stairs.

We entered the space outside the cavern, and I looked out over a calm sea. But that fear still remained with me. All I could think of was conveying my father back to the safety of the far shore. But in the next instant, he stood next to an angel that I knew was my mother. "You are waiting for the moving of the water," the angel said. "You will find peace there."

She reached down and coiled the water around her index finger. The sea swelled into a huge fury, waves roiled as a high mountain. Bolts of water ricocheted off the rock where we stood. A driving wind blew the boat into the rocks and splintered it. My father now stood with his angel inside the swirling water. The waves flew in white circles that surrounded them. They became the water, and blended into the white spume.

I jerked upright in my bed, grasping for air, my heart pounding in my chest, perspiration dripping off my face. The image of my mother and the angel stood at the front of my mind, blocking all else. I saw it rendered as white pigment on a black canvass. There was no sleeping after that jolt.

The conversation between my father and I, earlier that night, felt pleasant as I lay in bed, reflecting on things said. Dinner was over, and I hadn't even washed the dishes. We sat in chairs around the kitchen table. My father got a startled look on his face as if he had just remembered details from an unfinished conversation. He started talking.

"Godfrey, I'm so proud of you," he paused and nodded his head as if agreeing with himself. "My son, you growing into a fine man, you already gone further in school than I did, and you doing well. Keep out of trouble. You hear me?" He paused again, still looking at me. I thought he would mention Sydney and Xudine, but when he spoke, he referred to matters just slightly removed. "What you doing with Cyril's girl? What you doing with Yvette?"

"Nothing Daddy. We just friends."

He smiled, but his next words left me anxious.

"Godfrey, sex means different things to women than it does to us."

"What you mean? Yvette and I aren't-"

"Not yet, maybe. This is just a little warning, to let you know. Get you ready. Your mother and me for instance-"

It was the first time my father had mentioned my mother. In that context, I was left with a heap of untidy emotions. I had so many questions, but my misgivings refused to take the form of words. So, I remained silent. The bleakness of the last few weeks abated just slightly. This was what I had been waiting for. Now here it was before me- closeness to my father. I slept soundly that night and dreamt of him united in water with an angel.

I woke that morning to the light of the sun on my face and a strange feeling toughing at my heart. Unexplained tears ran down my face. My father had snuck out of the house early, to haul his fish-pots. I felt a little cheated, but not to this point.

The things he said last night, I wanted to secure that bond with him in the light of day. But that was no reason for tears. The idea that my father had finally opened his eyes and saw me as a man should have been a time to celebrate. So the tears had me completely baffled, until they came across the boat, *Lucky Joe,* bobbing on its anchor, empty. It didn't take them long to find his body. Ethan Soulages drowned in thirty feet of water one calm, sunny day. That's where the tears came from. I saw the death of my father long before it happened and didn't consciously know it.

His friend Cyril Ogilvie retrieved his body from the sea; his sister Grace had his body washed and dressed in his favorite gabardine suit. They laid him out in a box, balanced across two chairs. His friends came to the house. They drank rum and ate all the food. I took my turn keeping watch over his remains that night. My father looked fine, but I had to touch him. He was cold, cold as deep ocean water. He was now a part of the sea, as he was soon to be a part of this earth and this rock. Another lover of islands.

Around mid night it started to rain. Not the usual downpour that made rivulets. This was a soft rain. It fell gently, steadily, throughout the night. The inconvenience of death. Why do people die so unexpectedly? They should be able to send invitations. Please, please my friends, come watch me take this final breath. Let's have this last fete, enjoy my passage.

We carried the coffin across fresh black mud that stuck to our shoes. Four of us lowered the box into a hole in the ground where small puddles of brown water had collected. The rope slipped across my fingers, a soft enjoyable burn. Everyone from the Mang, Belmont, and Jananglais came: Anna, Cyril, Yvette and all her sisters, Tante Rose, Miss Olga, my aunt Grace with her children. Even the Rasta boys from up the road, the ones who called my father Mister Soul-ages. They stood off to one side with their leader, a fellow called Campesh. Ian stood with them. The preacher said a few words. Two people were conspicuously absent: Sydney and Xudine.

After my father was in the ground, people came up to me whispering how sorry they were. Yvette threw her arms around me in the presence of her father and whispered in my ear. "We need to talk." Everyone hurried away, except my aunt Grace, Ian, and me. We remained at the grave, staring at the box resting at the bottom of the hole.

Two men raised shovels. Tante Grace turned her back quickly, and covered her mouth. She moved off before the first clumps of dirt hit the wood. It was hard to watch them fill the hole. Ian and I started to walk. The final sounds of the burial followed us. We trudged the mud path, heading back to the house.

"He's gone, boy. Just when I thought-" The words stuck to my tongue.

"Jah loves, Godfrey," Ian said. "He never gives us more load than we can handle."

"I always wanted him to be my friend. I'll never have that." I swallowed hard to hold back tears.

"Not true. You'll see. Everybody knew him."

"Except me."

"You'll know him. His stories, you know…you know why he went to jail?"

We stood in the yard near the house. I wanted him to go away, leave me to crawl into my sorrow.

"You know the man better than me," I said.

"Me and you were too young to remember that, man. Campesh tells this story to every new convert to Rastafari. He recites it like prayers, the exact words, in all the same voices. I heard it told so many times, I'll never forget: 'the white man came to Grenada with notebooks and a tape recorder. He rented a room at Islander Hotel, and every day he came around asking all kinds of questions. Sometimes he even brought a bottle of rum to loosen tongues. Everybody told him all their business and even the business of their neighbors. The man got friendly with everybody. Even his white skin began turning brown. One day he went up to Ethan's house with his tape deck slung around his neck, took out his notebook, and started asking questions. "'Why don't you mind your own business?' Ethan asked. "'Go away; stop copying peoples lives, go live your own. Get out of here before I kick you in your ass.'"

"'Kick me. Illiterate bastard, this is scholarship, history.'"

"'Call it what you want, just get out me yard, man, before I throw you out.'"

"'Get your ass down here and try. Knock out a few of those rotten teeth.'"

'The white man threw down his notebooks and tape deck. People said that he liked to have a beer or two with his food. Well, that day he must have had quite a few because he got real vexed with Ethan. People heard the quarrel and started gathering to see. Ethan came down the stairs and stood in front of the man. The man put up his fists and started prancing like a rooster, then the fists began flying. The man popped Ethan in the mouth twice before Ethan could say Jackie Robinson. His lip started bleeding. Tasting his own blood threw Ethan into a rage. He moved toward the man, slapped both of the man's fists out of the way, and then Ethan hit him beside the head hard with his open palm. The man stumbled sideways and fell to the ground like a dazed chicken. But he shook his head and sprang up fast. He came at Ethan, throwing two quick punches, a left and a right that glanced off the same side of Ethan's head. Everybody was cheering now. Some making bets on the white man, others on Ethan.'

"'They fought long and fierce, faces, knuckles, peeling and bleeding. In the end, people said they called the police because they couldn't get them to stop. Even dousing them with buckets of water didn't help. It just seemed to energize them. When all was said and done, Ethan was arrested. At a trial in town, the judge with his white wig told Ethan to apologize to the professor. Ethan refused.'

"'I had a fair fight with another man," Ethan said.'

"'Apologize to the professor or go to jail,'" the judge warned.'"

"'I told you already.'" Ethan looked at the judge. "It was fair. Man to man.'"

"'Your Honor,' the professor stood up and shouted to the judge.'"

"'This is a court of law, sir," the judge said, "Sit down! No more disturbances, or I'll send you to jail with him. We can't have Negroes beating on white people. This will not do.'"

"'I'm an honest man," Ethan said. "I have no quarrel with anyone. But if you came into my yard-'"

"'I'll give you one last chance." The judge cut him off. "Speak. Say nothing except an apology.'"

"'Ethan remained silent, staring straight at the judge.'

"'Take him away. Six months at hard labor," the judge said.' Campesh always conclude the story by saying, 'I sat in that courthouse and watched it all. That was a junction for me. A solid example.'

"That's your father, man. Every time I hear that story... Campesh tells it better. Come to the house this evening, have dinner with us, we cooking a pot of Manish water."

"We'll see," I said, knowing that I couldn't be there. My aunt had already invited me to dinner.

"You alright?" Ian looked at me as if he saw something on my face.

"Yeah."

"See you late, Godfrey." And Ian walked away.

I went into the house and locked the door behind me. The hammer felt cumbersome as I took it from the corner and approached the spot where my father kept his money under the floorboard. Apprehension struck me. Leave that money alone, I told myself. Leave it alone. An odd rage consumed me, a rage against everything, against my father for leaving me in confusion, against life and time for being such miserable thieves. I felt the need to rush to the Jupa. Screw Xudine rough; let Sydney watch. I didn't care.

I still don't understand my rage toward them. I didn't suspect Sydney and Xudine of doing anything to my father. Still, everything turned berserk. My obsession to draw, the Ayahuasca memories, all seemed ridiculous. The day after my father's funeral, I dropped by the Jupa and no one was there. The Jupa looked forsaken, sitting there, far off the road. I looked around, peeked in the windows. Sydney and Xudine just went to town, I thought. They'll be back. The next day I revised that. They must be visiting friends in the country, should be back before too long. I allowed two days before returning to the Jupa. That's when the lump began to dissolve in my throat.

As I left the Jupa that day, a black schooner appeared at the mouth of the harbor. She headed straight for the banana boat tethered to the pier at the head of the bay. Halfway in, the helmsman spilled some wind out of her sails, slowing the yacht's progress, and then, he brought her about and changed course, straight for the channel into the lagoon.

I watched in awe. Most skippers would lower the sails, and drop anchor in the outer harbor. This allowed the Customs and Immigration people to come aboard, poke around, and drink a cola, or beer if offered. Then the captain would motor his yacht through the narrow channel into the lagoon. Not this one. With a crew of four, a helmsman and three others, they brought her in under full canvas. Eight sails flew.

Forward she flew three sails: flying jib, jib, and a forestaysail. Between the two masts, she flew three more: foresail, fore gaff-topsail, and a main-topmast staysail (a small sail way up in the riggings). The complement was crowned with two more aft sails, a mainsail, and a main gaff-topsail.

She keeled magnificently, stretched out across the wind. She sliced the water like a blade. The crew adjusted the sheets for a broad reach. The black hull slid past the other yachts at anchor. She made minimal waves. The crew took her way into the lagoon, near the spot where I stood. Winches whistling and grinding as the men released the sheets. For a moment, I thought they might run her aground. But they dropped some canvas, changed tack, and controlled her haste.

Everyone stood and watched. People along Lagoon Road, other skippers and crew on yachts at anchors: all eyes remained glued to these reckless fools. They brought the yacht around, pointed the bow into the wind. The remaining sails slapped in protest, beating at the rigging as the crew lowered them to the deck.

The swells from her wake rocked the other yachts. Anchor and chain poured out of her belly. The yacht called *BLACK DOG* sat out there, rocking gently on her own swells. I heard it took Customs and Immigration three days to clear them. Everyone onboard had to remain right there, and have no contact with the shore.

CHAPTER 11

If anyone knew of the whereabouts of Sydney and Xudine, it would be Anna, Sydney's sister. Anna ran her bakery from the brick house left to her by her father, Uncle Orisha. A group of children, organized by Yvette, were playing Mumblety-peg near the gap that led to the house. A few boys stood in the late evening shade, watching the skipping and the jumping. Yvette had this reputation with the children. Most of the other girls around Yvette's age had other interests. But Yvette loved to play with the kids and they all flocked to her. She looked unruly frolicking with the children.

"Godfrey," she shouted over the ruckus, "Remember? Tomorrow."

"Yeah, near the tree."

"Don't be late."

Yvette continued to sing that song and toss the stick with ease. Two of the children belonged to Anna. The sound of their voices followed me up the gap, past the patch of banana and the breadfruit trees.

I saw Anna long before she saw me. She stood in her kitchen, dusting and tossing a big lump of raw dough. The loose flour was all over her face and on the apron that covered her protruding stomach. Her husband, Ned, hadn't visited Grenada for over a year, but she was pregnant. She continued to wrestle the dough until I was at the kitchen door. She presumed the purpose of my visit and spoke to me.

"Ian isn't here. He's out liming with his Rasta friends. Ah keep telling him he's too young to be running around with dose ganja-smoking troublemakers. He doesn't listen anymore. He thinks he's ah man already. Ah keep warning him."

There was the sight and scent of fresh bread. One batch already out of the over sat ready, brown and enticing. Saliva moistened the inside of my mouth. This was the work of the person people frequently refer to as the woman with the sailor's tongue. I remembered when butter didn't melt in her mouth, but since the death of her son, life had changed for Anna. She started drinking rum and would quarrel with neighbors at the flick of a match. A palpable sadness mingled with the scent of her bread. I had intended to phrase my question tactfully, but the words poured out of me.

"What happened to Sydney and Xudine? Where did they go?" I spoke to her back as she continued to flatten the dough with the heel of her hand.

"Meh leg's killing me. Ah have to sit down. Let dis dough rise." She gave the dough one last punch and moved across the kitchen, sitting down heavily in a chair. "It was ah beautiful funeral. You saw how many people came. Dey left work and traveled," she smiled quickly. "Sit, Godfrey."

I sat down on the only other chair in the room.

"Dey left de same day we buried your father. Didn't say where… You mean, dey didn't tell you?"

The lump in my throat moved as I swallowed.

"You want something to eat? Get de butter, dere's bread over dere. Ah was wondering why Sydney gave me dis for you."

She reached into the pocket of her white apron, and took out a sealed envelope. I took it out of her hand before she offered it. She looked at me briefly and started talking again.

"Xudine is having ah baby, you know. Must be why dey left. And Karrol's death was too much for dem. How you doing, Godfrey? Things okay with you? You don't come around much anymore." She paused for a time, looked at me, and then looked away. It appeared as if tears might be welling in her eyes. "Ah loved your father. Always loved him, even wen we were kids. Dis fucking place, dis fucking ocean…" She shook her head vigorously. "Ah had de chance to leave Grenada once. Son of ah bitch, ah don't want to cry." Her effort to quash the tears thinned her lips. "If you ever get de chance to leave dis place, take it and run. Don't look back. Don't spend all your life here. You will find only sadness and pain." The last words left her mouth as if she had just spit out a seed.

"It's okay, Miss Anna. I'm all right. I understand."

I stood and started to move backward with the envelope in hand. The encounter with this woman left me jittery. It was as if I had swallowed a spider and it was still living way down in my stomach. "Tell Ian I came by." My voice came out like the croak of a frog.

I hoped she couldn't see the turbulence roiling all over my face, but I knew I was wrong; the confusion had to look like mango pulp on my chin. The moment I was out of sight I ripped into the envelope. The note read: "*Godfrey, get close and prepare for the battle of your life. The face in your vision is your Yumawalli. If you don't deal with it, it will deal with you. That's the way of this thing. It will hunt you blindly and limit the days of your life. It will stalk you in exactly the appearance you saw in your vision. Remember that face. This is our payment to you. You made wonderful things possible. Wish I had the strength to remain and help. But I'm old and tired. May the element of surprise give you an edge. Get close and kill it.*"

Oh my God! My father was right. The man is a lunatic. How can anyone kill a figment from a dream? At home, I locked myself in the house, and read the note again. And then I burned it. Took a stick match, struck it against the box, and put the flame to the paper. I watched the fire crawl and turn the note to black ash. The last lick of the flame burned my fingers. I dropped the last bit and watched it settle to the floor.

In bed that night, I hoped to dream, gather some insights into Sydney's message and Xudine's pregnancy. Am I the father of that child? They had to be some kind of connection somewhere that I was missing. Sleep eluded me, because my last encounter with Sydney tumbled around in my head like a stick in the waves. It both explained and obscured all that were bothering me.

He was standing in the middle of the path leading up to the Jupa, leaning on his walking stick and looking at me as I approached. I think he was blocking my route to the house and paving their escape. Xudine could have been packing as we spoke. I asked him the first question without salutations.

"Uncle Sydney, did you ever find the Black Lake?"

"Yes. We found it. It was not black at all. Because of its origins, they thought it might be black. They had a legend that said, if you drink of the Black Lake you could live forever."

"Well, did you drink?"

"Of course. We all drank. We lived on its banks. One day I went exploring along the shore of the lake and found a bunch of shiny stones. Diamonds. Just sitting there on the surface of the ground. I found a stick and dug around, found this big, red orb. It looked like a cricket ball left behind by some boys. My find had no value there, but in the outside world, quite another story. I placed my find in the same bag with my Bibles and tracts. By now, Xudine and I had formed a bond. I told her to keep a lookout for men with lights on the front of their head milking trees. We found a rubber taper who agreed to guide us out.

"We made it to Caracas, Venezuela, where I rented a safety deposit box and secured my find. I wanted no one to know. It would mean the end of her people. So, I took a few of the small stones, sold them secretly, and we bought a small house on a quiet street in Caracas. Men from the government, soldiers in uniforms, started coming around and asking questions. One night we slipped away, got on a ship to Trinidad, and then came here to Grenada. Hoping that no one would follow." He paused, looked around as if searching. But then the next words that came out of his mouth almost made me laugh. "The blood of some powerful shaman runs in your veins, Godfrey. Your Ayahuasca vision showed that. We suspected when Karrol told us about your dreams. Xudine's people need a powerful shaman to keep the faith. You helped us lay the foundation for that. We know where we belong now. But don't forget your journey, Godfrey. One day it will be made clear. Just be wary of the Yumawalli. It's a thief. I hope you didn't think I would tell anybody about the fire. It took courage, what you tried to do." That was our last conversation.

The next day began sunless, and wet. All I wanted to do was gain some understanding, come to terms with these riddles. I returned to the Jupa one last time, and looked around, at the place where I stood at the crossroads of time and saw that face that Xudine said would be my guide, but that Sydney called my Yumawalli. Now they want me to deal with it somehow. What body would such a face fit on? I perused the back yard, now wet and muddy with a few stray leaves strewn here and there. The house seemed forlorn as if it too understood my predicament.

I had plans for the rest of the day, and I still held on to a slim hope. The attempt to mend things with Yvette suddenly seemed crucial. She had agreed to meet me, but I knew she made this concession because of the death of my father. But the weather. It was near the end of the dry season, but the rain refused to wait its turn. The clouds hung for a moment over Richmond Hill, then drifted out in thin patches, bathing the valley in a delicate spray that ceased and resumed all through the morning. I rushed to the spot under the cordia tree as the weather die away. Yvette was waiting. Large red petals from the cordia flowers littered the ground. She looked slightly annoyed.

"I almost went back home. What's the matter? You afraid of a little rain?"

"I decided, Yvette."

"Decided what?"

She looked at me as if I was some kind of dog about to bite her.

"To leave school," I said.

"Godfrey, you damn fool. What did that leper and his woman do to your brains? What kind of job you think you going to get, garbage collector? Or maybe a porter, pushing a handcart around town till you gray?"

"Those are jobs that pays money."

She looked at me and shook her head. I suddenly felt like a small puppy.

"My father would never allow us to get married, Godfrey. Where's your plans, your ambitions. And come to think of it, why would I want to marry a man who comes home every day tired and stinking? Hardly have time for his children, can't afford to send them to a good school. Why would I do a thing like that?"

She spoke the words and turned her back to me, her fists clinched at her side. I understood her outburst, but she had no idea about my plans, or my ambitions.

"Yvette, they driving me crazy. I have enough up here," I said, knocking on my forehead with my index finger. "I can read and write, I can count. I am educating myself with the books my mother sent me.

I already know more than most of those teachers. I learn what I want to know, not what they want me to know. And I'll find good work to take care of us, and our children. You'll see. Fins told me I could be a very good artist one day."

I moved toward her as I spoke. I placed both my hands on her shoulders and turned her to face me. She yielded, just slightly, and I took her into my arms. She pushed me to an arm's length, and she smiled a half-smile, not with her eyes, just with her mouth. The gesture caused her to relax, and the fullness came back to her lips, softening them. I wanted to just grab her, spread her all over me like butter on bread, but she started to talk, slowly, with just a hint of renewed irritation.

"You said children? Lord! Godfrey! Fins, the leper, what are you doing with those people? Credentials, man, credentials are what you need."

She spat out the words, almost slapping me with them, but then she stopped abruptly, alarm flashed in her eyes, and she became rigid. I turned to see what stood behind us. A tall, slim man, skin as black as coal, stood there. It was like I had never seen him before. His features held definitions that chisels could have formed them. His long sculpted face held a wicked expression.

It was Yvette's father, Cyril. He stood a short distance away with a new machete in one hand. He looked reckless in khaki shorts, no shoes, and a sleeveless white undershirt. I held my ground as Yvette began to speak.

"What you doing, Daddy?" she spoke casually, in a high-pitch, singsong rhythm. He ignored her charm and kept me fixed in his gaze.

"Godfrey Soul-ages!" Cyril spoke carefully. He pronounced every syllable of my last name-Soul-ages. "Your father died in a fish pot; you going to die running." He charged at me with the machete raised.

I dodged around the tree, and Cyril slapped at me with the flat of the blade, striking the tree. The echo of steel on green wood reverberated and blended with Yvette's scream.

"Daddy! What you doing? You drunk. Stop that, leave him alone." She tried to move between her father and me.

Cyril turned on her. "Go home, girl! I'll deal with you later."

I seized that distraction to put space between the blade, and myself.

The rows of coconut palms and young banana plants beckoned and I ran. This was nothing new. Cyril occasionally found it necessary to chase me away from his daughter. This thing with the machete was new. I heard footfalls behind me, punctuated by cries, and fierce promises. It occurred to me that this could be serious. So, I ran faster.

I reached the bend in the mud path where it crossed Tante Rose's yard. Cyril lagged a little behind. My breathing was hard, and I didn't want to explain to anyone why I was running. I slowed, turned the corner, and went into a brisk walk. Tante Rose's old dog, Moocher, stood growling and blocking the path. It was a most inconvenient time to come across that dog. A stone or a small stick would send Moocher running, but no such tools stood at hand. And Cyril was still coming.

I avoided the dog by leaving the path and ducking into the banana field. I kept moving at a steady clip, hoping that my bare feet would avoid any broken glass or rusty nails. I headed toward the far end of the field, where it collided with a junction, near a hibiscus fence fifty yards away.

The long green leaves slapped me as I ran. Beads of rainwater washed my face, wet my shirt and pants. Strange refreshment. I felt relieved as I bounded out of the field onto the road, hoping to run into no one. Cyril was now shouting at the dog. I heard him as I caught my breath and waited for the second leg of this chase. However, I doubted that Cyril would make it past Moocher in time to catch me, because I was now out of sight. My confidence returned, and I proceeded to walk with intent. I heard voices. Two of them, two women coming up the road. Tante Rose, Yvette's aunt, and her friend, Miss Olga. They came strolling toward me, talking. I ducked out of sight.

The two women were opposites. Tante Rose had graying hair that she often dyed and straightened with a hot comb. Miss Olga was another picture: large, busty, with a head of black hair in braid so thick they resembled sections of a rope you could use to hitch a cow. People called these two women lesbians behind their backs.

The hibiscus fence was a perfect hiding place. I sat down and pulled my knees up to my chin. A lizard clung to a stem below a flower. Long, green, big bulging eyes, a wingless, shrunken dragon. The two women came right up to the junction, where they should have parted company. They just stood there, one smiling and the other talking. It took me a whole minute to grasp the thread of the conversation. Olga did the talking, her tongue smacking the roof of her mouth as if she was savoring something delicious. Tante Rose just kept nodding her head and repeating.

"Aha… aha… aha…"

"Girl, peculiar thing. Ah seen it all you know. Ah was up behind Islander Hotel in de bush, hauling wood for de fireside, wen ah looked out on de ocean and dere he was, pulling up de fish pots. He brought it up across de stern; it was loaded with fish, big ones. Ah could see dem flapping around. He wasn't dat far out. When ah notice he was alone, ah wonder what happened to Godfrey, because he always took de boy out with him. You know dat. When ah notice de ripples around de boat, meh eyes pop open big and ah drop de bundle ah wood.

"Ethan started looking at de water, turning around in ah circle as if ah pack of dogs were after his legs. De big sea devil came to de surface; horns stuck way out of de water. It kept going around and around de boat, and Ethan kept turning with it, like some kind ah rag in de wind. He bounced into de fish pot, and it tumbled back into de water. Ethan tumbled right in with it. Dey said wen dey found him, de rope was around his ankle and he was almost inside de fish pot. Wat would make ah man crawl inside ah fish pot under-water?"

"Only God knows, girl," Olga said.

"Olga, dey saying de sea devil was really after de boy. It looks like Ethan made ah deal and couldn't keep it. So, it took him instead of his son. He must ah really love dat boy." Tante Rose moistened her lips, and made that smacking sound again.

"And now de boy is courting your niece," Olga said.

"Don't worry, Cyril will soon put an end to dat."

The two women shook their heads as if in resignation, and then they moved off in different directions.

I had the sensation you might experience after a person with a bad cold sneezes in your face. This was exactly the kind of thing Tante Grace had tried to shelter me from that night of the prayer meeting for her brother. However they clothe my father's death, the facts remain. He died as he lived, mysteriously.

CHAPTER 12

Going home seemed dicey. Cyril might be waiting nearby, trap me in the house, start cussing away, waving his cutlass. I knew that game. Neighbors would listen and laugh. I decided to spare myself the aggravation, take a long walk. Visit my aunt Grace. Good place to hide. She always had some food ready. This would give Cyril time to cool down, and quiet the echo of his threats shouting in my brain.

Your father died in a fish-pot; you gonna die running.

I trudged up the muddy road; my memories teemed like red ants stirred from nesting. The advise of my Aunt Grace, all her words spoken to me at that prayer meeting for my father-strange how my legs moved in one direction and my thoughts in another. Shouldn't my brain follow the direction of my feet? I should be able to think forward. The wet mud slid between the cracks of my toes, and the chitchat of the two women joined the chorus in my head.

My aunt Grace had anticipated all this and had tried to shelter me from it. I did not live in her house, but she became my caretaker following the departure of my mother. She worked as a nurse's aide at the general hospital in Saint Georges, but she held fast to the conviction that the soul often needs more care than the body.

Soon after the death of my father, my aunt held a prayer meeting, to secure a place in heaven for her brother's soul. The event was loaded with emotion. After everyone had congregated at the old house, she opened the meeting with a prayer and a speech.

"All dis is more for de living dan de dead," she said. "My brother carries no guilt or sins to de house of God. You de living carries dose burdens. Learn to lay em down. Now, let's say ah prayer for meh brother, Ethan, in de hopes dat he would be safe in de hands of God long before de devil realizes wat happened down here."

They all bowed their heads in a mumbled prayer: Olga, Tante Rose, Cyril, Anna LaGrenade, my cousins, Julian and Alister, (Tante Grace's children), and many others. Some people came down from Perdmontemp. They filled the house.

Most of them honestly came to pay homage, and pray for a dead friend. Others came for the food and drinks that Tante Grace had assembled on a table in the corner. A framed black-and-white photo of my mother and father with Tante Grace standing behind them adorned the table. All three of them looked young and jovial. Tears welled up in my eyes. I knew they all assumed my tears came from grief, but my tears came out of a lost desire. The smiling face of my parents in that picture spoke to me like hieroglyphics on a tomb.

My aunt rested her hands on my shoulder, and I cringed. The prayer had ended; they all stood staring at me, and I could not control the convulsions heaving in my chest. She guided me out of the room. I went sheepishly. Alister followed us out onto the front stairs. She hugged me quickly, with one hand.

The voices from inside flounder through the refrain: "when the roll is called up yonder." They strained to do so much. Tante Grace turned to her son. We had spent sometime together, but no special relationship existed outside the family ties. Now he was speaking; the words came out of his mouth in little lumps as if rehearsed. "Godfrey, you will be all right you know. You feeling bad now, but that can't last long. Uncle dead, but you still alive. Mama said God has plans for you. That's why you here."

The tone in his voice, that attempted sentiment, both had a distinct effect. Our eyes met briefly. He lowered his head as if embarrassed, turned, and went back into the house.

"Well, now dat your fader is gone, you can move to Trinidad; live with your moder," Tante Grace said, "She always said she would be glad to have you."

She brought the aim of her attention to bear on me as she waited for my reaction. My aunt's words forced me to take a deep breath. I felt annoyed that her conversation now seemed to veer from my father, to my mother and Trinidad.

"Tante, when I was a boy, I dreamed like a boy. I saw my mother every night, in places with no names. Then I realized the equator was not a real place. That was a long time ago. I hardly ever think of her now. I have my house, my piece of land, and my boat. My father left all that to me. Can I forsake all that and run off? What am I going to do over there? My mother has her family and life. She doesn't need me around. I'm a man now; I need to make my own way."

Tante Grace smiled. I saw her jaw move, just slightly, and her eyes seemed to widen. When she spoke again, all the sympathy and tenderness had left her voice. She spoke openly, as if instructing me in the fine art of threading a needle. "Godfrey, you will hear all kind of things about your fader now dat he is dead. Pay dem no mind. Your fader lived ah rough life, drinking, gambling and smuggling. De people he knew were not nice people. Ah suspect one of dem may have done something to him but ah don't know. So don't listen to all the superstitious… you hear me, don't listen to dem. Talking, trying to sound important. De Lord giveth and de Lord taketh away. Dat's all dere is. Don't go asking questions, dat will only drive you crazy."

From inside the house, the mourners moved on to another hymn, *"Nearer My God to Thee."* My aunt's suspicion that my father may have been killed hit me like a stone. But her caution about asking questions? It seemed only God could give me the answers I needed and a question about my father and God took shape in my brain. It started with why! But just before it leaped onto my tongue, her voice came at me and forced the question to stick to the roof of my mouth like hardened molasses.

"Ah glad you want to stay in Grenada," she said. "You know ah love you like one of meh own. Your moder, your fader and me-we were de team."

A little burst of laughter erupted out of her, but she caught her breath quickly, as if the laughter might convey what she didn't want to express.

"We did everything together-played carnival, went to dances—that's before I found the Lord. Everybody was so mad at your fader wen we saw her belly getting big. We thought of throwing you away. We went to see Mama Viche up in Jan Anglais. She told us what to do. We picked de herbs and boiled de tea about five times, but she couldn't drink it. Every time ah see you, ah so glad. Look at de man you turn out to be."

She looked straight at me without saying another word. I found it peculiar, my aunt telling me about the choice to give me life, the undertaking of two young girls. The voices from the house filled the night. Her eyes were gauging me now, searching for what I don't know.

"Sorry we never told you much about your moder," she said. "De first night she spent in dis house ah heard her crying. Ah went to see wat's wrong. She started talking, telling me about de place where she grew up, on Saint Vincent. So ah sat and listened to her cry about her people and de place she called Blight."

My face twitched. Oh my God! I'm part Vincey? I almost shouted the word "WHAT!" The exclamation almost squealed out of my mouth, but before it could escape, my aunt was talking again.

"She came from ah little fishing village. Something like dis place. Dat's how she described. Dey called de bay Non-Such Bay. De village carried de name of dat man who brought breadfruit to dese islands, Captain Bligh. But somewhere along de way, ah T' got attached to de end of de name, and de place became known as Blight.

"De place lived up to its name during the world war. A fisherman found ah big round metal ball with spikes. He brought it in and all his friends came by, poking and prodding. One of dem suggested dey break it open to see what's inside. Dey brought ah sledge and struck de ball. Den, suddenly, boom! It exploded. For days, dey picked bit of human flesh out of de coconut trees along de beach.

"She was fourteen de year de jacks and anchovies ran heavy. Huge schools migrated into Non-Such Bay. De fishermen dropped deir seines and netted de biggest catch anyone could remember. But along with de catch, dey also netted two drums of denatured alcohol. No one knew wat denatured meant.

"De big catch sold for more money dan dey had ever seen. Den dey fried up wat remained and had ah great big feast. Dey feted all night, drinking dat alcohol from de drums, mixing it with cola and coconut water, eating fried jacks with breadfruit. Morning came, and Blight was silent, except for dogs barking and roosters crowing.

"De first screams came just as de sun peeped over de horizon. Den another and another. All de older people who drank from de drums were dead. Some stronger men and women just stumbled about blind. Down on de beach ah group of men lay chopped up from fights dat broke out as de rest of de villagers slept.

"Funerals went on for many days. Then after dat, Hurricane Janet came through, and mash-up de place. Your moder took ah bus to Kingston and caught de first vessel out. She heard dey were building ah big hotel on a hill in Grenada. She thought she might be able to find work dere. Ah spotted her one evening, walking up de road by Tanteen. She held an old brown grip in one hand. She looked lost. Ah recognized de Vincey accent wen she finally decided to speak to me. Ah took her home with me because she had no place to go. She became Ma Nellie's second daughter.

"God, she was bright, brighter dan a full moon. Your moder could've cooked food with words and numbers if she had to." Tante laughed quickly and was talking again. "She told me once dat ignorance can kill. Wen she got dat scholarship to study at de University of The West Indies in Trinidad, we were all so proud of her. But den you came. Dat only slowed her down, den she was off and running." Tante giggled this time, like a little girl, and threw up her hands. "Wen she wrote and told me she found the Lord, and dat she was studying to be ah minister, my heart soared." Tante tapped her breasts quickly with one hand.

"Godfrey, we know you were her gift to us."

I felt weird. Me? A gift?

"Dat's why she never tried to take you-to Trinidad, I mean. You see. All dose books she keeps sending you, dose piled high in de house, de ones your fader used to raise his nose at. Dat's her way of speaking without making a lot of noise. You will go traveling in dese islands one day, on one of those yachts or on a cargo vessel like your fader. Go to dat place called Blight. Some of her people might still be dere. Dey are things you need to know, but ah can't tell you, can't hear it from me, second hand. Dey need to tell you dem-selves. Let's go inside and get some food before dey eat all of it." On the night of that prayer meeting for my father, I said nothing to my aunt about the death of Karrol or my dislike for Vincentians.

* * *

Those old memories chafe on me like an awkward load on the back of a jackass. Now, for just an instant, I thought of avoiding my aunt's house. Go some place else to avoid Cyril. But it was too late. I heard her singing the hymn long before I saw her. Her voice challenged the nature of the day. *My God is a Rock in a Weary Land.* There was no turning back or sneaking by now. She stood in her kitchen door. She wore a frock. It went all the way down to her ankles, around the jelly shoes, the ones we called dog muzzles.

"Ah glad to see you," she said as I wiped the mud from my feet. "You here to play with your cousins? Julian's reading for his O-Levels exam." She spoke with pride. "Alister is here though. Alister, look who's here? Come in, come in. You just in time for some soup." She greeted me as if she hadn't seen me in years. Alister looked up at me and tried to smile. His mother must have been getting on his ass for some reason. He looked miserable.

"Let me show you this, Godfrey." He lifted three sheets of paper from a pile and handed them to me.

"What's this?" I took the pages from him.

Tante Grace looked at us with a mixture of sanction and annoyance. She moved across the room to a pot boiling on her new stove, and began spooning me a bowl of split pea soup with pig snout and some big dumplings. I ate the food slowly, savoring the brackish taste of the potage, and I scanned the pages. The words scribbled on the paper looked familiar, some kind of tale told to children.

"They told me to write an essay about life in Grenada, and that's all I could come up with." Alister sat in a chair in the corner as if banished there with a dunce cap. "They said that's a folk tale, not an essay. Can you believe it? They don't get it, and I don't think I should be explaining it to them. They are the teachers and I'm the pupil."

What did he want them to get? It was a story about a cow thief called Primus, who stole a white man's prize bull cow and slaughtered it for meat. I heard it for the first time when I was only seven years old. Alister sat there indignant, looking at me as I read the pages in earnest this time. He seemed to be looking for some kind of agreement from me. But as I read the last word, something happened. All these years and I had never truly appreciated what the tale was about. It was like being in a dark room and Alister opened a door just a crack, allowing a shaft of light to stream in. The story dealt with worth. The bull had more worth alive than as meat. And don't we all have worth, some kind of worth? Who bestows worth and what is it really? I felt stupid. All those years, I never got the true gist of the tale, and no one bothered to explain it to me.

"You see it now don't you? I can tell by the look on your face." Alister laughed out loud and clapped his hands.

"Yeah! I always knew the meaning of that story."

I couldn't let him know. My pride would be wounded. I had to leave, explore this new bug in my brain. I lied about a chore I had to perform and stood to leave. I assumed that Cyril must have calmed down by now, with the rain and all. Tante Grace handed me two avocados. The two pears felt substantial, could be used as weapons if needed. She grabbed my shoulders, forcing me to look directly at her face. Her eyes appeared mist and sad.

"Godfrey," she said, "you don't go to church with us anymore. You remember how to pray? God is a good God. Ask God to soothe your heart. Ask God to have mercy on you, pave the road in front of you. Ask and ye shall receive." She kept me fixed in that sad gaze for a moment and then she blinked twice as if something just flew into her eyes; she released me.

What could I to say to her? I lowered my head and spoke softly. "Thank you, Tante."

As I walked away from the house, I glanced back at my aunt, standing in the doorway. How could a person of such faith ever be sad? In spite of my new insights, the murkiness of the day still held me. I walked down the road, half expecting Cyril to come after me again. I felt even more certain about my decision. School bored the hell out of me, but my mother's books were shouting louder each time I looked at the bookshelf. I should share some of them with Alister.

The particulars of that day placed me in a deliberative mood. What's the worth of all these memories? My encounter with Yvette and Cyril; I knew that Cyril would calm down, and Yvette and I would be back where we belong. My visit to Tante Grace, my new appreciation of Alister, all of this seemed kind of ordinary. But the news about Xudine and the letter given to me by Anna, the one from Sydney, about the Yumawalli, all this threw me into a tailspin.

Could this be a dream? One so vivid you swear it's real. The kind that makes your heart beat fast, and when you come out of it you feel a mixture of disappointment and gratitude. What if I never woke from the influence of the Ayahuasca and I'm still dreaming on that cot in the back yard? Or locked away in some crazy-house? This mud under my feet, the rainwater dripping from leaves, the two avocados clutched between my fingers. Are they some minutiae from a lucid vision?

Just bury one fantasy with another. That double feature at the Empire Theater had to be the mulch. *Shane*, with Alan Ladd, and *Morgan the Pirate,* with Errol Flynn-that should do it. All the guys would be down there: Ian, Cosmus, those Rasta boys with no money, just hanging around, trying to sneak into the show at intermission.

At first, I thought of ripping up the floor and liberating some of my father's cash, but I decided against that. I knew how to get some money and keep my pledge not to spend any of that cash. The bunch of ripe papayas on the tree near the house spelled currency. A basket of fruit sold to the right yacht out there could yield five dollars in a matter of minutes. Throw in one of Tante Grace's avocados.

The arrangement would have been tempting to anyone. Three papayas, half-ripe, two small hands of yellow bananas, and topped of with the shiny green avocado. The offering sat in a wicker basket on the stern of *Lucky Joe*. Throw in the basket with the deal.

The *Black Dog* appeared to be the best prospect out there. Having just arrived, they had no idea what things cost. The oars felt rough in my palms. They sliced the water. *Lucky Joe* glided across the lagoon. The repetitive strokes, the sheer physical exertion, all this heightened my mood. Oh, what the hell! If I'm dreaming let it be.

The yacht rode at anchor fifty feet away, the hull, a brooding black, the wheelhouse and rails varnished, shiny even in the evening gloom. A Boston Whaler rode on a line off the stern. I allowed the oars to hang idly in the water as I glanced over my right shoulder.

The black hull looked ugly up close. Long streaks of quinoid brown tarnished the paint. Here and there, the bolts wept rust. Under the bowsprit squatted the ornate bust and head of a gorgon, painted white, except the hair. The snakes were in gold. The name stood out white in block letters-*BLACK DOG.*

Someone with wispy hair sat in the cockpit, under a white awning, back to me. It was obvious the person had heard the thrashing of the oars but remained unconcerned, not inquisitive one bit. Not a good sign. I pivoted the oars, and slid *Lucky Joe* parallel to the gangway.

"Ahoy, *Black Dog.* How you doing today?" I shouted in my best Yankee accent.

"The *Black Dog* would tell you she is doing fine if she could talk." The voice spoke with a Southern accent. Sounded like that actor from the movie, *TOM DOOLEY.*

The voice could have been a woman's or a young boy's. The person stood and turned. Something started way down in my throat, a kind of cough inside a bubble. I imagined the event would explode if it got the chance to leap onto my tongue. I strangled it somewhere down in my throat. An absolute shiver ran through me, made a rash on my skin. The speaker looked exactly like that face from the Ayahuasca vision. Finally, I remembered to breathe and came to a realization: this is a man.

For an instant, everything stood still and all the memories flooded my brain. The face looked as if a swarm of angry wasps had attacked it. Little craters pointed to the red dots that littered the pudgy face. A small, blood orange nose stood above the scraggly beard and the mustache that shielded his thin lips.

Nevertheless, the eyes reflected a soft silver-laden blue, quieting his misbegotten profile. A big smile exposed a mouthful of perfectly straight, white teeth. Clearly, this person had grown accustomed to such reaction. Embarrassment and confusion made my face ache. The fact that this person had misunderstood my reaction left me agitated. No explaining. He would never understand.

"Come aboard, come on. Let's see what you got there." He spoke as he walked across the deck, one hand slid through the droplets that had collected on the varnished rail. The other hand clutched a beer. "What's your name?" He was short for a man with such a big face and head. And he spoke again before I could answer. "Don't expect me to pay you too much. I'm a cheap son of a bitch," he said.

"My name is Godfrey Soul-ages," I said.

"Spell that," he said.

"S-o-u-l-a g-e-s."

"You mean Soulages, Soulages."

The man corrected me on the pronunciation of my name. He

sounded as if trying to say "so large," but squeezing the G and E sound up against his pallet with his tongue and at the last moment, dropping the S.

I handed him the basket of fruits, along with the bowline. He put down the basket, and wrapped the line around a cleat with a half hitch. I stood, balanced myself, and climbed up the gangway and over the gunwale onto the deck. The man stood with my basket of fruits hidden behind him on the wheelhouse. This is my name, I thought, who the hell are you to tell me how to pronounce it?

His name was Jack Trueblood. He bought the basket of fruits and gave me a sour-smelling beer. He paid me eight dollars in Grenadian currency, and then offered me a job. He told me that a man coming out there in this weather to make a buck deserves an opportunity. That's how Jack and I finally met with flesh on our bones.

Where are you Karrol? Are you looking down on this and laughing? Movies became the furthest thing from my mind that night. Jack and I had a confined and one-sided conversation. I wanted to remain close to this specter, try to make sense of what Sydney said. I allowed him to do most of the talking and I listened hard. I kept asking myself, Kill what? Kill this man who just offered me the greatest opportunity of my life?

I went home almost bursting with joy. How could I be this lucky? Who in the name of heaven could be looking over me? I wanted to sleep and wake up to the freshness of this new occasion. I rested in bed; listening to the melodies of the sweet, wet night. Crickets, tree frogs, an owl hooted in the distance, the neighbors laughed now and then as if they shared my joy. How far to morning?

CHAPTER 13

My first assignment on the *Black Dog* turned out to be a downright indulgence in monotony. Jack pulled the yacht into a quay, and he assigned me to pull three hundred feet of rusted chain out of the folksail, and wire brush, prime, and paint the links. Cyril kept strolling by our spot, not saying a word, wearing his swimsuit; goggles and snorkels rested on his head. He looked like Harry Belafonte in that movie, *ISLAND IN THE SUN.* The white women on other yachts threw him sly glances. He drifted by frequently as if assessing my progress. Bazil, the ex-policeman turned security guard, kept a stern, covetous eye on Cyril.

I hauled the metal links out, a foot at a time, down to the bitter end. I found the last link attached to the boat by a piece of mildewed rotten rope. What would have happened if all the chain came pouring out? I amused myself with an image of all the chain and the anchor trailing out across the bottom of some deep blue bay.

Jack hung around wearing a bikini bathing suit, watching me work, talking like a man just released from a solitary quarantine. He conversed in contrary snatches.

"Those fuckers call themselves friends. Ran like rats after that thing with the authorities. One of them could have remained to help me with this shit. One last trip and I'm done-my ex-wife, with her husband and two of their friends. She writes for a magazine called Tropics. She plans to do an article about the trip and this boat. Maybe, get a couple charters out of the publicity. That's the only reason I agreed to it. Just one week. After that, a trip to Trinidad to revamp this mother and I'm out of here, turning her over to a skipper. He can hire his own crew. You can deal with him if you want. I'm tired of this. Bought her for the tax breaks and ended up with a fucking headache."

His nose twitched like a rabbit's as he spoke. It disturbed me, made me unable to focus on his face, but he didn't seem to care. Jack frequently invited me to the Yacht Service's restaurant, where I was the only black face, except for the cooks and servers. The other white people looked at me as if I was some kind of stray dog that had wondered in. Jack just kept talking at me, his mouth full of food, chewing ugly and guzzling beer.

"I'll make you a bet. You have no idea. The *Black Dog* is way older than you or me. She was once in a movie. Something called, *In the Wake of the Red Witch*, with John Wayne. One of the few he dies in, by the way. She's more than thirty years old." He paused as if expecting some kind of applause, and continued to put the food in his mouth.

I was listening to Jack and searching for some bearing in his words. At first, I assumed he didn't want to eat alone, and was buying my company with food. But he must have been riling those other white people by bringing his black crewman into the restaurant. Either way, I didn't care.

He looked up from the food as if the flavor had suddenly changed. "You Grenadians are tame," he said. "You act so damn refined, civilized. You have no attitudes. Now black Americans-have it in spades. Not pun intended." He laughed and released the fork into his plate and pointed his finger. "Black Power hasn't reached you people yet. I don't want to be here when you people realize. So much wealth taken out of this land, and out of your black hides, poor bastards." He paused for a moment as if to catch his breath. I had a feeling that Jack had just insulted me, and every black person on the island of Grenada.

I had to respond. "Jack, Grenadians aren't poor bastards. Some of us fought in wars. Others are adventures, merchants going away to other countries. The man who owns that house over there," I pointed in the direction of the Jupa hidden behind the trees, "he followed a native guy into the Amazon and found loads of diamonds. So you see?"

"I'm headed back to the States," he continued to talk, completely ignoring my attempt to defend Grenadians. "My folks are getting old. I should spend more time with them, and my daughter. I invited her, but she didn't want to be on a cruise with her stepfather. This trip should be interesting, just four of them. They board in Saint Vincent in ten days."

His whole diatribe left me confused and irked. I wanted to also tell Jack about the Rastas I knew; how they would treat him if he got on the wrong side of them. *"Say It Loud, I'm Black and I'm Proud,* James brown strutting his stuff. Bunch of words compared to what a Rasta might do. However, I kept my mouth shut on that score and ate his food. I was getting very good at listening.

We worked on the yacht, at anchor and docked, for the next two weeks. We painted the hull, varnished the rails and deckhouse, sanded and oiled the teak deck. The *Black Dog* gleamed.

As we worked, we engaged in a rambling succession of conversations. We spoke about books and movies. I told Jack about a movie called, *"Taras Bulba,"* with Yul Brynner and Tony Curtis, which I once saw at Empire Theater, how I enjoyed the Cossacks horsemen. He told me the movie is from a book written by a Russian fellow who also wrote one of his favorite short stories. *"The Nose."* He told me about another story, where a man woke one morning to discover that he had turned into a great big bug. And then he shared a tale set in a town where the inhabitants started turning into rhinoceroses. Morbid tales. Those people had to be involved in Voodoo even if they called it by another name.

The America that Jack described sounded like a dangerous mix-like walking into a yard full of barking dogs and not recognizing the ones that might bite. I decided I would like to see this country just for the sheer adventure of it. So, with my first pay, I went down to the government's office and applied for a passport. In the spot where they ask for my profession, I wrote sailor. I wanted to be prepared.

For all the time we spent together, and all our talks about matters mysterious and rational, Jack had seldom touch upon his connections with women; he had a daughter named Pearl, and he was once married. Yvette had visited the *Black Dog,* and Jack was very polite to her. Still, I had a funny feeling; the man might be queer.

After work one Friday evening, three days before our departure, for Saint Vincent, Jack and I sat in the cockpit of the *Black Dog* with a couple of beers. In the dwindling heat of that day, Jack Trueblood posed a question that would completely change my impression of him.

"Godfrey, where can a guy get laid around here?"

"Laid?" The question staggered me.

"Yes, laid. I see all these beautiful young women around here, white ones, black ones. You think I'm a dead man? Your Yvette is a real fox, as they would say in the States."

He winked and that left me jittery, as if something slimy might be crawling on my skin. Jack had use the word "laid" and "Yvette" in the same breath. I was taken aback and at once relieved. He had eyes for women. I was delighted for not having to carry the stigma of working in such proximity to a queer man. Damn rumors and jokes would have been crushing.

"Godfrey, you look a little embarrassed by all this. Right now, I don't have the time for a relationship. Some of the guys who work around here have been known to help-out a friend, you know. Get a woman for…you know…a clean one." The words left his mouth as little fragments. He took a sip of his beer as if to clear his throat. He turned aside. I felt trapped between a mounting uncertainty and a blistering arrogance. I was on the brink of speaking when he cut me off.

"It's no sin you know. At one time, the Catholic Church ran whorehouses, and even Saint Thomas Aquinas recognized the necessity. He even wrote about it."

Jack brought his beer to his lips again, and took a long slug. He emptied the bottle, placed it on the seat next to me, swallowed loud, and smacked his lips.

"I mean, if you don't know how, or would rather not be involved in anything like, I wouldn't-" He smiled, threw his palms wide open. He looked at me with his seawater eyes and waited.

I felt insulted. The idea that he thought I couldn't speak to a woman. My pride bubbled forward and I agreed to do this thing without saying a word. In earnest, I had heard of only one woman. Nevertheless, I intended to find her, and bring her back to the yacht just to prove to Jack that I was a man who could handle situations. The woman I had heard of lived in Saint Georges. They called her Qwill. I had seen her a few times when I hung around Fins' shop, and I had heard stories from Cosmus and others.

The moment it turned dark, I took the Boston Whaler into town. I motored by two cargo ships at the pier discharging their cargo. I surmised that along the wharf would be the best place to look. But what would I say?

I tied the boat to the wharf, started designing my approach as I walked. It was as if everyone in the rum shops and those lined up in front of Empire Cinema knew my errand. I walked by, self-conscious, wondering what Fins might be doing. I stood away from the crowd filing into the movie, on the fringe of the glow radiating from the floodlights outside the cinema.

A giant billboard to the side sported a picture of a stallion and Audie Murphy with a drawn pistol. The letters above his head read *SIX BLACK HORSES*. I hadn't seen the picture yet, but I knew it would be good. Audie Murphy's pictures were always good. A faded poster of another of Murphy's film, *To Hell and Back*, was on another billboard. I had seen that one, a war movie, and I loved it. Everyone claimed he played himself in that one. Must be fun imitating your past actions.

The woman came running down the road so fast, I started looking for what might be chasing her. She was tall, fair-skinned. She carried a pair of men's shoes in one hand. I was struck dumb by my good luck. It was Qwill. She ran right up to me, looked at me quickly, and then brought her index finger up to her lips as she moved behind the pillars of the billboard, and bent down.

"Qwill! Come back, Qwill. Qwill, where are you?"

I heard this pitiful plea long before I saw the man. He came staggering down the street, his bare white toes on the black asphalt, his clothes disheveled, a crewman off one of the cargo ships, drunk and on the town. He swayed in front of me. The stink of stale booze whiffed across my face.

"Say, blokes, have you seen Qwill? She stole my shoes and ran," the man said. He lurched too and fro, eyes red, face slack and gawky.

"Yeah. She went that way."

I pointed past the line of people filing into the movie. The man staggered on repeating his mournful lament. "Say, blokes, have you seen Qwill." The crowd broke into a hail of laughter. The man staggered on down the Carenage. "Come back, Qwill. My shoes. I have the money. Qwill."

I slipped behind the pillar with Qwill the moment the man staggered pass the line of people. "Wat you want? Payment for not telling him? Ah don't have any. Dat cheap limey, snatched his money back de second he got wat he wanted," she said.

"Ah don't need your money."

"Good. What you want den?" She looked me up and down. "You dat boy who was following Fins around like some kind of puppy."

"Ah have ah, ah have ah job for you."

"Job?" She laughed, exposing a mouthful of teeth with a little rot across the top gum line.

She covered her mouth with one hand to stifle the sound. She stank of perfume, her breath warm, minty; she was chewing on a wad of gum. Sweat left a soft gloss on her skin. She looked like any other woman. Could have been someone's mother. I liked her. Now she measured me with her eyes. "What's dis job?" Her face scowled. "Ah don't mess wit kids."

Kid! I can show you... The scent of her perfume forced me to swallow, and the next words that left my lips lacked certainty. "Not with me. Not for me. Ah working for ah white fellow, on ah yacht. He asked me to find you."

"Ah white fellow. He asked you to find me?" She poked herself between her breasts with one finger. "What's his name?"

"Well, not you exactly. You know."

"Where's dis yacht and dis white man?"

"In de lagoon, near de Yacht Service. Ah have ah Whaler over dere."

"Okay! Let's get ah couple things straight. Don't expect anything from me, and don't think dis makes us friends. You hear me?" She glanced down the wharf.

Qwill slipped away from the shadow of the billboard. The loafers dangled at her side from two fingers planted in the heels. I felt relieved as we moved away from the theater and the wharf. I had no idea it could be this easy. I started the motor, slapped it in gear, and placed it at half-throttle. The motor purred softly as we rounded the stern of the cargo ship.

"You hang around him for ah long time. Most of his friends don't last dat long."

"Wat you talking about?"

"Fins. He was once my friend, too."

"Dat fool. I don't want to talk about him."

"De snake jumped up and bit you, huh. Leh meh tell you. Every year around de time his mother pass on, same thing. Ah bottle of rum and chasing his friends off. It's hard to do anything for him." She fell silent and looked into the dark water sliding by the hull of the Whaler.

I delivered Qwill to Jack, told them I would be back. I was a little late for one of the few times Yvette would be allowed out after dark; I had this great story to tell.

A mixture of feeling took hold of me as I motored across the lagoon. My pride bubbled up at my success in bringing the woman to Jack. But something besides Qwill's speaking about Fins troubled me. What other kinds of stories could she tell if she sat me down? I couldn't shake an image forming in my head: Jack on top of her, thrusting and moaning. Would she close her eyes, or would she look at him, the way Xudine stared into me without uttering a sound. I told myself, say nothing of this to Yvette. She just wouldn't understand.

An hour later, I motored back to the Black Dog. Qwill sat in the cockpit, waiting. No sign of Jack. She didn't allow me to tie off. She came down the gangway and stepped into the Whaler the moment it came alongside. She still held the sailor's shoes in her hand. For a moment, I thought she might loose her balance and tumble overboard. But she sat down hard and spoke briefly. "Drop me off, over dere." She pointed at Lagoon Road, fifty yards across the water. As we approached the shore, my curiosity was killing me. I decided to use politeness.

"Sorry it took me so long to get back," I said. "I had no idea how long ah ah. You know."

She just stared at me with what I saw as disgust. Toward whom or what, I couldn't tell.

"What happened?" I asked the question just before the Whaler reached the shore. I couldn't let her escape without knowing.

"Let's call dis ah wasted night. Good-bye, Godfrey." She waved her fingers at me, and a ghost of a smile darted across her face just before she turned and vanished into the night.

CHAPTER 14

Jack crewed the *Black Dog* sparingly for the trip to Saint Vincent. I would be first mate, and he borrowed a cook, a meager woman with red hair called Marilyn. She came off an old yawl called *SCARAB*, registered out of Brisbane, Australia. Marilyn spoke in snippets. She seemed to shrink, almost making herself smaller when you looked at her. The woman had no obvious bruises, but you could tell she knew pain. She instructed me in the proper way to set a table. I marveled at the need for so many tools. One knife, a spoon, and maybe even a fork, seemed quite adequate to consume food. During the seating lesson, Marilyn whispered something that made me even more inquisitive about her.

"I was born in Africa," she said, "and I'm not an African. You have never seen Africa, and you are an African. Interesting what makes us who we are?"

"I've never called myself an African," I said.

"You should. That's who you are more than anything else," she said. "You look like some of the kids I grew up with." I almost asked her where she grew up, but she walked off, and all I could think of were images from Tarzan movies.

This was my first real job, and I considered it with great pride. Cyril stared me down as he released the bowline and tossed it onto the deck of the *Black Dog*, while Bazil released the stern.

"How long you gone for?" His question caught me by surprise. He shouted to be heard above the drone of the diesel engine. This was the first time the man had engaged me direct conversation.

"Ten days, sir," I said.

"When you come back, I'll have Yolan cook up a fish broth. We can drink some coconut water. Take care, Godfrey."

The yacht pulled away from the dock, and I watched Cyril standing there behind Lennox and Bazil. It was as though the sun had burst out from behind some dark cloud. What made him finally extend this gesture? He had never taken a trip off this island. I knew that for sure. Could this be some kind of jealousy, or did Cyril finally see me as a man worthy of his daughter?

We cleared the point off Balis Ground, motored through the channel, and out into the outer harbor. Stevedores were unloading a cargo ships. I imagined the shoeless fellow who had chased Qwill working on that ship in bare feet. Or did he have another pair of shoes? The harbor and the cargo ship faded in the distance as we motored away. This would be my first journey outside of Grenada. I had been out to sea before, but never moving away from land this fast. Stories to tell.

One thing Yvette said to me kept reverberating in my head. *"Without a complete education, you have no future, Godfrey."* We'll see about that. Captain of one of these could be a good profession. Owning one of these would certainly show everyone who the son of Ethan Soulages turned out to be.

The yacht received the wind in her sails as we cleared the lee of Grenada. We headed north under a steady breeze, Jack, Marilyn, and me. Other islands surfaced on the horizon: the Sisters and De Ronde, then Carriacou and Union Island. I sat on deck, watching flying fish swoop over the waves. Whales did a graceful ballet, broaching out to port, blowing plumes of white water and twirling their great tails to plunge back into the deep. Dolphins rode the bow waves just below the bust of Medusa. A great rush of contentment welled up in me as the BLACK DOG plowed the sea north.

Jack left Marilyn at the helm and came forward to the spot where I stood. I had this inkling that he might slap me on the back, but he didn't. The man had become very gracious with me, I assumed because I did the listening and he did the talking.

"Good thing they ran like rats, those so-called partners. I enjoy your company more."

I felt pleased standing side by side with Jack. Saying thank you seemed stupid, so I remained silent, wondering what happened with him and Qwill.

"I've always enjoyed the company of young people," he said. "Wish my daughter was here. She would have enjoyed this." A hint of sadness crossed his face and was gone like the ocean slipping by the hull of the *BLACK DOG*.

"This old tub needs some work to remain seaworthy. After this trip, we'll return Marilyn to her husband, head south to Trinidad. Get the work done, prices are cheaper and the quality of the work better than anything in Grenada." He stood gazing at the Caribbean Sea stretching north.

I felt important. I was Jack's confidant, first mate, and best friend. He would take me to those places I had dreamed about for so long, all those exotic names I had seen on the charts. I even envisioned sailing to the States on the *Black Dog*. He had to take her back there someday. Sydney's warning about the Yumawalli seemed absurd.

The prospects of the trip to Trinidad, seeing my mother and her family, not having to stay, showing her that I was a man on my own, those thoughts fortified me, made my heart soar. What would it be like to sneak up to my mother's house or go to her church one Sunday? Sit to the rear; watch her and her family for a while without announcing myself?

Silly, stray thoughts, like a playful puppy. Finally, I hit upon a plan, one that would show her what kind of man I became. I would tell her about the place called Blight, the village where she was born. Go there; see what it's all about.

We spent the first full day in Saint Vincent preparing for the guests. Jack went shopping for gin, rum, wine and ice. Marilyn and I went down to the market, where we bought breadfruits, bananas, dashines, and other condiments that would last the trip. All the necessary preparations were finished at the end of that day. I spoke to Jack that night, informing him that I'd be taking a day off to visit a village across the island.

"What are you going to do there?" Jack asked. The Johnson motor droned on as he ferried me to the wharf the next morning. "You have other family members there?"

"I don't think so. My mother lives in Trinidad these days. Just want to see the place, check it out. She left in a hurry, long before I was born." A hint of unease played around Jack's seawater eyes. He spoke jovially.

"She left in a hurry? Why? She robbed a bank?" He looked at me quickly, and then said something that sounded kind of dreamy. "Sometimes it's best to leave the past alone." A little smile played around the edges of his eyes. "A few years ago, I got this zeal to go searching for my biological roots. I didn't have to look far. My adoptive parents had an idea where my biological mother might be. They steered me right into her arms. Terrible mixed blessing."

"What does it feel like?"

"What?"

"To be adopted."

"It's complicated. Remind me. I'll tell you. What's the name of that place again? Might have to come rescue you from the natives." He laughed without heart. I jumped out and pushed the boat away from the dock. He pointed one finger, winked and gunned the outboard. At first, a taxi appeared the way to go, but that seemed expensive, so I decided to ride the buses. Should be just like Grenada. Somewhere near the market they would congregate, the conductors would collect the money and seat passengers, while the driver sat casually at the wheel.

They all seemed to ignore me when I got there. Could be too early to catch a bus headed back into the countryside. Two boys in khaki pants and blue shirts walked briskly, on their way to school I supposed. Women stood near the stands of fruits and vegetables. All the buses had radios blaring the latest road march for the upcoming carnival.

"Wat you looking for?" An old man sat out of the early sun, on a wooden crate under the west eave of the market building. My first impression: stayed too long at the rum shop. Pickled his brain.

"The bus to Blight," I said.

He wore a stained pair of dungaree slacks and an old, white T-shirt with VAT 19 on it. "Blight?" He shouted the name and looked at me with bloodshot eyes. A little goatee danced under his bottom lip as the words left his mouth.

"Go over there. Buy me a cold Fanta. I'll tell you about dat place."

"Tell me what? I don't have to...all these people-"

"Dey will show you de bus. But people walk into dose Carib and Garifuna woods and never come out."

I decided to spend twenty-five cents on the Fanta.

"What you going dere for? No one lives dere anymore, Grenadian."

"Why you calling me Grenadian?"

"Ah can hear you Grenadians from miles away. Years ago ah lived dere. On de wharf. Right near de fire station, de closest house. Miss Butty still have ah rum-shop dere?"

He lifted the bottle to his mouth, and shrugged, as if to dislodge something. I wanted to tell him the closest house to the fire station burned down years ago before the firemen could spray one drop of water on it. My first impression of the old man took a hit. He could have been a young a Saga Boy in those days.

"Dat was almost twenty years ago. Just after de Second World War," he burped loudly and looked at me as if searching for some sign of disgust.

"Meh mother came from Blight," I said.

"Dat bus over dere," he pointed. "No one lives dere. Hurricane Janet mashed it up, man. Dat bus still pass near it. De government build all dem new homes, moved everyone across de bay, to Tourama Point." He leaned closer to me and whispered. "Even some of dose big shots in government believed de stories about dat place."

"Stories? What stories?"

"Dat will cost you five dollars."

The old man had done a fine job of wheedling me out of that Fanta, but five bucks? I thanked him and moved toward the bus he pointed out.

"Go then, go and see," he shouted at my back. I made sure of my situation by conferring with the conductor. The fellow nodded, and looked at me just a little too long.

The ride up the coast was ordinary. The bus ripped past women balancing baskets on heads covered by bandannas, small children at their sides. A man rode a bareback jackass down the road, a cutlass held in one hand. He reminded me of some ancient warrior with a stained blade, the constant fighter beating back weeds and pests, twisting these lands to their will.

The words of my aunt Rose resounded in my memory. *Jacks and anchovies ran heavy that year. The two drums read denatured alcohol. No one knew what that meant. The police from Kingston kept finding scraps of bones and skin lodged in the trees.*

The history of this woman who gave birth to me dominated everything. I had this undying need to understand her and what she did. The bus roared past Soufriere, and Georgetown, heading toward Tourama Point. I was heading north and thinking south. Going south, toward that imaginary line, always held a certain fascination for me. The first time the word "equator" came into my vocabulary, I knew it had to be a place, a real place where the inhabitants compared everything. Even after I searched it out in the dictionary, I still imagined it to be the place of the big zipper that ran across the middle of the earth. At the equator, you could pull the big zipper, divide the world into two equal halves, pull it apart, and climb in. A short cut to China. Marco Polo didn't know shit, climbing mountains, and crossing deserts. What the hell for? Use the shortcut.

I was ten years old the year I received my first Bible and a dictionary from my mother-for Christmas-part of her once-a-year package. A return address was usually on the boxes, but I never used it. Never wrote her a single letter or thank you. During the years, the mystique of the South Atlantic took on new forms. I knew it as the place where people went and never returned. Some would be lost at sea for sure, but others just went and remained in places like Trinidad, Venezuela, Aruba, and Curacao. Some would write to friends and family, but others just stayed gone and silent.

Sydney spoke of crossing the equator to arrive at the place where two waters, the fresh and the salt, tumbled onto each other like frenzied lovers, creating a brackish current that influenced ships for hundreds of miles off shore. He called it the mouth of the Amazon, the place where the river kisses the sea. Sydney's tales of the Amazon and the South Atlantic, what should I believe? What's fact? What's fiction?

The bus came to a halt near an overhang of foliage near the road. "Why you dropping me off in this bush, near nothing?" The question shot out of my mouth like some kind of blame.

"Blight." The conductor pointed to a hole between the undergrowth. They looked at me with suspicion as I made my way off the bus. "Follow dat road straight down," he said. I handed him twenty-five cents. "Be back here before four if you want to sleep in Kingston tonight."

The waves cresting on the sand blended with the roar of the bus as it drove off. The wind in the trees replaced the noise of the engine: soft groans blending with whispers, mournful, down below. The conductor's last words as he swung onto the running board sounded like a warning.

A dry path shaded by briars and a few banyan fig trees led down to the beach and the place called Blight. The vegetation was at war, and the banyans seem to be winning. Large clumps of branching roots snaked out, seizing ground, a twisted amalgamation of gray trunks. Epiphyte from the banyans enfolded some briars. Soon the briars would be dead, strangled, replaced by the steadily inching roots of the tree brought here from so far away.

The sea stretched out blue to the eastern horizon. Whitecaps after whitecap tumbled into a wide bay squeezed between two fingers of land. Along the path, butterflies and bumblebees flitted from flower to flower. Birds chirped from the bushes. Trees dallied under the influence of a steady warm breeze. The sun blazed down from the clear sky, and everything cast stubby shadows. At first glance, the whole thing seemed ordinary. Then I saw the rest of it: old houses consumed by tangled greenery, spread across a gradual slope that stretched down to the beach.

In a country with so many poor people, no one leaves galvanized tin and boards to rot. Nevertheless, in this place, they did. All the roofs seemed to buckle and cave in on the remains of the houses. Tall palm trees towered over the dilapidation. Nettles and vines, blooming shrubs covered the ground. Only one house, down near the shore, seemed livable. A half circle of coconut palms shaded it. Two dogs dashed at me, barking loudly as I advanced on the house carefully. A figure sat on the tilted porch. A voice called out to me before I could make out the person sitting in the chair.

"Who is dat coming here? Dead or alive."

"Godfrey Soulages, from Grenada," I shouted over the barking of the dogs.

"Anoder Grenadian? Oh! Dat's you, at last? Wat took you so long, Maji Chatoyea?"

The strange words came out of her mouth like a reproach. I decided to use the common dialect in speaking with her. She had to be mistaking me for someone else. What other Grenadian, though? I sought to put things straight. Obviously, this old person was confused.

"Meh moder was born around here. Her name is Clara Wilson. Ah wonder if you knew her. I'm not Maji."

I turned my head, waltzing with the dogs as they barked and circled. I inched toward the base of the porch, keeping one eye on the dogs and the other on the old woman. She sat calmly, as if praying. Strips of rags stuck out of the cushion she sat on. Her eyes were closed, and she held a stout stick between long bony fingers.

She was a frail creature. Cheekbones stood out on a long face that could have been beautiful at one time. Her gray hair, braided in strands, circled her head like a crown. She wore a homemade flour-sack dress that came down to just below her knees; Baking Four in faded red letters stretched across the front. Old leather slippers and blue socks covered her feet. The old woman sat motionless in the wicker chair. I had the impression that she might be assessing me somehow. She raised the stick suddenly and brought it down hard on the porch.

"Mash!" she shouted, and a stream of spittle flew out of her mouth.

The two dogs ceased barking and went into a soft whimper, tucking their tails between their legs. They squirmed across the mixture of sand and dirt that was her yard. As the dogs slid under the porch, they continued to whine, looking back at me as if to say, "See what you caused."

Her sudden movement and force of voice jarred me. It was as if she orchestrated with the dogs to take command of the situation. The departure of the dogs gave me some hope of getting some information from the old woman. But my confidence wilted as she spoke to me with stout ease.

"Come closer, come up here, Maji Chatoyea."

She raised her head, and the lids of her eyes furled back. Her eyeballs were completely white, milky orbs in brown hollows above a wide nose. She stared me down with the vacuous gaze of the blind. I felt foolish and even more disconcerted. I should have known by the way she sat there with that stick in her lap. Her face had a vaguely familiar look.

"You frightened of me, Maji? Ah don't bite, you know. Come, come up here, let me feel wat you look like."

I took two doubtful steps up the porch, still watchful of the dogs, wondering, what the hell am I doing here with this old woman? The stairs squeaked under my weight. What did she have in mind? I stood before her, waiting.

"Come, come, stoop down here." She motioned with one hand as she placed her stick to one side. "Ah seen you often in my dreams. Chief Chatoyea said one day all Garifunas would come back to Yurumein. You are de first. Ah need to lay my hands on you."

The old woman smelled like a potpourri: earth, dry leaves, and an obscure whiff of food. The combination completed a sickish sweetness that forced me to breathe shallow. She used both hands; first she ran them over my hair softly, and then she came back to the middle of my head, squeezing hard, down to the scalp, massaging. She moved across my forehead, gliding gently over my ears, and then to my eyes and nose. Her fingers lingered on both of my cheekbones, but eventually they moved down to my lips and chin. Her bony palms made me itchy and anxious.

"You de one all right; you nice looking, too. Black Carib for sure. The blood of Joseph Chatoyea runs through your veins."

I stood, took two steps away from her and rested against the banister. It felt weak. I decided not to lean. Joseph Chatoyea meant nothing to me.

"You came all dis way. You returned to Yurumein. Let me get you ah glass of lime squash."

"No thank you, Miz-You called me Maji. My name is Godfrey. What is...?"

"Meh moder called me Veronica; at school dey called me Veronica Wilson, but dese days, everybody calls me Miz Vero. So many names. My grandmother, the Garifuna, she told me Maji in de old tongue means water. It was de name we called our fader. He came ashore in chains after the slave ship hit the reef, and den he married a Carib woman. The mother of Joseph Chatoyea. Dat's who we are. Today they call this place Saint Vincent. The Caribs called it Yurumein. So many names."

"Wat does it mean, Miz Vero? Garifuna, Black Caribs. Dey all dead and gone."

"No, Maji. On de mainland to de west, thousands of dem live there. You came because the spirits guided you. Looking for what you want to know, looking for something you could only find here, in de place of your ancestors." She gently rested her hand on her breasts and coughed. "Ah know you didn't eat any supper. Your journey was long. Ah can't eat in front of you and not offer you some."

The old woman reached for her stick and stood. She walked to the door as if she could see. I thought of following her into the house, but one dog crawled up on the porch, placed itself between the door and me, rested its head on its front paws, and eyed me like a coiled snake.

The sunshine blazed across the beach. It shucked thin shadows off the coconut palms, stretched them long across the dingy sand. Little waves clawed at the shore. Am I wasting my time with a lonely old woman? What's with all these old names? Maji, Garifuna. Garifuna I had heard of before, but just in old stories about African warriors who joined the Carib Indians to fight the slave owners.

The old woman came back through the door carrying an enameled plate filled with fried fish and slices of bread. She sat back in the chair, and rested the plate on her lap. An army of little red ants crawled all over the bread, spreading out from under the fish, scurrying to the edge of the plate.

"Have some, Maji," she said gesturing at the food.

"Red ants all over de food, Miz Vero."

"Don't worry. Dey won't hurt you. Dey good to eat and if you don't like dem, just brush dem off."

I took a slice of bread and a chunk of fried fish from the plate. The old woman lifted a chunk of fish with crawling ants to her face. She placed the food into her mouth, and a swell of nausea bubbled in my throat. I held the fish and bread in one hand, unable to eat any of it. I bent slowly and dropped the food of the edge of the porch. The dogs charged the food the moment it hit the sand.

"Don't feed dem, Maji. Dey get spoiled dat way." The old woman continued to chew, and I couldn't take my eyes off her face.

"Your moder must ah left ah powerful scent." She spoke and chewed loudly over the words. One red ant crawled across her chin. She flicked it off with one finger like nothing. She swallowed a large chunk of bread and fish, her throat moved up and down.

"Your moder lived right here, in dis house. She was meh only surviving grandchild. She stayed with me for a long time after her parents died, but her soul and her heart... One morning ah got up and she was gone. Never knew what happened to her until your father came.

"Ah told him about de Black Caribs and how we came to be called Garifuna. Ah told him about de Mmandwas, our religion, and de Maji priest dat was our daddy. How dey captured him near ah river in Africa. Although he was ah Christian just like all of dem, dey sold him into slavery anyway. Am de last one here. All de rest, buried in de ground, over dere." She pointed with her stick, to a cluster of trees on the bluff. "All of dem, all of dem except me. Am too weak to walk over dere. Ah can only see de place in meh mind. But dat's all right. All of dem know it now. We must live dis life and den return to God with all our human experiences, help God to see mankind again." She smiled for the first time, exposing blue gums with scraps of brown teeth.

She held the smile, which gave her face a sly look, and then she shifted her head to one side as if gauging me. I have always thought I wanted a long life, but now I was doubtful. It took the old woman a long time to speak again. It was as if she was arranging what next.

"Ah blind, Maji Chatoyea, but ah still see far. You came here looking for answers, and you don't even know de first ting about de questions. How can dat be? Let me tell you dis. Wen dese rocks came out of de ocean many years gone-bye; dey had no dirt on dem. Just bare rocks. It was de dirt of Africa on de wind that gave dese rocks skin. Dis is African soil. We had to come here and live. You, Maji, and de Mmandwas, seeds planted, like all de other plants on dese islands: breadfruit, cocoa, and nutmegs. Still, so many tings happened here, and ah don't know why. Oh! Not just de bomb and de poison in de drums. Other plagues.

"Seaweed floated up here one year, so much it filled de whole bay, mounded up along the beach high as a mountain. De sun baked it, and it stunk to high heaven. We took most of it into de bush and buried it. De turtles stopped coming to lay deir eggs in de sand. Den people started talking about seeing de devil riding ah white horse along de beach.

"Fishermen went out day after day and came back with empty boats. A multitude of sea crabs invaded de houses dat same rainy season, biting people in deir sleep, den ah woman gave birth to something dat looked like ah snake.

"Hurricane Janet was really de final blow. It came late one evening. We all knew de storm was coming. De sea swelled up, sending waves crashing onto de beach. De water came up to de coconut tree over dere. De wind howled across everything. Four o'clock dat evening looked as black as midnight, and de wind and rain just kept lashing away. If you stood outside and de wind didn't blow you down, just de water in de air alone would drown you.

"De storm knocked some houses down, tore de roofs off oders, snatched up trees. Lashed everything to bits. Wen it was over, no one rebuilt. De government got money from people in England. Some of dose politician in Kingston got rich, built some new houses near Tourama Point, and everyone just picked up and moved. One by one, dey moved over dere." The old woman pointed a bent finger at the houses across the bay.

Tourama Point looked insignificant in the distance. A few fishing boats bobbed at their anchors. Two yachts were moored upwind in the lee of the peninsula. She gauged me, following my actions with her ears I suppose. She spoke again, softly, with intent.

"Ah know wat you thinking. Wat you looking for."

Her words caught me off-guard. For an instant, it sounded as if she had peeked inside my head. But how could she? I knew I had always wanted to see Blight, ever since my aunt told me about the place. I had imagined it a thousand times, in a thousand ways. But now I stood there before this old woman, wondering-what she knew.

"What am I looking for, Miz Vero?" I asked.

"Maji, you looking for de marrow in de bone?" She smiled. "Sorry ah can't help you. You have to find your own way. Don't worry. Just keep dreaming. De matter is only so thick. Ah heavy load though. Ah carried all dat for so long; now it's your turn, Maji Chatoyea."

I saw sadness at both corners of her mouth. Her lips began to tremble as the last words came out. I felt compelled to say something. Nevertheless, the proper words eluded me. Instead, I heard myself say, "Suppose ah don't want any of dis."

The old woman laughed out loud, a dry cackle from deep in her stomach. But then she started to cough fitfully, stopping and starting, tears run down the side of her face. The plate of fish bones and scraps of bread slid off her lap, and crashed to the porch. The dogs rushed it, growling as they snatched at the scraps. She cleared her throat, hacked up a great wad of mucus, and spat it across the banister into the sand. She took a deep breath, and the amused laughter returned, softening her face.

"You know de truth, Maji. It's in your veins. You can feel it. Even your moder couldn't escape it. You came here to hear about the Garifuna, to listen to meh mouth. Ah waited ah long time to tell you." She shook her head from side to side. "We came from some powerful people. In times of war dey could give warriors de power to turn bullets into water. Dey knew de true purpose for life and living. Now here it is. Yours to carry. Long time ago, God created humans, and placed dem on de earth. Dey lived so long, God lost track of dem, knew almost nothing about dem as time went on. One day he looked down on dis terrible situation, den he created death to bring humans back to him, in a form dat he could consume, learn of deir experiences. Be close to dem again."

She paused as if waiting for me to speak, but just before words left my mouth, she cut me off.

"Take your time, Maji. Take your time. De birds sing, de dogs howl at de moon; no one asks dem why. Ah link in de chain, de bidding of your ancestors. Dey will come to you, asking favors, bringing gifts. Remember deir many faces. Never turn your back."

Forgetting that she could not see my physical response, I nodded. All basic replies eluded me. What kind of shaman could not grasp the babbling of an old woman? She continued to speak as I wrestled with all her slippery meanings.

"Ah wish ah had more to give you, something dat you could hold on to, help you to remember all of dis. One day you will have to do wat am doing, passing it on." She paused and reached into the pocket of her dress. "Here, take dis, before you have to catch your bus."

I reached out and took the small box from her hand. It felt insubstantial.

"Don't open it, not yet," she said. "Keep it for a while or you might be disappointed. Dere is some papers and other old stuff. You will know when to open it. Dese people dat take care of me? Dey waiting for me to die. Dey wants to get deir hands on de money dey tink ah have stuffed in meh mattress. Ah have ah big surprise for dem."

The old woman laughed again, and then she stopped and turned serious. The small cardboard box wrapped in twine felt odd in my hand. It was small enough to fit into my back pocket without leaving a bulge.

"Life is not de bully, Maji. It only challenges de strong. If you lucky enough to be blessed with dat summons, rise to de occasion; do de best you can, and life will always be good to you-treat it before it has de chance to treat you. Now go catch your bus before you have to walk all de way back to Kingston. If you ever come back, ah probably won't be here. Find meh grave and put some flowers on it. Then you can let me know how it all turned out-your life, ah mean. If you stand next to meh grave and talk, ah'll hear you. Go on now."

Reluctance besieged me. I walked away from the old woman, assuring her that I would return. She laughed, and that response bothered me. Halfway up the path to the main road, I looked back, expecting one last glance. It could have been a trick of the light, or the angle around the trees, but the house was no longer there. I had a nagging urge to rush back to the stop where the house first came into view, but I heard the sound of the bus in the distance, and I ran toward the road.

The driver and the conductor looked at me as I climbed into a seat at the back. They were the only people on the bus. I felt tired, drained, as if I had worked long and accomplished nothing. The memories of the old woman sat heavy. The small box in my seat-pocket pressed hard against my backside. Beads of perspiration ran out of my hair and down my neck. I decided to do as the old woman asked-not open the box. The bus rushed down the road toward Kingston. And I was speculating on the superstition of old Grenadian, about Ladables, Loupgarues, and other nymphs that walk among us. Did I just spend some time with one of them?

CHAPTER 15

The ride back to Kingston seemed shorter than the ride to Blight. I walked from the market to the harbor. *BLACK DOG* stood at anchor near the peninsula to the south. The late evening sun gleamed through strands of yellow and black clouds across the western horizon. Why didn't my father mention Veronica Wilson? What would Yvette think about all this? What would Jack think when I tell about my day in the country?

For the first time since I have known Jack Trueblood, I saw him sit and listen. I told them the details of my day as we ate dinner that night. Jack and Marilyn, the cook, were chewing their food casually. I felt a sense of ease as I related the encounter with the old man in the market, the reaction of the people on the bus, and meeting my great-grandmother and her dogs.

When I got to the part of the story where the old woman called me Maji, Marilyn seems to perk up as if she wanted to interrupt me, but she waited. And when I was finished, Jack spoke first.

"Christ, Godfrey! You should have asked her who owns all the land," he said. "If you are her last surviving heir, you could inherit quite a bundle." I decided not to mention the box or the fact that my mother is Veronica Wilson's next surviving heir.

Marilyn was standing across the galley, preparing to wash the few dinner dishes. "It's interesting that she called you Maji, Godfrey. I remember that word from my grandfather's stories. He was a soldier in Her Majesty's Army, in Tanganyika. But he used that word twice. Maji-Maji. Some kind of revolt long before I was born. They had to put it down. It was a kind of religious cult. They claim to have the power to expel witches, Europeans, and turn bullets into water. My grandfather called them the War Charm Cult. He found it amusing to have shot so many of them. It always troubled me that he took such pleasure in telling us about it."

Those were the most words to cross the woman's tongue in my presence. She seemed inspired by my story of the encounter with the old woman. Now she was speaking as if to Jack. She was fumbling with the dishes, her back to us. The radio was playing a song from some hit parade.

"Isn't it amazing? Every group of people on this planet has a story to explain their origins. You think that's where all religions begin? We have Adam and Eve, and his great-grandmother told him her story." She turned to face us, water dripped from her fingers onto the floor. "Looking back and not seeing her or the house, that's interesting. In Africans where we lived, they called that kind of visitation Egungun. A relative or close friend returns from the dead to deliver a message." She smiled, wrinkled her brow, and turned back to the sink.

"Just a bunch of mumbo jumbo," Jack said, as if the whole matter somehow threatened his interests or beliefs.

Those words again, from the mouth of the old voodoo woman, Mama Viche. Calling a thing by its name, and not recognizing it. What would she say about all this?

"Godfrey, you believe in any of this?" Jack glazed my recollection like a shadow slipping across the sun. *You believe in any of this?* I stood in that moment, conveying nothing from inside. A little voice whispered, ask me if I believe in my fingers or my toes? I shrugged, pursed my lips, and that seemed to satisfy him.

* * *

Around nine the next morning, a small group of white people surrounded by lots of bags stood on the wharf. The assemblage appeared to be more than the Whaler could carry in one trip, but as I motored toward the dock, I realized that I was mistaken. It would be a tight fit, but workable.

The group was comprised of four people, including a tall older man with graying hair pulled back in a ponytail, and a short, younger woman with an unusual manner. She spoke in bursts; she appeared as though she might jump out of her skin. She kept dwelling on the beauty of everything. As I loaded the luggage, she spoke directly to me, as if searching for confirmation of her own observations. Her admiration for the ordinary appeared skittish. The two others were blond, blue-eyed; they resembled aging athletes. They were all wearing shorts. Which of these women is the writer, once married to Jack, who had a child by him? My curiosity tasted sweet.

I ferried the four passengers, with their luggage, out to the *Black Dog*, where Jack and the Marilyn waited. The introductions were composed. They all spoke in turn, except the small woman, who continued to prattle about the beauty of it all. The tall, older man and the little agitated woman were a couple, Carl and Elaine Holman. Elaine was Jack's former wife, the travel writer. This was the first time Jack had met her new husband, the naturalist artist, Carl Holman. The other couple was Joel and Marla Shotts, friends of Carl and Elaine, from New York City.

I helped them move their luggage to the cabins. We lingered around the harbor for some time, allowing the guests to get settled. Finally, Jack started the motor and gave me the signal to hoist the anchor. We headed back south. Bequia would be our first stop.

The *BLACK DOG* sliced across the channel between Saint Vincent and Bequia at a leisurely pace. I hoisted three sails, and Jack killed the motor. As the yacht quartered the serrated current and mounting waves, I had an annoying sensation of leaving something behind. The memory of the unopened box stashed in my suitcase only aggravated that strange ache. Saint Vincent became indistinct, gray and misty as the *Black Dog* made distance. Two hours later, we came around the northern peninsula and headed up into Admiralty Bay.

The fishermen and boat-builders of Bequia were hard at work. Two bright dinghies under sail tacked and reached across the mercy of a head wind, trying to make the far shore. Some crafts sat at anchor, others hauled out of the water, propped up on the beach. A half-finished vessel sat on land, just off the sand, baring her unpainted hull in the midday sun. Just like *Miss Irene* under construction at Balis Ground. The shipwrights hammered and chopped. I took in the vista of houses tiered up the slope of the volcanic island, one above the other, staggered on the hill.

I stood on the port side, holding a stanchion for support. Bequia was a smaller Grenada. I came to that belief just looking at the shoreline, and measuring the pace of life around Admiralty Bay. A car and a truck, a crowd of people surrounded a boat moored at a jetty near the head of the bay. A fisherman selling his catch, for sure.

The *Black Dog* motored straight into the head wind, sails slapping. I walked toward the bow, testing my sea legs, preparing to lower the sails and drop the anchor. I stepped up on the deckhouse and reached for the main halyard. I looked forward as my hand reached the nylon rope fastened to the cleat on the side of the mast, and I felt an actual chill; in the bright, hot sun, the hairs on my skin stood up. There, riding at anchor with the other crafts, she looked used. Without a doubt, it was *Miss Irene*. But she sported a new name across her stern, one word: *CALYPSO*.

Everything rolled back on me, hit me like a closed fist: Karrol and me, the vessel being built, the way he died, all the talebearers' superstitions about a soul for the vessel. But I shook off my anxiety and released the main halyard. The white sail came sliding down the mast, onto the deckhouse, and I bundled it, tied it to the boom, and then I brought down the staysail and jib. I bagged the two sails, and went forward to stand-by the anchor.

On Jack's signal, I dropped the Danforth. The chain reeled out across the derrick until I engaged the dog and Jack reversed the engine to set the anchor. We rigged an awning over the cockpit, and Marilyn served lunch. After lunch, Carl, Elaine, Joel, and Marla left for a taxi tour around Bequia. They planned to visit Port Elizabeth and Spring Bay on the far side of the island.

I washed the lunch dishes in ten minutes. Our guests wouldn't be back for almost three hours. I would be transporting them back to the *Black Dog* at that time. After that chore, the rest of the day belonged to me. What could I do with my time? Life around Admiralty Bay didn't look too exciting-no movie theater. I decided to continue in that book

I had started to read, *Not so narrow not so deep*. That should keep the presence of that vessel cornered.

The charter came back from the ride around Bequia later than planned. Carl and Joel seemed thrilled. They met the captain of the *Calypso*; his invitation for drinks and a few hands of poker appealed to them. Their wives scowled. At dinner that night, the women's displeasure triggered a small squabble.

"Did you see how he looked at me?" Elaine asked.

"Christ, Elaine, you think every man looks at you like that," Carl said.

"She's right," Marla said. "He looked, and that swagger. Bring us along? You think he wants to play poker with us. Did I say that?" Everyone laughed, a little nervously, except Elaine.

"I'm not going over there," said Elaine.

"Look out, Godfrey. She has issues with black men," Carl said.

"You're such a mean bastard." She flashed him a look. "You don't even know the man. How can you play? He might be a cheat."

"Just an existential exercise, sweetheart. Small price to pay. Might be fun to see how he does it," Carl said. "Twenty bucks, nickel-and-dime stuff."

"Twenty dollars doesn't sound like any nickel or dime to me. You treat the whole thing...one of these days." Elaine swallowed hard.

"Most of those guys are harmless," Jack said. "He just needs an audience, you know, try to impress with tales of his exploits. That could be fun, Elaine. Use some of that for spice in your article."

"The magazine wouldn't publish fiction."

"What? You guys concoct that shit all the time. I saw you write an article on Corsica from our apartment. Including pictures of the birthplace of Napoleon. You never set foot near that island," Carl said.

"This is a great opportunity," Jack interrupted. "A night of free entertainment, raw Caribbean. Godfrey will take you over. He'll stay until you get bored. Right, Godfrey? Now, who's going? Talk to my first mate." Jack looked at me, a reluctant look on his face.

"I don't want this to reflect badly on you, Godfrey," Elaine said, "but I would feel much more comfortable if you would go along, Jack. And take your gun. Just kidding, just kidding, about the gun I mean."

Sounding superstitious and old-fashioned in the presence of these Americans was the last thing I wanted to do. An itch ran up and down my spine. The past I shared with the vessel felt like a load. What could I tell them-my friend drowned at the launching of this vessel, and the prevailing rumor said his death gave this vessel a soul? What could that mean to them? What would they think if I admitted my history with this boat? I chose to remain silent.

Four men, Carl, Jack, Joel, and myself, I felt a certain pride being in their company. But my old uneasiness persisted as I motored the short distance to the gangway of the vessel. The craft sat high on the water, obviously, no cargo in her hold. The long gangway stretched down to the waterline. A young, fair-skinned man about my age met us and took the bowline. The captain of the vessel stood on deck dressed in a white shirt, a blue blazer with shiny buttons, and khaki pants.

"Welcome aboard the *Calypso*, gentlemen," he shouted. We climbed the gangway. "I see you left the women behind. That is wise. This is no place for ladies. The lingering smell of cargo sometimes turns their stomachs. You must be Captain Trueblood. I'm Solomon Gates." He extended his hand to Jack.

They both stood pumping each other's hand as the rest of us filed along the deck. My first impressions of Captain Gates? Lean, sun-washed. In spite of his effort with the clean clothes, he still looked rough. Jack turned and introduced me. Captain Gates looked at me for a single second before he turned aft. I felt humbled by the insignificance in his glance, but then he asked, "Soulages? Are you Ethan's son?"

He asked the question as we entered the cockpit, and then he continued to talk without waiting for an answer.

"It's good when a young man travels in his father's footsteps. Sad to hear about your father. He was one hell of a sailor, and a good man. Godfrey, this is Nausin. Make Godfrey feel welcome, Nausin."

"Yes, Daddy."

A folding table with three bottles, a few glasses, and a bowl of ice sat near the stern. Two other black men sat sipping drinks in the glare of a kerosene lantern. They knew my father? I remained silent. Jack glanced at me as we all entered the cockpit. The introductions were brief. Everyone stood, shook hands, repeated names, and then fell into an awkward silence. One of the crew seemed to carry a frozen smile. Captain Gates left everyone in the cockpit and went below.

I climbed onto the wheelhouse, and sat next to Nausin. He looked a little like Karrol. Fair skinned with a long face, like some white people. Questions teased my sanity. How would he react if I ask the most pressing one?

The vessel seeped a blend of decay, cement, and brine. The pungent smell wafted up from the bilge and cargo hold, stale but intriguing. The men chatted in short sentences, nodding frequently. They all seemed ill at easy.

"You live onboard here all the time, Nausin?" I asked.

"When I'm visiting my father. I live most of the time with my mother, on Key West."

"Tell me, ahh, ahh, you ever hear any voices, like somebody crying or laughing, on-board here?" I spoke softly.

"Voices? What you talking about?"

Now that I had let it slip out, I felt trapped. I had to continue.

"All these vessels have a soul, you know. They get one the day they are launch them." He was looking at me as if I had grown a second head. A little smile tugged at one corner of his mouth.

"A soul, huh? You mean, is this vessel haunted?"

"Not exactly. I think it's the opposite." I felt a bit foolish for speaking those words, because now a grin covered his entire face, and he was shaking his head vigorously.

"You islanders, really ridiculous. All this superstitious shit?" His declaration raised my ire.

"What kind of name is Nausin any-way?" I shot back.

"Greek. Nausinous. Son of Calypso and Odysseus. That's my namesake." He spoke with a certain pride, and looked at me with conviction of my ignorance of Greek mythology. I had read the myth about Odysseus in captivity on the island with the beautiful Calypso, but knew nothing about them having children. The sound of his father's footsteps coming back through the hatch rescued me from our little confrontation.

"Okay, fellows," Solomon Gates said. "Make yourselves at home, don't forget the drinks over there. Hope you brought a lot of Yankee dollars." He reached into his pocket, and brought out the largest bundle of bills I had ever seen.

"To simplify matters," he continued, "turn your bills into chips. This is the bank." He placed a box on the table. "Reds are twenty-five cents, and blues are a dollar. Exchange them for cash when the game is over. If you have any chips left, that is. No table stakes. You can wager anything, anytime. Just keep it friendly. Know the depth of your pockets."

Jack chuckled. "We just penny-ante guys, Solomon."

"No penny ante here. Dollars, quarters, and a bit of the inscrutable."

"The inscrutable?" Jack said.

"Yeah, like pride," Solomon Gates said.

Jack counted out fifteen dollars, one ten-dollar bill, and some wilted ones. He stuffed the money into the box, and reached for the poker chips. He counted, piling the chips, one on top of the other. Solomon looked at him suspiciously, with just one eye. All six men sat around the table with chips and cards before them, cigarettes burning short near half-empty glasses. The original strain ebbed down to some friendly banter as they completed the first hand. It took less than five minutes.

"Ah thought you fellows said you could play dis game?" the smiling black man said, hauling in the pot. "Straight can't beat a full house."

"Captain Gates, I admire a man with command of the Queen's English," Carl Holman said. "Where were you educated?"

"I studied at Florida State University, marine biology."

"You are a marine biologist? How did you end up on this…"? Carl Holman allowed his words to trail off as if he thought better of completing the thought.

Solomon smiled as he handed the deck to Jack.

"Ante, gentlemen," Jack said.

He dealt the cards. Everyone picked up their hands, examined them, and Carl threw two red chips into the pot. Solomon spoke as his two chips hit the pile accumulating in the center of the table.

"Destiny, Mister Holman. Cause and effect, effect without cause. But I hold no grudges."

A rooster crowed in the distance; a dog barked. The chips made a clicking sound as each man in turn threw his bet into the growing pile.

"They perceived me as some kind of threat. Only threat I felt in America came from white men," Solomon said.

"Yeah," Jack agreed. "The fear of black people in the United States is somewhat irrational."

"Oh, it goes deeper," Solomon, said. "You white people have always hated the idea of intimacy across racial lines. Primordial survival instincts, I presume."

"I don't give a shit who screws whom," Jack said.

"Unless she's your daughter or your sister. That was my offense. I had a relationship with one of my graduate students. One day the police came to the house where I rented a room, near Tallahassee. They found a bag of ganja in my underwear drawer. I don't know how it got there. They tried me for possession. Instead of throwing me in jail, they deported me. So, I guess, I came out better than some. Could have been a stout rope over a strong branch."

His last words hung in the air. In the distance, a halyard slapped repeatedly against an aluminum mast. A group laugh came floating on the night wind from somewhere across the bay. A radio from far off blasted a calypso, the Mighty Sparrow complaining about political malice in Trinidad.

Jack spoke this time with a big smile on his face, his words tinged with mockery. "Captain, we didn't come here to be apologists for the assholes of North America; we came to play poker and drink some of your booze."

Solomon Gates laughed in a way that could have been taken as an act of contrition, or concurrence. But his next words came in like a man wielding a blade. "I like you, Captain Trueblood. You see things plain and you speak to that. For a moment, I thought you might be one... You know the ones, whenever the subject of slavery or the dehumanization of black people come up, they would say things like, 'I never owned a slave, so how does that concern me?'"

Jack looked up from his cards as he called the bet, eyes blinking in nervous flutters.

"I can't speak for these other guys here, but I've never said boo to a black person. The closest I've been to any black person is with Godfrey over there, and we've only known each other for about six weeks. I'm an adopted child; I've no idea whether or not my ancestors benefited from the exploitation of black people. Why should I shoulder any of the blame?"

"Captain, you misunderstand."

"Are you guys going to play cards or bullshit all night?" Joel said. "Nothing we say here will bring about change. The world is full of assholes-present company excluded, of course-white ones, red ones, black ones, yellow ones, and we have to live with and tolerate the bastards because it's illegal to shoot them. The bet is to you, Solomon. May I call you, Solomon?"

Solomon laughed as he called the bet and made a two-dollar raise. "You are truly a gentleman, sir. You may call me Solomon. One thing that bothered me to no ends when I lived in America was how everyone instantly tries to get familiar with you. You meet someone, and two minutes later, they're shortening your name."

Cigarette smoke curled through the air. The men sipped their drinks and called the raise Solomon had made. The game fascinated me. I had seen it only in the movies. In westerns especially, every poker game seems to end with a gunfight. The tone of their conversation left me itchy. My shirt stuck to my skin. I came off the deckhouse, and stood behind Jack, trying to get a better look at the cards and to put some space between Nausin and me. Jack had lost most of his chips; just three or four remained before him. The silent man seemed to have most of the round plastic disks.

"If I may ask, what did I misunderstand, Captain Gates?" Jack asked.

"Captain Trueblood, it's a rare white man who has given any thought to race relation or its resulting human tragedy. You take all your privileges for granted, as if God has given you some rights he had denied other persons. Everything that Europeans has done throughout the ages, in the name of God and country, who do you think are the inheritors?"

Jack threw his hand into the discards. "Deal me out for a minute." He stood and brushed by me. Beads of perspiration glistened on his forehead.

"I remember having a similar conversation with a fellow some years ago," Solomon continued. "I told him you white people should learn to behave. You know what he said to me, 'I'm a white man. I don't have to behave. Niggers have to behave.'"

"As I said before, assholes everywhere," Joel said as he hauled in his first pot.

Jack walked over to the bottles and poured himself a drink. He stood looking at the quarter moon. A fish jumped, fracturing the surface of the water. Jack looked troubled. Nevertheless, when he came back to the table, sat down and bought some more poker chips, it was obvious that he was vexed about events not going his way.

Jack picked up the cards dealt to him, looked at them, and bet a dollar. "Captain Gates," he said, "you sound as though you believe white people are the devil."

"Not at all, Captain. You remember my lover from Tallahassee? She left the States with me. We have one child, Nausin, over there. I've lived long and I've paid attention. Some black people are just as mean and nasty as any one else.

"Let me tell you a story, about the man who built this boat, Laslo Pope. A poisonous neurotic, so stuffed with arcane beliefs, Shakespeare could have written about him. Laslo made his money in the oil fields of Venezuela. He was never married and had no children that we know of. He once attempted to convince me of the value of blood sacrifices.

"Now I'm not a man with a great deal of belief in rituals, those things tend to bore me, but I listened to him. He took the pains to quote from the Bible and other books he had read. Made an interesting and speculative argument about the rite in ancient cultures. In the end, the man shocked me. All the time I thought he was talking about animal sacrifices, he meant humans."

For the second time that day, I felt the hairs on my skin stand on end. I never had a person to associate with what happened to Karrol, but now I did. Laslo Pope. The conversation made me feel like stone.

"We picked up a load of provisions in Grenada. A night crossing, headed to Trinidad. Your father had just quit, Godfrey. He said he had things to do at home. Halfway there we found two stowaways hiding in the cargo hold. Laslo drew his pistol, marched the two men up onto the deck. I thought he was just trying to scare them. I stood at the helm as he ordered both of them forward onto the bowsprit. When he told them to jump, I almost laughed. It was a ludicrous idea. All we had to do was turn them over to the harbormaster once we made port. They looked like two scared rats.

"One fellow boldly refused to jump. Pow, pow! Laslo shot him in the chest. The man tumbled overboard; the vessel sailed right over him. I heard his body bash into the hull, and the other stowaway began to cry like a child. He dropped to his knees, and hugged the stanchion. This just infuriated Laslo. He walked toward the man, kicked him square in the face. The man tumbled into the sea. I shouted and brought the vessel into the wind. Laslo came aft, pushed me out of the way, snatched the helm and returned the vessel to its course. No member of the crew said a word. Around six the next morning, we sailed through the Dragon's Mouth, and motored across the Gulf of Paria into Port of Spain.

"The atmosphere on the vessel felt thick. We unloaded our cargo and waited for the load back. One night, we got into a poker game just like this, playing draw. The other guys had some money in the pot, but all of them folded after the draw. Just Laslo and I remained. He had drawn three cards. I drew one and got the perfect card: a six of hearts for a straight flush.

"I knew he either had a full house or a four of a kind. 'I would bet this vessel on these cards, he said. 'I would have to call you,' I said to him. 'You have nothing to call me with, Solomon. As first mate on this vessel, I don't pay you enough. He laughed for a minute, and then he turned serious. 'On the other hand, you do have something to wager: that white woman of yours.' I thought he was joking, but he stared me down, cold.

"We had the other fellows witness the deal. He laid down four aces, and I became the owner of his vessel. I gave him fifteen minutes to pack his belongings. A fellow like him would never give up his position of power and privilege without a fight. Big dogs you know. He went down to his cabin calmly and I got ready, waited for him. He came back brandishing his pistol; I gave him no chance. I sank a gaff hook into his spine as he came through the hatch. His pistol discharged, fell out of his hand, and hit the deck. I threw a halyard around his neck and hauled him up into the rigging. He kicked and squirmed; and then he pissed his pants.

"We waited awhile before we let him down. The police arrested me and questioned the other members of the crew. They got the whole story about Laslo Pope. In the end, after a few palms were greased, they concluded it was obviously self-defense. So you see, Captain Trueblood, our creator has endowed us with about the same measure of humanity. No more, no less. It all comes down to how we choose to employ it.

"I was a fool to tell my wife about Laslo. She didn't find the tale amusing, not one bit. It seemed such a great story at the time, assuring her of my precise interpret of the cards. She left me a month later and filed for a divorce. Said she could never look at me the same way."

Everyone sat silently as if waiting for more. They held their cards and made no bets. They just kept repeating the word check, check, check, until Jack threw two disks into the pot. They threw down their cards. Solomon said nothing else, and the quiet man called Roy spoke for the first time.

"Don't forget ah was deer for all ah dat, Solomon. You speaking de truth enough, but ah remember standing at your back."

"You calling me ungrateful, Roy?" Solomon asked.

"Oh, nothing like dat, ole friend," Roy said. "Just play de cards," and they both smiled as if sharing an inside joke.

The whole affair astonished me. I had never known Laslo Pope, can't even recall if I had ever set eyes on him, but the account of his death left me with a sense of loss. It was as if I had found an item, and then lost it before I could realize its importance. So, that's why she has a different name.

The card game lasted for just a few more minutes. Solomon Gates announced that they would sail with the tide. He said the words as if they had some real meaning. The story of Laslo Pope left a kind of awkwardness, not quite a stigma, but something close to it. We all said good night and tried to leave without looking pressed. I glanced at Nausin as we moved down the gangway. I waved one hand at him, and he nodded.

Back on the *Black Dog*, Joel and Carl couldn't decide whether to laugh or cry about the events of the night. They spoke about the encounter on the vessel in the same way as I spoke to my friends about movies we had just seen. Different interpretations of the same occasion. The women had already retired. Joel and Carl went below to join their wives. Laughter came from aboard the *Calypso*. Jack looked at me, and I wondered if the laughter was at our expense. Who won or who lost? Must all human transactions be so hard-hearted?

Jack and I made a quick check, and secured the yacht for the night.

We stood on deck, looking over at the vague contours of the vessel. A small gust swept across the night, and halyards slapped against the masts like hands imparting an ovation.

"The Tobago Cays tomorrow," Jack said. "Spend two or three days there. They should like it. Then on to Petite Saint Vincent for the weekend. They usually have a steel-band and dancing, I hear." He spoke softly as we moved aft to the cockpit.

"You like to dance?" I asked.

Jack chuckled and shifted our conversation with his next breath. "You believe any of it? All sounded so farcical. Two murders, wagering his wife. Things like that don't go on down here." He angled his head as if in hope to receive a secret. "Well, do they?"

"Don't know anything about that kind of… yeah murders, people murder sometimes. For example, that vessel, it had another name. *Miss Irene.* They built her in Grenada, near that big manchineel tree on the point, Balis Ground, near the Yacht Service. You know where I mean? The day they launched that vessel, I lost my best friend. He was found in the sea, the next day, with no water in his lungs. They took his life to give that vessel a soul."

"Jesus Christ, Godfrey." Jack threw up his hand as if to block the smile on his face. "You guys, one story after another. Murder maybe, but a soul for the vessel?"

"You can't be drowned with no water in your lungs."

"I'll give you that."

"Laslo Pope believed in human sacrifice. You wanted to know what I thought."

"Throwing stowaways overboard. I wonder how many times that motif has appeared in the annals of shipping stories?" Jack spoke and slapped his palms together.

"Laslo Pope is still dead," I said.

"Or did he even exist. Goodnight, Godfrey. Don't have any nightmares," Jack said as he moved through the hatch to go below.

Laslo Pope must have existed. It was the only way my world could make sense. I sat for several minutes, staring at the obscure shape of the *Calypso.* A litany of unanswered questions circled me like gnats. A feast of conjectures and imaginings burst in my brain like sparks from a flame. What if he killed many more? What if he was some kind of mass murderer who killed to satisfy some kind of bloodlust, and then tried to validate it in the name of sacrifices?

The light of the moon penetrated the near dark, and to the west, beyond the entrance to the bay, everything was still, black, and inching. Laslo was dead, but his essence remained. I imagined a face laughing and laughing at Laslo's folly. He made this deal with the devil, expecting to live forever in the flesh, only to discover that he was tricked. His only life would be in the trifling imagination of the living.

I went to sleep that night thinking about Laslo Pope and two kinds of *Calypso*, the music and the vessel. But the dream refused to allow me the luxury of ignorance, and the third Calypso became clear.

In this dream I was standing in a thickening miasma, on a long strip of land when Karrol came to me. He was dressed in one of those white robes. A section of the garment was folded over one arm. He looked big and stout, not the disfigured image I held in memory from the day they pulled his body from the sea at Balis Ground.

Leather slippers covered his feet. 'I'm with the Goddess Calypso. Not like Odysseus at all. I'm staying with her. Living with her.' I wanted to ask him questions, speak to him, but before words could leave my mouth Karrol walked away, across the water. Covetousness gripped me as I watched him vanish in the mist. I came awake the next morning feeling more peaceful than I had in a long time.

CHAPTER 16

On deck the following morning, I was eager to look at the vessel, make peace with those old memories. But she was gone. I looked around the bay and out to sea. "*We sail with the tide.*" The conversation around the breakfast table, about the night on the *Calypso*, was mixed with scant mockery. The whole thing made me edgy. Right after breakfast, I weighed the anchor, and Jack steered the *Black Dog* for the far western point of Bequia. I stood on the bow, scanning the horizon to the north, toward Saint Vincent.

We cleared the western point of Bequia, and started motoring east against a rough head sea. I moved aft. Elaine stood next to Jack at the helm, grabbing onto him with every heave of the yacht. She was turning pasty, pallid. A greenish hue came into the skin on her face. There was something odd about these people.

Elaine and Jack, do they ever talk about their daughter? Or is she some unmentionable stray, castoff into the world to make her own way? I felt a kinship with this person I had never met. What could she be like?

Joel, Marla, and Carl stood way forward, holding on to the stanchions. The ocean sprayed over the bow, and over them. Elaine seemed relieved when Jack altered course. Joel helped me set the sails, and the *Black Dog* quartered the swells, gently. Jack brought her around to a steady heading, southeast toward two rocks in the distance, Quatre and Baliceaux.

Another rock called All Awash stood out to the east, challenging the Atlantic. Plumes from breaking waves shot into the air, billows from a battle. I thought of another bit from Greek mythology, and I wondered whose labors Homer would say were being performed there.

The *Black Dog* sailed into the lee of Mustique. They say English royalty hides out there. The place looked like a lonely rock, not unlike All Awash. I found it strange that anyone would want to spend time on that boulder instead of on a place like Grenada, Saint Lucia, or some bigger island. Banished, jailed, I thought. Napoleon on Elba. Do these people have hopes and dreams? What are they? If they possess all, everything in the world, do they stop dreaming? Or do their dreams transform into caricatures of themselves riding on the backs of the poor and the bridled of their domain? Do their soft-feathered dreams sometimes turn into nightmares about some budding Guy Faulks?

I looked at the small islets of Petit Mustique, Savan Island, and Petit Canouan to the west. In that instant, I knew how space aliens must see the Earth-a small islet in the vast ocean of space. They pass by and barely glance at it. A bird shit on the rock, and a seed regrets its place of deposit. No one stops, except perhaps lost adventurers or banished souls.

The Grenadines dotted the southern horizon, gray, blue, curling white caps across a shimmering sea of islands and reefs. Canouan, the big one, stood silhouetted against the southern horizon like some paper cutout. Beyond that, Channel Rock, and then Mayreau.

And out of sight, further south, Sail Reef, Palm Island, and Union Island. I saw all this as I stood behind Jack, looking at the chart laid out on the table near the compass. I looked at Union Island again, and there at the southern tip was a point of rock with that familiar name: Miss Irene Point. Who was this Miss Irene?

To the east, Petite Saint Vincent, and then Petite Martinique, sister islands standing close. The ocean ran between. The border between Saint Vincent and Grenada is the narrow strait. We would visit a number of these places: the Cays for three days, Palm Island for lunch on the fourth day, and then on to Petite Saint Vincent for dinner and dancing that night.

I released the anchor into the clear blue water at the center of the Tobago Cays, just in time for a late lunch. Two other yachts occupied the channel. The anchor sliced down to firm white sand and the yacht fetched up against the tide. The Atlantic slid by the sleek black hull racing to join some other water, with another name, against some other shore. The *Black Dog* bobbed at anchor as everyone sat under the awning, ate tongue sandwiches, and potato salad, drank Carib beers.

After lunch, Carl pulled out pencils and a notebook. He sat on the foredeck, running the pencil across the paper. I walked by, sneaked a peep. He had reproduced an exact view of the Tobago Cays on the sheet of paper, down to the last detail, spelled out in notes. Arrows pointed to the color of sand, shrubs, and the angle of light. This fascinated me. I made a mental note to speak to Carl about drawing.

I listened to the Americans speak about themselves, and I wondered if privacy existed for them. Carl and Elaine were married for about five years. Joel and Marla for ten. They talked about their friends, their businesses, with no discomfitures or regrets. Everything in the open. Naked people. I thought they were fully capable of walking down a street with no clothes on.

The occupants of the other yachts were preparing to go somewhere, east toward Sail Rock I surmised, to snorkel, and explore the sea life among the coral heads. I thought of Karrol, the times we went down to collect the white sea urchins, the time he told me the black ones were responsible for building the reefs. Just the black ones, the laborers. I wondered how Karrol knew those things.

The remainder of that day, everyone lounged around the deck. They drank beers, sipped gin and tonics, continued their idle conversations, and grumbled about the separate features of their lives. I learned a few things about the world and those people. The world is not as large as some would have you believe. Most people's lives are furnished with refuse and regret, while others live in servitude to scraps of joy, yoked like mules to the plow of pleasures. I thanked God for my ears, and I marveled at the simplicity of it all. Their lives were not that different from the peoples I knew. Tante Rose and Miss Olga all over again.

"Godfrey, is this a job or a career?" Marla's words jolted me out of my chewing on the comparisons of human existence.

"A career?"

"What the hell am I talking about? Do people down here have careers?"

"I don't know; I'll just see. I would like to travel, go somewhere beside," I said.

"That's good," she said.

"Don't listen to her, Godfrey," Joel said. "Stay here. Remain in paradise. Someone must be the guardian." He nodded his head slightly, as if enticing me to agree.

"Pay no attention to him, Godfrey. He has no idea what it means to be poor," Marla said.

Her words struck me at a strange angle, because I never thought of myself as poor. The four guests sat in the midday sun, baking and basting their skin like hams. I seized the opportunity to approach Carl on the subject of art. He looked at me long and hard, as if I had asked about the size and style of his wife's underwear.

"Have you ever done any drawing, Godfrey?" he asked.

"Some, in school," I said.

"I've practiced this for more than thirty years. Some of my labor sells for thousands of dollars." His voice trailed off. He took a sip of his drink.

"Carl, he's just inquisitive. That's why you and Pearl never got along. You don't understand young people," said Elaine, and she glanced at Jack.

"Why do you have to bring your daughter into this?" Carl asked. I don't mean to be insulting to Jack, but that girl is headed down a bad road. Some of those friends of hers. Remember the one with the ring in his nose. Had the balls to tell me I should buy a camera instead of wasting paint. Little prick."

"Just give him a quick lesson instead of getting all worked up," Elaine said.

"Godfrey, she thinks I'm being inflexible. Soulages? You have the name of an artist. If I remember right, the fellow came from the school of abstracts. These things are never as simple as they seem." Carl took another sip of his drink and licked his lips. "This thing called art. It's a powerful tool, used by politician and statesmen for centuries, one of the greatest propaganda machines in the history of mankind. From Alexander the Great all the way down to modern times, Stalin, Hitler, even some of the good guys. All the commissions given to artists, to sculpt statues, make molds for coins. You think those bastards just love art? All designed for the consolidation of power. Did you know that Franco hated Picasso? Hated him to the bone."

I nodded, struggling to comprehend his gaggle of words. The conversation seemed to have gone astray, and all I could think of was Pearl, this person, not here, but still here. Is she a girl with a little girl's body, or is she a woman like one of these? Clad in skimpy bikinis that barely cover their ass, wisps of pubic hairs sneaking out near the edge of their crotch. I put forward a question, attempting to retrieve the conversation.

"You ever heard that African saying: "a child will inherit seven traits of the person he or she was named for?" Whom was Pearl named for?" I asked Elaine.

"Jack's mother-his adopted mother," she said.

Carl smiled with just one corner of his mouth. He obviously took offense to me changing the slant of the conversation and speaking to his wife instead of to him. Jack ignored the whole discussion. He reclined on the aft deck, reading a book by Jacques Cousteau. The man looked greased. Sun tan oil, white balm on his lips; he looked like a white Jab Jab, straight out of carnival. He would be an interesting figure to paint, just like that. I stored the image away for future reference.

"Old age must be getting the best of me," Carl said. "I have no patience anymore. Without exception, someone would walk up to me, at one of those gallery shows. A lawyer or a doctor usually' 'Carl, those are quite good. I do some painting in my spare time. It relaxes me. I have always wanted to devote more of my time to it.' I would bite my tongue, all the while thinking, you asshole. I have always wanted to perform surgery or argue a case before the Supreme Court."

"Christ, Carl!" Elaine said.

"What! Get off my ass, will you. I'm only trying to give Godfrey some perspectives on this thing we call art. Here's your first lesson, Mr. Soulages. It's what we call an aptitude test. Draw that island. Any style."

"Carl, why are you trying to humiliate him?" Elaine asked.

"Elaine, why are you being a mother hen?"

She flashed Carl an angry look and turned away.

"Here, Godfrey."

Carl handed me a pad of paper and a few pencils. Their squabble over this simple matter left me anxious. I sat and started to draw lines across the paper, and remained out there on the deck for the rest of the evening, doodling. Finally, all the light was gone. When Carl asked to see the results, I closed the pad, indicating I was not finished. He looked puzzled, but then he smiled.

The next day I took our guests snorkeling. I instructed them to stay away from the pink fire corals, and to keep their hands out of holes in the reef. An eel might be waiting. I sat in the Whaler like a lifeguard, watching the four of them. Marilyn came along, and Elaine stayed aboard the *Black Dog* with Jack. She said she didn't feel like swimming. She needed to make some notes for the article on the trip so far.

Snorkels and bright-clothed asses played above blue water. Flippers thrashed about, fragments of conversations and laughter drifted to me. They swam against the tide, and I looked on. On the eastern horizon, a ship was heading north, a small speck. Where is she headed? What cargo? Another vehicle, traversing this long, circular road. Look what Columbus started.

The last day of our stay in the Cays, Elaine and Marla planned to go ashore on one of the islets to walk on the beach, languish in the sun half-naked, and warm their bare feet in the sand. They planned to get some color to their skin.

The two women had formed an alliance after the night their husbands had deserted them to play poker. I took them ashore and promised to look out for them. They would hail *the BLACK DOG* when they were ready to be picked up. But fifteen minutes after I dropped them off, they stood on the beach waving their arms and shouting.

At first I thought, Oh shit! An accident. I shouted to Jack and started the Whaler toward the beach. As I approached the shore, I noticed both their feet had turned black. The sides of their feet looked as if they had stepped into big piles of black cow shit. On closer examination, I saw it was oil. Along the eastern side of the beach, small tar balls hid in the sand, rolled up, disguised in clumps. The moment you stepped on them, they burst like little black tomatoes. I took the two women back to the yacht; Jack used thinner to remove the oil from their feet, fuming as he rubbed at the black smears.

"Nothing safe in this world. Some tanker flushing its bilge or holding tanks, kind of shit will destroy everything. Soon one species disappears, then another and another."

Elaine was looking at the back of Jack's head as he rubbed on her feet with the rag. She reclined in ecstasy, closed her eyes, and spoke as if with regret.

"To think, ignorance could destroy all this, and just so we can drive our cars. That's a damn shame. I must include this to my article."

Her husband, Carl, stood to one side, watching Jack rub on her feet, frustrated, holding back, as if barely able to keep from snatching the rag out of Jack's hand. Marla cleaned her own feet, and looked on at Elaine with a puzzled concern.

At 11:30 the next morning, we sailed the *Black Dog* to Palm Island. One other yacht sat at anchor: *West Wind*, a white sloop-registered out of Falmouth, England. Palm Island is no more than a high sand bar with a few palm trees surrounding a hill. Young bayberries and sea grapes crawled along the flats near the sea. The emerald vines strove to hold this place together against the winds and tides of the Atlantic. What would happen to these buildings in the first hurricane-wind, rain, and the storm surge? Those forces would pummel the buildings into splinters, and blow them away like straw.

They went ashore for lunch, toured the new resort under construction and swam on the beach at Palm Island. I remained aboard the *Black Dog* working on my art lesson. The six of them returned from their excursion around 3:30, and I presented my assignment the moment they came aboard. It had taken me almost three days, but there it was. The sheet of paper rested on the chart table, and everyone gathered around to see what I had done.

"Well, I'll be!" Elaine said, looking as pleased as if she had done the drawing. The others remained quiet.

The composition was simple. The island looked like an island but not the same island in the Tobago Cays. I proportioned it in relation to harmony and balance with the beach, the sea, and the shrubs. The real composition began beyond the sand, at the spine of the rock. There, I added an extra touch: a line of figures, holding hands, across the top of the knoll, nothing like real human beings, more like stick people. Carl looked at the paper for a long time. When he spoke, it was as if he couldn't quite believe his eyes.

"Godfrey, I don't know what to call this. This is yours. Uniquely yours. Some call this uncultivated, primitive art. The Haitians do stuff similar to this. You certainly aced your aptitude test. You have pencils and paper; those are yours. Keep them." He gestured at the pencils and the pad as if I had tainted them. "Create, man, reinterpret. There is a space between art and nature. Find that place, and there you will know liberation of the soul. Go get 'em tiger! Now, how about a gin and tonic?" Carl turned from me. He was finished.

In the middle of the afternoon, we motored over to Petite Saint Vincent. That resort was already built. Little bungalows and beach huts dotted the palm-lined shore, and one big structure with a veranda sat up on a hill, overlooking the bay. It was probably a restaurant, dance floor, and bar. Out on a point, away from the structure, near a high bluff at the southern tip of the small island, sat Petite Martinique.

Four other yachts sat at anchor. A man in a rubber dinghy came motoring out the moment we dropped anchor. Dressed in shorts, his skin brown, he pulled alongside the *Black Dog* like some kind of Customs official. He shut off the motor, stood up in the dinghy, and started speaking.

"I'm Gordon Laridon. Who's your captain?" Jack waved at the man. "I'm told you don't have reservations for dinner. Come join us anyway. This is an invitation for all aboard. Come dance with us tonight. Put on those blue suede shoes. Be ready for a fete. You see over there?" He pointed to a small cargo vessel moored to the jetty, and a group of people with instruments walking up the hill. "You should change your mind about dinner. Our cook came from Paris. I'll see you all later," Gordon said. He pulled the starter cord on the outboard twice and motored away.

For dinner that night we ate dashines, breadfruits, and red snappers stewed in an onion sauce. Jack brought out three bottles of white wine. Marilyn called the meal her West Indian special. They ate and praised her cooking. The music on land started before they were finished with the wine. The steel band tuned up softly. Satin steel, rolling off the island on a soft westerly wind.

They drank all the wine before heading for shore. Empty bottles sat on the table. Elaine seemed to have had the most. She started dancing around the deck and almost tumbled overboard. Carl grabbed her arm roughly, and scolded her. She pushed him away. I finally took everyone ashore, and then motored back to the *Black Dog* to finish my work.

It took me less than thirty minutes to wash the plates, pots and pans, and tidy the galley. Nighttime had settled in. Flecks of light from Union Island to the west, and Petite Martinique to the northeast, they twinkled in the dark. In the distance to the south, and across the channel, a steady light burned on the northern tip of Carriacou. Some smugglers hiding their loot, I speculated. I motored into the dock, tied up the Whaler at the far end, and started up the hill to the dance.

I spotted Jack first, moving stealthily away from the festivities, going toward the rocks that overlooked the narrow channel between Petite Saint Vincent and Petite Martinique. Moments later, Elaine came striding out of the building, and walked in the same direction. I continued up the hill, unsure about what that might be all about.

A mixed crowd littered the dance floor: island guests, people off the yachts at anchor, crews and captains, black and white, all dressed in garish clothes. They all moved about in awkward gyrations to the beat of the steel drums. I settled in with my back to a wall, near the bar.

"Godfrey?" Carl shouted, gesturing me over. "Join us." Carl stood with Marilyn, our cook. "Have you seen Elaine?"

"Not yet," I lied without understanding why. Carl looked at me. I stared back at his face. Gordon Laridon strolled up.

"May I have this dance, fair lady?" he asked Marilyn.

They joined hands and swooped to the edge of the crowd. They began throwing arm gestures. They acted as if attempting to dance with a minimum of feet and hips.

"Let me buy my favorite art student a beer," Carl said over the pitch of the band. He moved closer and leaned in to speak. "Are you married, Godfrey?" He didn't wait for an answer. "At least it's safe for her here."

I turned from looking at Gordon and the cook to face Carl. His voice sounded grave.

"They mugged her, not raped, just mugged. In New York, just before we were married. Forgive me, man, but those niggers were bold. Took what they wanted, knocked her down, dragged her, took her purse, bruised her up. At times, I think she married me because she just needed to feel safe. Have a man around."

I looked at Carl, and nodded in agreement, not knowing exactly what I was agreeing to. He shifted his weight from one foot to the other. Why did he ask me for forgiveness? Are the sins of other men also mine to bear?

A black man dressed in starched black and whites handed me a beer. Carl paid him some money. I thanked him and returned to looking at the dancers again. Joel and Marla danced like bad soccer players, throwing elbows, shuffling around as if trying to keep the crowd at bay. The steel band came to an abrupt halt. The crowd clapped and yelled.

This time the band came back with a slow ballad, something about a yellow bird in a banana tree. Pure bullshit. I've never seen such a bird in any banana tree. The dancers fell into each other's arms, and waltzed around the floor as the pan-men pounded out the folk ballad about love to die for.

What a strange ritual. I knew how to dance, but I had never been to a dance like this one. I placed my back and elbows on the edge of the bar, trying to look relaxed, watching the dancers, sipping my beer, hoping that Carl wouldn't start with that strange talk again.

Jack appeared out of nowhere.

"Can I buy you guys a beer? Bartender!" Jack raised one finger in the air and continued to speak. "I ran into Ralph Sims, off the *GULCONDAR*. Once he gets started, it's hard to shut him up. I met him on Saint Thomas two years ago."

"Have you seen my wife?" Carl interrupted.

"She's out there, admiring the stars. Walked right by her on the way in."

Carl strolled off to find Elaine. Jack turned as the bartender came up. He ordered two beers. I nudged him and whispered in his ears that his fly was open. A swift smile crossed his face. I found it hard to measure: was that pride or remorse? The band poured out the melody as Jack and I stood sipping the beers. Could I ever looking these people in the eyes again?

I saw Carl first. Far across the dance floor, he came lashing through the crowd, pushing people as he moved, his ponytail whipping. He bounded straight for where we stood. I bumped Jack's elbow and pointed. He turned just as Carl reached us.

"What the hell have you done?" Carl shouted, his face red as a beet.

He tossed a weak punch at Jack. Jack ducked and moved. The bartender shouted. Gordon Laridon rushed off the dance floor, and threw himself between Jack and Carl.

"What's going on here?" he asked.

Jack moved away, his head down. He maneuvered toward the door; a few dancers stopped to watch. The music seemed to grow louder. Carl followed Jack outside onto the veranda, and I went after them. Joel and Marla, Gordon and Marilyn: they all came outside. Gordon and Marilyn stood near Elaine, who was sitting in a chair with her legs spread wide. She said nothing. Carl came up behind Jack.

"You son of a bitch. You raped my wife!" he shouted.

Jack half turned to face Carl just as Carl's left hand came up, swinging wide, and faster this time. It connected with Jack's mouth. Jack staggered, took two steps back. His hand covered his mouth. He said nothing at first. He didn't even look surprised.

"I'm going to kick your ass, you puss-face gremlin!" Carl shouted. His lips compressed as he sized up Jack, and prepared to throw another blow.

"That's the way you want to handle this? Let's go." Jack crouched into a boxing stance.

Elaine leaped out of the chair. "Stop! Stop! Stop that! No one raped me, you fool. You treat me like a child," she shouted. "I'm so tired of all this shit. You know why I told you he fucked me? Just to see the look on your pompous face."

She took off, running toward the rock bluff. Jack and Carl stared each other down like gunslingers.

"Somebody should follow her. Talk to her," Joel said.

"I'll do it." Marla started after Elaine.

Everyone milled around, looking uncomfortable. Finally, they started gravitating back toward the sound of the band. Jack moved off, skulking, putting space between himself and Carl. I was about to follow Jack, because I wanted to know what to expect in the next few days, but Marla's voice shrieked from the hillside.

"Help! Help! She fell in. She jumped in. Somebody help her!"

The few people remaining on the veranda froze, as if awaiting some command. Jack and I ran for the Whaler, and sped toward the passage between the two islands. We saw no one in the water. The ocean slid by the hull of the dinghy. Everything appeared unbroken at a glance. A group of people had arrived on the bluff. The wind scattered their voices as they shouted down to us and called her name from above.

The vigil on the cliffs lasted most of the night. They acted as if they expected Elaine to rise from the waves. I joined a group searching the rocks with flashlights. At first light the next morning, they began a search of the water. All the yachts in the bay joined in. They formed a flotilla. Some tourists on one yacht operated a big camera from a tripod, as if shooting footage for a movie. A group of divers from Petite Martinique found her fifty yards offshore, in deep water.

Gordon Laridon declared that she drowned in Grenada's territory, and the police from Carriacou took over. I stayed away from the body; didn't even glance at it. Image picture of Karrol and my father, after divers had pulled them from the sea, the memories prevented me. The body was placed on the police launch and taken to Hillsboro, Carriacou. Carl went with them, shouting all the way that Jack Trueblood was responsible. They should arrest him.

Jack steered the *Black Dog* at a safe distance behind the launch. No one spoke a word all the way into Hillsborough. At the jetty, the Customs authorities informed Jack that they would hold an inquiry at Saint Georges, on Grenada, in two days. They debated what to do with Elaine's body.

I had no idea that being dead so far from home could be so inconvenient for the living. Carl would have no part of transporting Elaine's remains back to Grenada on the *Black Dog*. Marla and Joel seemed confused. They elected to stay in Carriacou with Carl and the body of his wife.

CHAPTER 17

We headed back to Grenada on the *Black Dog*, Jack, Marilyn, and I. He hurried her along, propelled by both motor and sail. Grenada surfaced out of the gray-green mist on the southern horizon. I stood on the foredeck, listening to the ocean wash by. A stanchion held tight in my right hand. Would there still be a trip to Trinidad? I felt a twinge of guilt for thinking of such matters.

The *Black Dog* plowed on down the coast, past the towns of Victoria, Gouyave, Grand Roy, and Grand Mal. Four hours after leaving Carriacou, we pulled into the Yacht Service and the lagoon. The place looked routine. I searched the dock for Cyril. I doubted my senses. So much had happened in the last few hours. I spotted Yvette on the far shore. She stood, watching us drop the anchor. Everyone here should have heard the news by now. Their indifference to our arrival felt like blame.

Marilyn packed her few belongings in a hurry. Jack handed her a wad of bills; I hauled the Whaler in and dropped her off near her husband's yacht. She acted like a rat escaping a sinking ship. Yvette still stood on the far shore. On closer inspection, I noticed something. Everyone seemed to be holding their breath. They walked around the dock with their heads down as if sad or ashamed.

I motored over to where Yvette stood. She grabbed the bow as it drifted into the shore. Her eyes were red and puffy, as if she had been weeping hard. I tipped the motor, and ran forward to help her control the boat.

"What's the matter? You that glad to see me?"

She fell into my arms. Words poured out of her mouth in sputters as she gripped my shirt. "He killed Bazil, Godfrey. He's dead. Oh God! They are going to hang Daddy."

"What you talking about? Who killed Bazil?"

"Daddy shot him with a spear gun, Godfrey. He killed him. They had a fight."

Everyone around the Mang was talking, but they would go silent the moment Yvette and I walked by. We tried to imitate the custom my father had with his sister, after returning from a trip, but that fell short. It appeared as though someone had poked a hole in the universe, and the universe was sucking everything unsecured into that wound, trying desperately to stop itself from bleeding to death.

I decide to find Ian. He would know the truth. I found him loitering near Cyril's house with some of his Rasta friends. They were guarding the place in case some of Bazil's friends decided to seek revenge on Cyril's family. Ian spoke to me as we sat in the yard. We were just show; we had no weapons to defend the women if Bazil's friends really came.

"I never trusted that man, you know. He's a coward, that Lennox," Ian said. "He could have prevented all that shit. He was right there."

"What you mean he was right there?"

"He was there when the whole thing started, Godfrey. I was working on *Ring Anderson*. Cyril just completed a job and was waiting for his money. Bazil wanted him to wait outside the gate. He didn't like Cyril sitting around the dock half-naked, told him to wait outside. Cyril refused, said he would wait right there. Bazil threw him in a chokehold just as Lennox came along. Cyril pleaded with Lennox to have Bazil release him. Lennox didn't even look at them. He walked right by. Bazil dragged Cyril to the gate, and threw him out, out onto the ground in a heap.

"Cyril hauled himself off the ground. You could see he was in a rage. He took off running to his house. He came back carrying two spear guns, cocked and ready. I saw him running back and I knew it: someone was going to die. Cyril charged through the gate and no one stopped him. Bazil was on the dock near *Ring Anderson,* joking and talking to Lennox as if he was proud of what he had just done to Cyril.

"I heard Cyril's footsteps pounding up the dock. He came into view and Bazil turned to face him. Bazil looked at Cyril as if he intended to laugh. He kept glancing at Lennox, and then back to Cyril, looking at Lennox and back to Cyril. Cyril stood with the two spear guns cocked and ready, pointing straight at Bazil and Lennox. Bazil should've jumped over board, run, anything. Instead, he moved between Cyril and Lennox, that funny look still on his face, and then he made a little move with his head and legs, as if starting to dance.

"That's when Cyril pulled the trigger. One shaft sank into Bazil's side, right up into his ribs. I felt it myself. I know I screamed, but I don't remember hearing the sound. Then I saw Bazil down on one knee, clutching the shaft with one hand and the other hand pulling on the cord attached to the spear gun that Cyril still held. Bazil looked surprised, as if he expected nothing. When Cyril turned with the other spear gun, Lennox was already moving. He scrambled aboard *Ring Anderson* and ducked below the deck. I could hear him shouting, 'Lend me your gun. Lend me your gun.' Bazil was laying flat on his back. I knew he was dead. Cyril just turned and walked away. They say he walked all the way to the police station, and just sat down."

Ian kept coiling his deadlocks, and then he would switch and run his palm over his face. "I lost something," he said. "Seeing a man killed, watching with your own eyes. Something happened to me. Everything changed. I realize how flimsy humans are. Just like a bubble. Just poke the right spot and puff, everything is gone, spirit in the sky, let out."

We spent that night hiding in Cyril's house, Ian and I. We armed ourselves with machetes. Yolan and her aunt, Rose, made sure we slept in the front room, separate from Yvette and Yoelina. I had no idea that Ian had something going with Yoelina. Nothing happened at Cyril's house that night. The next few days I tried to comfort Yvette, went everywhere with her. I kept saying to her, everything would be all right. But I didn't believe it.

The girls and their aunt hired a lawyer called Cline, to defend Cyril. I found my two encounters with the legal man quite intriguing, but also quite sad and ominous, so final. So it was said, let it be written and done. Who are these wig wearers? Keep putting things off and telling people to come back later. What would they do to Cyril?

The inquest into Elaine's death came next, but it concluded moments after it started. Not enough evidence to support criminal intention. An accident. No one to blame. Carl flew into a rage. Outside the courthouse, he almost got into a fight with Jack. "I'm going to sue your ass for all you own, that garbage scow included. Then I'll scuttle the motherfucker. This is not over. You little puss face gremlin."

I had no idea how he would carryout that threat. He flew out of Grenada the next day with Elaine's body. Two days later, Jack followed them back to the States, but within a week, he was back in Grenada, hiding onboard the *Black Dog* like a flea.

Jack fell into a terrible funk. For weeks, he drank, and hardly ate, or slept. I hung around because he was still paying me. No one came to see him, and no one sent him messages. I brought him food. I also escorted Yvette to the courthouse, where the wig men were prosecuting her father.

The same day they sentenced Cyril to life in prison, a fat letter came with the mail that I was collecting for Jack. Up in the left corner of the envelope was some writing about the district court, in Miami, Florida. Jack read the letter, and his face went from red to a milky white. He wrote a letter and enclosed it with the legal papers. He addressed it to a man, Horace McNealy, in Boca Raton, Florida.

Jack must have started drinking early. By the time I came back from eating supper and visiting with Yvette and her sisters, he was drunk. His stringy hair looked greasy, matted to his scalp. His eyes and face were bright red. He squinted as if blind. The man had turned into this thing I hardly recognized. Lord have mercy, I don't have to kill him. If I just wait, he might die on his own.

I stood at the cabin door, looking at him. He poured himself a shot of the Scotch whisky, and with one quick flick of his wrist, he tossed it at his face. I thought the liquid would just splash in his eyes, but he opened his mouth. His face scrunched up as he swallowed and began speaking to me.

"I've always known that bitch would be the death of me. Have a beer, Godfrey."

Jack nodded at the icebox. Something told me to get back into the dinghy and go. But I ignored that urge, stepped into the cabin and reached for the beer. Peculiar smells hung over everything. Jack hadn't taken a bath in weeks. I could smell his breath from across the cabin.

"I was out of it, away from all her shit."

He slammed his hand on the table. The bottles jangled; three of them toppled over and rolled toward the edge. I darted for the table and righted the bottles. I stood in the center of the cabin, trying not to look directly at him.

"She lured me back, Godfrey, right back into her bullshit. When I was married to that bitch, she screwed everybody, and she always seemed to procure men I knew. She always blamed it on alcohol or dope. We have a child, and I'm not sure if I'm the father."

Jack shook his head and looked away. His eyes focused on the cabin wall, behind my back. He took a deep breath and exhaled as if expelling something from his lungs, and then he was speaking again.

"You know, even after she left, I was still fucked up about all of it. I just wanted to see how low she would go. That's why I tolerated it. What the fuck was wrong with me?"

I was standing there, listening to Jack. And that urge to bolt took hold of me again. I remember another man telling me his story, and it turned out to be so much more than I bargained for-diamonds, Yumawalli and that far-off jungle. Some of Jack's pain made strange sense to me. Death, what a thing? We humans wallow so much in our recollections of it. It can move us to the height of rage or drag us down to the pit despair. I stood there not knowing what to say to him.

"In spite of it all, I still love women," he said. "I would like to get off on that woman you brought aboard that night... if we had the time. What was her name?"

"There's always time for that."

"We are leaving, Godfrey. Tomorrow. Tomorrow evening."

"Going where?"

"Trinidad. She needs work, to keep her seaworthy." Jack didn't look at me. I had a strange inkling about the way he avoided my face and spoke to the floor. "In her shape, she can't make a trip back to the States," he said.

The plan came to me in a moment of silent clarity. I moved away from the *Black Dog* that night and the details seemed very practical.

Walk away from the yacht and this crazy man in Trinidad. Catch transport to Venezuela. Sydney and Xudine can be found. Caracas: that's the first place to look. A hobbled, disfigured black man, and a beautiful Arawak woman shouldn't be hard to find. In my father's money belt I stuffed three thousands dollars, latched the contraption to my groin and started on my adventure. A map to the place where he found those diamonds was really my goal.

CHAPTER 18

Yvette came down to the dock to see us off. The tension between us seemed evident as she hugged me and whispered in my ear. "I'm so happy for you. You'll be gone for a while. Your mother, be with you brothers and sisters," She went silent, her hands clasped across my back. "Come back quick," she spoke the words and laughed against my cheeks, then pushed me to her arms length and looked into my eyes. My deception felt like weights, but I couldn't speak of the plan. I distracted myself by thinking of the message and the few provisions my aunt had given me for my mother.

I watched the island fading in the distance, and Jack instructed me to hoist three sails-staysail, main, and jib, but he kept the motor at full throttle. The sails slapped at the riggings as I hauled them up the mast. The *Black Dog* was pointed west, motoring at the setting sun. It didn't take long to escape the lea of Grenada. Fifteen minutes out, the trade winds ballooned the sails, and Jack made a course change.

A night crossing, should take about twelve hours. The moon, the stars, and a wide ocean; I felt like writing a song. My imagination took me away. Jack and I could become pirates. Pick up a few cutthroats on the way, sack a few vessels, and sell the plunder on the Spanish Main. Sheer crap, I thought immediately. What the hell is the Spanish Main any way? And I already had plans to find diamonds in the jungle.

I moved aft, and entered the cockpit. Jack stood at the helm.

Trinidad was southeast, but he had set a course almost southwest. When I inquired, he shrugged it off, said we were heading west toward Los Testigo, and from there, we would catch the Amazon current back to the Dragon's Mouths. Should be there by morning.

"You have the first watch," he said, "I'll relieve you around midnight."

He swung himself through the hatch and disappeared below. I hoped he wouldn't take out his bottle of Scotch, leave me to man the boat all night. The sun dripped over the western horizon, and the air immediately took on a slight chill. Minutes after the sunset, darkness came and a few stars sprinkled the sky. I imagined nothing like this. A full white moon hung low on the horizon to the east. The hull plowed through the waves as I held her on course.

Sitting at the helm of a boat at night on the ocean? Boring. Thoughts of my plan sustained me as I negotiated the fray between the yacht and the sea. All the other men who came this way, doing the same thing-Portuguese, Spanish, French, English-all seeking their fortune. And here I'm, an African, me, the great adventurer. The stars know my name as they did all my ancestors. Am I not a child of God?

I watched the moon rise high over the horizon and wondered when Jack would relieve me. He returned, sipping on a cup of coffee. I went below, switched off the cabin light, and crawled into the bunk with my clothes still on.

Yvette came into my awareness. She was more substantial than the body she had allowed me to handle, for the first time, the night before. Lord, what a gift. That's what she called it. In spite of her reversal, I could still smell her, taste the salt on her skin and the sweet water of her mouth.

The idea of sex first came to me as we were treading up the sand in the half-light of the quarter moon. It was the first time we had such freedom. I knew I couldn't holdback if the occasion presented itself. Between my attempt to soothe her distress over her father, talking about the trip to Trinidad, and what might come to pass, we suddenly arrived at a tiny moment, weighted with a baffling silence.

I must have touched her, but I don't recall where. I remember her precise reaction: something collapsed. I'll always remember that moment. I knew exactly where we were headed, but when we arrived, it still surprised me. The silence between carried us along. There was no going back. Women. What beings. God must have placed the best part of herself inside of them. Such a gift to men.

The main event took less than fifteen minutes. Such a short time, such confused bliss. Ecstasy combined with hard physical memories, the warmth of her naked skin, and the accepting smell of her breath as it left her nose and mouth. The sweet work. The sound of waves lashed at the sand and rocks. Animals screeched from the screw palms and beefwood back off the beach. Yvette transformed. In the midst of it all, she became someone else, a new person.

After we were through, I wanted to settle down and gaze at the stars, listen to the waves and the sound from the bushes, talk about the future and what this meant. But immediately she tugged her panties on, and then dragged her bra across her chest. When she took up her shirt and pulled it over her head, I realized she was really getting dressed.

"What's wrong? You putting your clothes on."

"You expect me to lay here naked with you all night."

"Yeah. What's wrong with that?"

She chuckled harshly, and then reached out and touched my hand without looking at me.

"Godfrey, this feels too good. I don't think we should be meddling... and anyway, you gone. I don't have to worry. I've a feeling I might not see you for a while. Trinidad, you know. People go down there and not return for years."

I moved to a sitting position next to her. In the dim light, the shadows of the trees danced around us. Yvette looked remarkable, hesitant, but I was mistaken that she might be spicing her words with caution.

"You chewing on your words, Yvette. What you really saying?"

"I don't know why I'm telling you. You going to be gone, and it's none of your business anyway."

"What? You trying to bamboozle me?"

"Lenox offered me a job at the Yacht Service," she said.

"What? Doing what?"

"Typing, filing, office work."

"And then he ask you to work at one of his parties, and you in his house. You can't trust the man. Guilt is a terrible thing."

"I know why he's doing it. I'm no fool. But the money still spends, and I need to help my family, need to get Daddy out of prison."

"What you going to do, break him out?" The words poured out of my mouth with instant regret, but she ignored me.

"There are many ways to get a man out of jail. Force is only one."

Her tone surprised me.

"Why did we, ah, ah?" I made two little gestures with one hand as if throwing something at her.

"You going away. That's my gift to you. It's all I've," she said. I was moved, but saddened-seemed so ordinary as if she had handed me a cup of soup. What the hell, so be it, we all have our memories to keep.

These recollections hop-scotched across my brain, preventing meaningful sleep. They became part of a restless thought-dream. I languished near sleep and wakefulness, swimming in reminiscences. The motion of the schooner interrupted this dawdling. Something was not right with the motion of the Black Dog. My eyes came open in the dark, and I threw my feet off the side of the bunk and reached for the light switch near the door. My feet splashed down into a pool of cold water.

I leaped off the bunk; my heart pounded in my chest. In the main cabin of the schooner, I stood in water up to my ankles. I threw the switch twice; nothing happened. The sail slapped around as if Jack had dozed off and pointed the bow too far into the wind. The ocean lapped at the hull, completely discernible from the heavy rain falling on the deck. The raindrops sounded like fish frying in a pan.

My mind juggled the obvious. Jack should have waked me for this squall. Where is he? This water; the yacht must be sinking. Did he fall overboard? Moonlight slashed through the cabin as the boat pitched. I waded to the hatch leading into the cockpit. The hatch was latched from outside.

"Jack! What's happening? Open the hatch." His footsteps sounded across the cockpit. I expected to hear the metal click, but instead, Jack spoke.

"She's going down, man. I can't afford to pay for all the work she needs. That son of a bitch is suing me. My daughter hates me. I'm a piece of meat and the world is full of hungry dogs."

His voice sounded weird and-wonderful.

"Jack! The hatch. Open the hatch, there's water-"

"I'm sorry, Godfrey."

Those words. I felt warmth coursing up my spine and into the back of my head. Then it was in my throat and on my tongue. I swallowed. A metallic taste filled my mouth. The water climbed slowly up my chin. What a terrible dream. Wake up! Wake up! I knew I had to move, dream or whatever, but my feet refused. Then, in the diffused moonlight spilling through the porthole, I saw Karrol Lagrenade standing in the water on the other side of the cabin.

"It's time, Godfrey," he said. "Time to show them."

Time. Time for what? The question formed in my head, but before I could speak, he pointed. I looked forward and saw a stream of light, but when I looked again at the spot where I had seen Karrol, nothing. I waded through the water to the skylight near the bow. Jack had nailed it shut. I kicked at it until the Plexiglas broke, and I squeezed my head through the frame, wondering if my shoulders would fit.

Rain lashed my face as I climbed to the deck. The yacht pitched and rolled through the phosphorescent waves; she groaned like a wounded beast. The sails still struggled to drag her forward. Jack stood at midship, holding onto a stanchion. He wore a yellow oilskin. In one hand, he held a gun.

"You should have remained below, Godfrey. Now I have to use this," he said.

"Shoot me? Why?"

"Double indemnity. The insurance company...pays twice as much if..."

"You mean?" The idea struck me with a mixture of amusement and rage.

Out of the corner of one eye, I saw the boathook strapped to the deckhouse along the handrail. The visualization technique that Fins had thought me blazed. I saw the whole plan to save my life before I made a single.

The yacht slammed into a wave and I flung myself. The jib slapped at the rain. The sinking vessel pitched upward onto the wave, and Jack went off balance. My hand landed on the boathook, and the straps broke as I had seen it in my mind's eye. I took all my chances in one burst, and the blow connected. A shot rang out, and a jolt ran up my arm. Oh God, I'm shot, but I yanked the pole back and struck again blindly. Jack crouched and grabbed his shoulder. I heard the gun hit the deck.

"Son of a bitch," he shouted.

The pistol slid through the scupper, hit the top of a wave, and disappeared in the green glow of the starboard light. Jack stood, holding his shoulder, confusion raged on his face. He made a slight move toward me. I braced myself against the motion of the yacht and made ready. For the first time I realized I was in complete control. The shot had gone wild. Bring it, you nasty son of a bitch. Fierceness took hold of me. I stepped away from the rail and onto the deckhouse. Jack sized me up as if to attack.

"You make one move toward me and I'm going to beat you to death. You, you...throw your ass over-board. Son of a bitch." I held the pole up high, cocked and ready to strike. Jack lowered his head and took two steps back.

"What now?" he asked.

Water dribbled off his beard. He stood with his hands slack at his side. He looked small and miserable.

"She's sinking, Godfrey. We have to get off," he said.

"Get the Whaler," I said.

Giving him that order felt pleasant. I still gripped the boathook in one hand. My voice sounded unfamiliar. Jack moved aft and into the cockpit. He stooped down and picked up a bag from the floor. He turned suddenly, threw the bag at me, lowered his head, and came charging straight ahead. I stepped to one side and swung the pole hard. It connected with the side of his face, near his chin. The blow yanked him straight up. He grunted just once, and crumbled to the floor of the cockpit.

I thought he might be dead; on closer inspection, I saw he was still breathing. The *Black Dog* pitched to starboard and did not right herself. The sails slapped at the wind and rain. The schooner no longer made headway. She drifted backward and sideways at the will of the sea. A broach of panic made my chest tight. I moved fast.

I hauled in the Whaler and threw in the bag of supplies in. Two choices stood clear before me: get the motor and the gas tank or get Jack. The sea was irate, gray blue, ebullient in the half-light. I looked back at

Jack on the floor of the cockpit. For a second, I thought of getting the motor, cutting the line, and leaving him. I recalled Sydney's words: *Get close to it and kill it.* But my conscience refused to let me leave him. I stepped into the cockpit, heaved him onto the deck, pulled the Whaler alongside, and rolled him in. He hit the floor of the Whaler with a thud. He neither groaned nor moved. He rested in a pool of rainwater.

I jumped into the Whaler just as a wave washed over the cockpit. It was as if the boat made one last effort to snare us. The sails and stanchions whipped through the water near the dinghy, forming a small cage of wire and canvas. I pushed off, and the tide swept us clear of the hull. The *Black Dog* groaned and pitched backward. The stern went under first, and the bow pointed straight up into the drizzle, at the moon glowing lackluster.

For a long time, the yacht stood like that, held up by the sails ballooning like domes, refusing to surrender the schooner to the sea. The rain ceased; the wind quieted as if in observance. The moon cleared the low-hanging clouds and shined down on the crippled yacht. I watched her as all her crevasses accepted the sea. One last shriek bellowed out of the hull, as if Medusa protested. Finally, the jib gave way with a loud pop, and the *Black Dog* slid under the waves.

The spot where she went under looked ordinary. The ocean rolled toward me from the distance. Not one thing floated to the surface. She took all that she possessed to the bottom. I settled back, dazed. That bastard wanted me to be inside that hull. He must have smiled when I brought aboard the stuff my aunt gave me for my mother. How long would it be before we were rescued? Had Jack sent out an SOS? What position did he give?

The waves pushed the dinghy along the corrugated surface of the sea. My fingers hurt. I looked down and found the boathook still clamped in the palm of my hand. Jack lay on the floor of the dinghy as if dead. A slow rage boiled in my chest, and my heart began to pound. How dare you just lie there? I had an urge to hit him with the pole, wakeup, speak to me…look at me, you miserable bastard. But I decided to wait, let him come around on his own. I'll deal with your ass in due time.

CHAPTER 19

Near daybreak, Jack came awake in a startled flash. His hands flew out to the rails of the dinghy and he pulled himself into a sitting position. I sat near the bow wondering, what he would do. He coughed. A cursory smile appeared on his face, and he laughed, cringed, and one hand reached for his jaw where I had struck him with the pole.

"Didn't realize you had it in you," he said, massaging the side of his face.

"You fucked-up, Jack. Really fucked-up, man."

"No sacrificial lamb are you, Godfrey Soulages. How does it feel?" He smiled.

"What the hell are you talking about? You almost killed me."

He laughed out loud this time. His face scrunched up, and his lips flared ugly. He made a noise with his mouth. A small school of flying fish skipped off the top of a wave, flew by, and splashed down a short distance away.

"Is that your best, Godfrey?" he said. "Man, you stood up; you fought like a warrior. Now where's the poetry in 'you almost killed me'."

"Fuck poetry. Man, what the fuck?"

I brandished the pole. He looked at me with almost a care. A wave crested to port, flouting the emotions of the sea.

"Decide, Soulages," he said. "You could have left me on the *Black Dog.*"

I saw Jack Trueblood for the first time. The miserable sight provoked me in a whole other way. I once admired and respected the man. Never again, never again, I told myself, would I give undue respect to anyone because of skin color. What a backward kind of prejudice. I should have followed Sydney's advice and killed this Yumawalli.

"I could have let you drown…but I found it hard to shoot you," he said.

"Thanks, Jack. Thank you very fucking much. Why did you do this? Because you told me so much about you and Elaine?"

"What the hell! Think about what happened here. You are not dead. What the fuck, you-you black son of a bitch. You angry because you grew the balls to save your own life?" He stared me down as if demanding a response.

Something in his outburst left me speechless for a second.

"Did you send out an SOS?" I asked.

"No, Godfrey. Lightning struck us. The radio went dead. Everything happened too fast. Don't worry. Oil tankers from Venezuela, cruise ships, cargo vessels from Trinidad. We are in the shipping lanes. I hope they spot us before one of them run us down, chew us up in its screws."

"Lightning, huh? That's what you saying."

"You were asleep," he said. "How could you know? She sits in three hundred fathoms of water. No human eyes will ever rest on her again. Lightning struck us." He folded his arms and hunched against the stern of the dinghy. He acted as if attitude could make his words true.

The motion of the dinghy prevented me from falling into a restful sleep. A mixture of thoughts and images, about the old woman on Saint Vincent and the people she called Garifuna, wrestled for the space inside my head. Agitation took hold of my brain as the early morning sun peeked over the horizon. The images and thoughts formed a situation of their own. Not dreams, not thoughts, but something reminiscent of a chaotic movie playing behind my eyelids. It was less than restful. I had no idea how long this lasted, but when I opened my eyes again, into the full glare of the hot sun, Jack was staring at me.

"You were hard at work there," he said as if trying to start some kind of conversation. Tiredness and thirst gripped me. I reached into the sea, intending to wash my face and drink a little as if from a stream.

"Don't do that," he spoke as I cupped my hand through the water and moved it toward my face. "In this sun, the salt will blister your skin, and if you drink, it will kill you."

I felt a twinge of gratitude.

"Here." He handed me a canvas bag. "Drink sparingly."

The bag contained water and food. A few cans of sardines, bread and crackers sealed in plastic, a couple oranges, a couple grapefruits, and three containers of fresh water. It looked like a big lunch. I understood just how completely Jack had planned this.

"Man, you were wiggling and groaning, tearing at your clothes. What were you dreaming?"

"Nothing. Don't worry about it." I hesitated to share the slightest with him.

"Must have been painful." He looked at me and waited.

"What do you dream, Jack?"

"You tell, me tell." He spoke as if imitating a West Indian accent. The sound coming out of his mouth softened the moment.

"Okay," I said.

"One rule," he leaned toward me, the yellow oilskin wrapped around him. "No stopping if it becomes embarrassing. You know dreams."

"Rule?" What rule?"

"Call it what you want." He smiled and threw up his hands as if fending me off.

Rude bastard. I sensed condescension, and that's when I decided to have some fun with him. How could he tell if I was revealing my dream or making it up? Out of gratitude to him for warning me about filling my belly with salt water, I decided to play the game.

"Alright. You remember my great grandmother, on Saint Vincent?" Jack nodded his head, looking slightly disappointed.

"I would rather hear about the fellow who found diamonds in the Amazon," he said.

"Sorry, Jack, I made that up. Nothing like that happened." The lie felt good coming off my tongue.

"You spoke about him in such a natural way. No way you could have been lying. I would have seen it."

"Well, I was. Now let me tell you how I dreamt about the old woman. How do I put this? I woke inside this dream. I was asleep on that beach, the one near her house, and I could hear her saying, '*wake up, wake up, Maji. The tide is coming in'.*   "She was looking down at me with milky blind eyes; she spoke words that didn't come from her mouth, but I could hear them inside my head: '*Dey waiting for you, Maji. Why you sleeping on de edge of dis water wen dey waiting for you? You know dem? Dis Atlantic Ocean remembers dem, too. Wake up, and come. You earned your scars, Maji'.* Then she was gone.

"I found myself in another place, just like that. It resembled an African village or what I thought an African village might look like— you know, from those Tarzan movies. Small fires burned all around, but there was no ground. It was as if we were up in clouds formed by wood smoke. My eyes burned. I could hear and smell fresh water. I saw faces in that place, faces I knew. Sydney, my father, Karrol, Cosmus, Tante Rose, Tante Grace, Yvette, Ian, Cyril. But in the way of dreams, I knew these villagers were not the same people from Grenada. It was as if they just borrowed the skins of those Grenadians. Then the old woman was back, and her eyes were healed."

Jack sat, staring at me intently with his bright blue eyes as if he had a burning question.

"What?"

"Nothing," he said. "Go ahead."

"I knew the old woman was there to shed my blood. The idea mesmerized me. I felt it in my groin, a sexual twinge. Will it hurt? The question came to me mixed with the voices of the villagers chanting something that sounded like an apology for slavery. I can't remember it exactly, but it went something like this: 'We are Africa/Some days we pray for forgiveness/ At other times we wonder if we can even call our deeds sins/You charge us with rebuilding temples long burned to the ground?'

"They waited for an answer to what I didn't recognize as a question. The old woman poked me in the ribs. '*Give dem de answer, Maji.*' I heard her speaking inside my head again, and I felt betrayed, wondering why she was not speaking for me.

"I floated on the sweet chastising tone. The old woman left me where I stood; she walked to a fire, filled a bowl with ashes and came back to stand beside me with a small black knife in her right hand. Her voice spoke some fragmentary dream words out loud.

"'The world begged/-No one volunteered/-so, we assumed, fools that we are/-Sorry we missed the obvious/-This world has a poor record in the preservation of living messiahs/-But a great desire to spawn them, let them come of age, acquire the gift of tongues/-Do we have to remind you, Maji Chatoyea? You earned your scars. That's why you here.'

"The old woman stood before me with the blade clutched in her hand. She made three quick perpendicular swipes over my heart. She dropped the blade and grabbed at the ashes in the bowl. She crushed the ash into the cuts on my chest. The pain, excruciating. That's when I recoiled, ripping at my shirt, searching for cuts or blood. But there was nothing, except the memory and you staring at me."

"Is that all?"

"Yeah. What you expect? Your turn."

"Diamonds in the Amazon would have been so much more…Give me a minute. I'm roasting," he said. I had no idea that Jack had paid any attention that evening as we ate dinner at the Yacht Service.

He peeled off the yellow rain suit and started rigging it across the dinghy, using the boathook as a spine. It seemed to take him forever. The man was stalling for some reason. A band of white clouds drifted up from the horizon. Inch by inch it boiled up and covered the sun, big chunks that resembled curdled milk. I thought of rain, and minutes later it started as a drizzle, and then became steady, cold, chilling, and driven by an incessant wind. We huddled under the only cover. The rain lashed my face. My teeth chattered. I detested being this close to him. I wished I could make him vanish. He smelled like a wet dog.

I endured the rest of that day and night hunched close to Jack. The ocean tossed and pitched the boat. Discomfort overrode any chance of sleep. Toward morning, the rain ceased, and I heard Jack mumble. He spoke almost directly into my left ear.

"It doesn't have to be this way, Myra. It doesn't have to be this way." I almost pushed him away, but then I realized he was only dreaming. He kept repeating those words, off and on, all the way into morning, and then he went silent.

My head ached, and my joints refused to move. The sun stood high above the eastern horizon, and blazed across the early morning. It didn't take long and again I was hot and dry. In spite of everything, I was glad. Sweat trickled down my skin. I thought of trees, cool shade trees. I looked east, west, north, and south, nothing but water: clear blue, a perfect bubble. I imagined someone poking it, pop, and there before me would be land, and people, rescued by the act of some great conjurer.

Nothing broke the perfect circle of the horizon. I thought by now someone might miss us or a ship might appear. However, on further consideration, I realized that no one would come. If we were found, it would be strictly by accident. Jack came awake as I shifted my position next to him. He looked up when he noticed me staring at him. His lips had cracked; his skin had turned the color of beets.

"You were talking in your sleep. Who is Myra?" I asked.

"My biological mother," he answered.

He rubbed his hand across his face, flinched, and looked at his palm as if it belonged to some stranger. Then he gazed off across the miles of water.

"What doesn't have to be this way?" I asked.

"What?"

"In your sleep last night. You kept repeating. It doesn't have to be this way."

He looked away, a little disappointed. "It's a recurring dream. Happens every time I'm stressed. That day in Saint Vincent, I started to warn you."

I regretted asking the question. That tone of familiarity annoyed me. I yearned to crawl back into the comfort of my own imagination and wait to be rescued. But he was speaking.

"Until I was nineteen, it never bothered me," he said. "Adoption was just a word. I have always known. But that year my girlfriend's sister lost her baby. Everyone started talking about Tay-Sachs, and genealogical inherited diseases. I started searching for my mother right after that. My adoptive parents warned me, and then they helped, grudgingly. It's amazing what you can do with enough money."

Jack's blasé declaration about money aggravated me. His voice sounded like footsteps on loose gravel. The son of a bitch sank the yacht because he wanted chances, and now he's talking about money. I wanted to kick him in the ass. Break sticks in my ears.

"They told me exactly where to start…in Miami, about two hours from where we lived. I found her in a bar on Biscayne Boulevard. She was a skinny little woman with rotting, cigarette-stained teeth. She drank beer out of those stubby glasses, drafts; she chewed the filters off cigarettes and piled them in an ashtray in front of her. Her eyes bothered me; they looked exactly like mine. I watched her without saying anything. I went back day after day. Finally, I couldn't take it anymore. I'm your son, I told her. *'Buy me a beer and stop being a fool. I'm no one's mother,'* she said.

"We had some drinks, and then she purchased a six-pack to take home. I followed her back to the old hotel where she lived. I came back daily for over a month. She refused to acknowledge the papers. My parents warned me and stayed hands off.

"Myra refused to ride in my car. She would stop as we walked down the street. She spoke to imaginary people. They told me she suffered from schizophrenia. I always thought I would come down with it one day. Those monsters in her head would relocate, once she was dead, find refuge with me.

"One day she turned on me. *'Who are you? What do you want? If am your mother, I already gave you life. What more do you want?'* I had no idea how to answer that, so I asked her about my father. *'He's in heaven',* she laughed out loud, exposing those disfigured teeth. *'Go away',* she told me. *'Stay gone or I'll have to call the police.'*

"I never saw her after that. I went searching many times and could never find her. No one knew where she went. Ten years later, I received a letter from a lawyer, in a little town called Stevensville, in western Montana. She turned out to be the only heir to some land. They called it a ranch. The lawyer who showed me the property, offered to take it off my hands, and that made me suspicious. The place didn't look like much at the time. It was just an old house way out, near the base of the Bitterroot Range. I remember lots of cats and dogs running around. Nothing special: a house with a beautiful view on a chunk of land. All that changed when that utility company made me an offer. They wanted to run a power line across the valley.

"That shit haunts me still. I should never have gone searching. I should have left well enough alone. If I had done that, I would not be here with you now. Never would have had the money to buy the boat." He threw up his hands in a wide gesture and avoided my gaze.

"Have you ever heard of a Yumawalli?" I asked.

"Yumawalli? Sounds like a candy bar."

"Group of Arawaks called the Palikur thinks you are a Yumawalli."

"Pass me the water? I've never heard of Yumawalli or Palikur. How could they know me?"

He took a sip and settled back, quietly on the stern. I told myself that if I survived this, never again would I trust anyone on sight. I decided to construct my own rules for living, not cower under a set of strictures created by a bunch of thieves and liars who think less of me than of their dogs or cats, people who live by two sets of moral and ethical standards-one for people who look like them and another for people like me.

For a moment, I thought of telling him about Ayahuasca and the dream where I first saw him, but that seemed so unwise. We ate the last of the food, drank some water, and slept through a calm night. Around ten the next morning, a ship appeared on the horizon. We watched it, small, crawling across the distance, unaware of whether it was headed in our direction. We rigged the yellow rain gear onto the pole to make the dinghy more visible and waited. It took the ship less than thirty minutes to reach us.

The big, black hull sheltered us in its lea. The ship was called *Agamemnon*. They lowered two lines and hoisted the Whaler onto the deck, lashed it down and were on the way again in a matter of minutes. The parity I felt a short time ago vanished instantly. It had everything to do with numbers and whiteness. Jack acquired a different status the moment we set foot on the ship. They dropped anchor in the outer harbor at Saint Georges, and towed the Whaler behind the launch that took us to the pier.

Jack was placed in an ambulance and taken to the hospital. Flimsy bastard. Only three days on the water. What could be wrong with him? Beyond a little sunburn. Actually, I expected him to insist that they take me with him. Instead, they left me on the pier, didn't even offer me a ride home. People looked at me as if I was something brought back from the dead. For the first time, I saw it bare, my exact worth, a mere curiosity, and it infuriated me. I wanted to shout at them, "Look at me. I'm a man. I fought, and I'm alive today." I turned to start walking home, and there stood Yvette. All the anger drained out of me. Such a lovely sight, standing there dressed in nice clean clothes as if she had just come back from church or some function. But it was Tuesday around noon. She came up to me and threw her arms around my neck.

"I thought… I might never see you again," she spoke into the fold of my neck, near my ears. "Those three days, very long and the nights longer. You okay?" She pushed me to arm's length and inspected me like some position just returned.

"Yeah, I'm good," I said.

"Let's go home. I'm on my lunch break. Chitchat about the *BLACK DOG* already started around the Yacht Service."

"What they saying?"

"You know, insurance money and all that. Speaking in the hush, hush tone. You know how people are. Blacks and whites, all the same."

We left the Carenage walking hand in hand. I felt an urge to run over to Fins shop; thank him for everything and the gravel he placed in my craw. But I continued to walk with Yvette. The wet paper money around my waist felt like a weight.

CHAPTER 20

It took the authorities two weeks to get around to me. At the inquiry, requested by the insurance company, my story matched Jack's perfectly. I was asleep below when I heard a loud bang. I came on deck to find the vessel sinking. We were lucky to get off before she went down.

Scream it to high heaven. Tell the suckers what really happened. But I saw no benefits in that for me. The insurance company would keep the money; the law would handle Jack. I wanted to deal with him personally. I wanted to stare the motherfucker in the eyes, deal out my own retribution.

I envisioned Jack with two big suitcases full of money from the insurance company. I pictured myself knocking him down, kicking him in the ass as he tried to crawl away, ugly little bastard. I saw myself making off with the cash. Just like in the movies. How stupid of me.

The rudiments of a plan took shape. I knew the bungalow at the Calabash Hotel where Jack went after the courthouse. I decided to recruit some help. Ian and I spoke quietly, in the yard, near the brick oven that his mother used to bake her bread. Bleached dreads hang on both sides of his face; he had grown in many ways since the death of his brother, Karrol.

"I need help with something. There might be some money in it." A baby wailed loudly and furiously from inside the house.

Ian looked at me. "Tell me one thing," he said. "Anything to do with that white man from the yacht? I've a couple friends."

"No one else. Just me and you."

"Okay. He's only one man."

Ian carried a butcher knife. I carried a short machete, swaddled in burlap, and tucked behind my belt, below the tail of my shirt. The plan called for swift action. Ian actually fine-tuned it. No hesitation. He sounded like one of the soldiers in movies we had seen. I knew what we were headed to do and I justified it by repeating a kind of mantra to myself. In a world of liars, cheats, and murderers, choices are limited. You can either join them or prepare to be their victim.

We gave Cosmus twenty dollars to use his old Zephyr taxi for about an hour. He looked at us funny when we decided to do our own driving, but he decided to let us takes the car. Ian and I completed the details of the plan as we drove to the Calabash Hotel. We parked on the far side of a wooded trail that led to the back of the scattered bungalows.

We made our way through the bushes to a spot near the back window of number 10, the last one at the edge of the trees. My palms were wet. My legs shook slightly. I glanced at Ian, crouched beside me.

"You ready?" he asked.

I forced my legs to carry me across the grass. Ian followed on my heels. I peeked through the back window and almost knocked down a rake leaning near the back edge of the bungalow. The place was decorated sparsely: one bed, a table, and chair with a lamp. Jack was nowhere in sight.

"Wait here. Let me go around front." I was about to peek into the front window when a voice shouted from across the lawn.

"Hey! What's up, fellas? Looking for someone?"

The voice came from a white fellow walking toward me. Not Jack. This fellow was thin, with a big nose and not much older than Ian and me. He wore blue swimming trunks and a towel thrown over one shoulder. My stomach constrict, I felt the machete slipping in my belt. One hand went instinctively to my waist and steadied the blade.

There was no one else around except Ian, waiting out of sight. The fellow looked bold, the way he spoke and kept walking toward me. Go away, man. Mind your own business. The thought crossed my mind, but no words left my mouth. I imagined all the privileges, the good life, fearing nothing even this far from his home. A measure of trepidation and rage took hold of me.

"Hey! Help me out," he said. "Know where I can score some ganja?"

Who the fuck? The way he moved and the words coming out of his mouth. Messing with my plan. I decided to just wait, let him come. One hit with the blade. Open his throat and haul his ass inside, no witnesses. That's what they say in the movies. I eased my palm toward the handle of the machete. Just one more step. But Ian came into view, carrying the rake. He engaged the fellow with calm and balance. He spoke like an English gentleman, and the rake in his hand seemed out of place.

"We are here to do some yard work and clean up. The guests in this room must be having lunch." I glanced at Ian, such calmness, and I was almost jumping out of my skin.

"No. He left a few minutes ago. For the airport, heading back to the States, he told me."

"Well, thank you," Ian said. "We'll continue then."

"You fellows must have some idea where I can score some smoke? Rasta man like you, have a spleef to share with me?" He sized up Ian.

Ian just smiled and spoke softly. "Just go down to the beach, man. Ask any of the fellows down there. They'll help you."

"Okay then. Thank you." He moved away down the path to the main building. I stood looking at the back of his head, and my hand refused to be still. I was amazed at how close I came to chopping him with the blade. The comprehension sent a chill up my spine. Ian must have noticed the uncertainty on my face.

"You all right?" he asked.

"Let's go, man. He gone," I said. My anxiety subsided as I started to walk.

We made our way back to the car without one word passing between us. Ian drove. His eyes remained steady on the road and the other vehicles. Halfway through Grand Anse, the silence ballooned in my throat like a rancid belch. I had to say something.

"Who was that?"

"I don't know," Ian said.

"No matter how old they are these white people act as though they own the world."

Ian took his eyes off the road; glanced at me for just an instant.

"What you think of all those foreigners? Coming down here, buying up land and houses like the cheap goods at some Syrian's store," I said.

"They have money." He spoke without looking at me.

"What's more important? Money or people?" Ian didn't answer right away. He kept his eyes on the road and the flow of buses and cars.

"Well," he said finally. "I'll say both are important. You and Campesh, he asked me that same question one day. You two should talk. His question went like this. Which is more important, capital or labor? I didn't tell him exactly what I was thinking because I knew he wouldn't want to hear it, but I'll tell you. I see the question like this car. One is the fuel and the other is the car. One can't do anything without the other."

"I'm surprised at you, Ian. Labor is more important, man. The most a man can do with money is wipe his ass. He can't eat paper. But labor, land, and a little rain, you know what I mean?"

"Well, don't say that to the rich. They might laugh at you Godfrey. Grenada is not the entire world, you know. There's enough food out there to feed many generations and the rich have the money to buy it."

I felt put down, as if my thoughts and claims were so trivial.

"You don't understand, Ian," I said. "Grenada is my world, my home."

"Yeah. I understand, okay. We Rastas don't just smoke weed you know. We read books and talk about everything. If matters keep going like this, one day there will be no place left to plant food. What would we do with our labor then, when foreigners own everything, even the water company? They might force our government to pass a law making it illegal for us to even catch rainwater. No competition, even from God."

"Shit, you so crazy, Godfrey? Who would try such a thing?"

"Powerful greedy people."

"Oh, I forgot to tell you. My mother got a letter from Uncle Sydney."

"Where's he? Where are they?"

"Caracas, but that was weeks ago. He gave me that piece of land and the Jupa. Said he was heading back into the rain forest. I read his letter; it reminded me of an old, sick...you know what I mean, returning to a favorite place to rest his bones."

We parked the car on the road near Cosmus' house, shouted to him that we were back, and left before he came out to get the key. We walked past Brewster's shop, where a few guys were already hard into the strong rum. What a direction my life had taken since the death of Karrol Lagrenade one year ago. Could I have saved him by just saying more? Would that have changed all our lives, make the sun shine brighter?

"Ian, you ever blame me for what happened to Karrol?" Ian turned and looked at me briefly; then he lowered his head.

"Blame you? How...for what? You weren't even there. Going back for more Oildown? Haven't eaten breadfruit in a long time. Oildown have another taste now."

"We waited too long to have this conversation." I said.

"What you think it would have accomplished?"

We walked on down the road, an anxious silence as our only companion.

"You know Ian, the day that Karrol died I had this feeling, a funny itch that something was about to happen. I should have told him."

"Tell him what? If you had found the words, you think he would have believe you?"

"Who knows, he might have."

"And then what? You are fooling yourself with all the supposing, Godfrey. Why beat up yourself? It'll never bring Karrol back."

"So what if I tell you I've that same feeling right now?"

"Yeah. I believe you. It came from that look on your face when that fellow wanted to know where he could buy ganja. Let's talk about something else, man. These kind of things just make me real vex you know."

"Okay, okay."

Ian made long strides as if in a hurry. I kept the pace. The next words came out of my mouth for no reason but to oppose the near quiet.

"I think I found it," I said.

"What! You lost something?"

"No, no, not like that, man," I said.

Ian looked at me and raised his brows.

"You remember when you first learned to float on your back in the sea?" I asked.

Vexation, condescension, I spoke quickly to combat the rising wave on his face.

"That's where I am, in a place looking at life from a new angle. You remember how we were as kids? Living the don't-care, free of worries. For some reason, I thought I could go back to that, bring back those times. The day we lost Karrol . . . I'm telling you, Ian."

"Godfrey, you loved my brother and for that you are twice my brother, what ever the hell that means. You understand what I'm saying though? On the other hand we should learn to cuddle our demons. Sounds like you found something alright."

"No. That's not it. No God. No religion. I'm just looking at the world with fresh eyes," I said.

"Well, can you use those fresh eye to help me fix a roof?" he said. "The jupa needs some work. I want to move out of my mother's house before the rainy season. Have a place where I can live with my girl, now and then." He cocked his head and smiled.

"Just get a ladder and the stuff you need. How bad is it?"

"I already have the stuff. It's not bad," he said.

"Let's get started, man, right now. Shouldn't waste time. Rain, you know, never waits."

At the Jupa, a ladder, two sawhorses, some sections of board, and a can of tar sat outside the garden abandoned by Sydney and Xudine. I wanted to push that strange energy out, exert myself, hammer on something.

We grabbed two hammers, one each, and a crowbar, climbed the ladder onto the roof, and started removing sections of the galvanized tin. Where to from here? My thoughts drifted to the incident at the Calabash Hotel. The young fellow, an innocent really, but it was so cathartic to realize that I too could be a killer, that I was capable.

"Godfrey! Didn't want to leave without saying goodbye."

The voice came from below. There on the ground stood Jack Trueblood dressed in a suit, nice shiny shoes, a tie and all, looking like some kind of businessman. Ian and I exchanged surprised glances, and continued to tear the nails out of the rafters.

"I'm a man who always pays my debts," he said to our backs. "You don't have to come down."

"How did you find us?" I asked.

"They gave you up like that," and he snapped two fingers. "Everybody around here know exactly where..."

"Well, if you always pay your debts, give me some of that insurance they paid you."

"You think I've the money in my pocket?"

I turned and looked down at the man standing below us. Ian ignored the conversation and continued the work. Jack shifted his weight and gestured with both of his hands, palms up as if throwing something up to us.

"What you keep in your pocket; in your wallet, that's not real money," he said. "Real money now..."

"Why you standing there talking all that shit, Jack?" he seemed a little surprised at my interruption.

"I told you when we first met, you are a person worthy of some opportunities. I intend to give...not money. In a year or so, you would be just as broke as...go on, live your life... some day soon. I've some loose ends to wrap up."

His words sounded like permission, to what I had no idea.

"Is that all, Jack? We have work to do."

I shifted my position on the roof, turned as if to ignore Jack, and in the next instant gravity realigned my entirety. I heard Ian voice. "Oh! Shit," he said.

My feet moved, gone as if they were not mine, then my hands flailing, the hammer flying and hitting the tin roof, sliding down and off. I felt buoyant as a feather. Thoughts of wings came to me. And then one final assumption, I'll be the second man to die from falling off this roof.

My experiences slapped at me as I fell. Chief amongst them was the vessel, *Miss Irene/Calypso,* floating near Balis Ground. The details came, not as a procession, but as a stamp, a big rubber stamp inked and slammed onto a clear surface. Life so far. And in the next instant I hit Jack. Pain shot through my back from landing on what I assumed to be his head. We fell and rolled, came to a stop just before slamming into the trees near the edge of the garden.

"Oh! Shit," Ian shouted again. "You alright." He moved towards the ladder and came down fast.

I got up slowly, grabbed jack's arm and tried to bring him to his feet. He pulled his hand away, groaned, moved and pushed himself to a standing position without my help. He looked smashed up. No blood though, welts on his face, grass stains on the jacket and pants, shirt pulled out and the tie wedged to one side like a noose around his neck.

"Well, now you owe me one," he said and began dusting himself off, straightening the tie.

Ian stood near the ladder looking at us. He pointed at his own lips and spoke over Jack's comment.

"Godfrey, your lips… Bleeding," he said.

I brought my hand to my mouth, and at the same time I swiped my tongue across my lips; the savory taste of my own blood brought me out of my panic. Jack stood looking at me with a half smile on his face as if waiting for a response to what he had said. The sudden development left me speechless, but Jack's words and demeanor reminded me. I'm still engaged in an asymmetrical struggle with this man.

"I don't owe you anything," I said. "We might be close to even."

A smiled moved across his face. He stood looking at me as if searching for the right words. "You take care then," he said and pointed his index finger at me like a gun. He turned, and limped away down the gap.

"Well, Godfrey," Ian said, I turned and faced him, "carnival is just a week away. We should be able to finish this before then. He started back up the ladder.

*　*　*

Three years has past since my adventures with Jack Trueblood et al, and the world seems different, nothing like the place that Karrol and I once inhabited. Now that I had the time to think of it, trying to follow Sydney and Xudine seem so foolish. How could I have found them in the vastness of the Amazon? Who would have led me to them? I imagined a guide cutting my throat after a few days, stripping my body of all valuables and leaving my remains to insects and animals. Killing me would have been an act of kindness.

Not one day goes by without some aspects of my past coming into play. For instance, Yvette heard about a small yacht for sale, a craft designed for day charters. I pooled the money my father had left in the floor with the cash my great grand mother had given me in that box with her will, and I had enough to make a down payment on the yacht. I get between six to eight charters per month. Ian accompanies me on some of them. We make enough money to keep the bankers happy.

I know that one day Jack would return. My newly acquired intuition told me men like him seldom make promises they don't keep. I've learned to trust my instincts, sincerely embracing the mystical and the mysterious. These have opened doors for me. They say life is for learning. I've gained some understanding since the death of Karrol Lagrenade. I will remain one with this land, acknowledging its mystique and dreadfulness, nurture what I've grown to be, and continue the struggle to maintain an open heart, and keep it as open as this wide, blue Caribbean sky.